The Cow
at the Window

Alex Niven

Library of Congress Control Number: 2014917317
ISBN: Hardcover   978-1-4990-9005-5
                 Softcover   978-1-4990-9007-9
                 eBook   978-1-4990-9006-2

Print information available on the last page.

Rev. date: 03/26/2015

To order additional copies of this book, contact:
Xlibris
0-800-056-3182
www.xlibrispublishing.co.uk
Orders@xlibrispublishing.co.uk
663255

Contents

INTRODUCTION

Where to start!

Well! Having been a vet for a very long time it is reasonable to assume that many interesting cases have drifted under my stethoscope.

I began recording cases; animal and human, early in my career and used them as the basis for many talks.

At last I have yielded to the many requests that I should share these tales with a wider audience.
It was always my intention they would eventually be published in some format; although my original idea was to leave them behind as legacy of our experiences, as part of the record of our family history.

A word of warning!

These stories which have to be termed as fiction form part of my life experience.
Most are so true as to make me relive them each time I cast an eye over them.
Some make me smile while others still tug at my heartstrings.
Not all of them are happy, bunny hugger stories.

The tales include a variety of different animal species and also jump around from one time period to another.

> Only a few examples are included in this volume: *The cow at the window*, which is the first volume in the series of our family adventures in veterinary practice.

The tales in this volume are a mixture of different areas, different practices and indeed times.

> I have lumped most of them together as having taken place in Drofter for the sake of continuity.
> I do, however, protect that great practice by declaring that none of the mistakes or bad stories did in fact take place in Drofter.

People and animals have shared in building these adventures and I thank them all for forming an important part of our lives and for sharing my journey towards my final resting place in the glory of God.

Please feel free to let me know what you think of my stories as constructive criticism is always of value.

Perhaps the titles of the subsequent volumes will tickle your fancy as to what is to follow:

THE BULL WITH THE BENT WILLY

RABBITS IN THE BEDROOM

Johannesburg Feb 2015

DEDICATION

To The Lord of the Universe who blesses all of us.

For Theresa who becomes more special every day.

To Melissa and Andrew who are genetically perfect; it comes from your mother's side.

"So faith, hope, love abide, these three;
but the greatest of these is love."

1 Cor 13:13

ACKNOWLEDGEMENTS

My grateful thanks go to

The superstars:

> Tom and Elsie Shanks for their amazing kindness and generosity.
> Jim and Val Brodie for their friendship, support and love.

My many Veterinary colleagues who unknowingly contributed to these stories including:

> Alison, Angelo, Crocky, Dave, Grant, Jimmy, Len, Terry, and others

Nurses:

> A huge bouquet to Angie and Elaine: the salt of the earth.
> For Carol, Caroline, Jenny, Judith, Pauline, Sara, Sanscha, Trudy, etc for the part they played.

Patients and Owners:

> Thanks to you my brothers and sisters.

My daughter Melissa and that great author Jassy MacKenzie for their constructive advice on the manuscript.

Thanks due to all at Xlibris for their encouragement, patience and professionalism

CHAPTER 1

CHANG'S STICKY THING

MY FAVOURITE STORY centres on a pair of remarkable characters.

The two-legged one was Ms Rodgers; her Pekinese dog, Chang, was the other.

Chang and Rodgers, what a double act! Ms Rodgers was a bit of a practical joker whose sharp sense of fun often caught me out, especially when she strayed into those areas that make a young man blush.

Revenge came at last, and it was sweet! It occasioned a story that is now part of Drofter folk lore and must never slip into the grey area of urban legend. Chance is a funny thing, and when it comes along it must be grabbed with both hands. It was my chance, my turn to make the old lady's cheeks turn even pinker that the highly coloured blusher already decorating them.

Ms Rodgers was a vivacious character.

She must have been a real cracker as a youngster and her still lively mind, and great sense of humour, made her popular with our staff. She was one of those people whose inherent beauty, and oh - so - smart dress sense, always suggested her to be in Sunday best.

Chang was a real dog with a rich, thick, red coat that ended in a glorious, if somewhat twisted, bushy tail that even Reynard the fox would have been proud of. His aristocratic personality gave him an air of assurance, a bearing that suggested his superiority. He enjoyed people, but was not a lap dog as his involvement with two-legged animals was that of equals, of friends.

Our hero Chang was drifting into the wrong side of middle age and he had developed; as most of us do who creep past the halfway mark, a leg problem. His arthritis was of more concern to his human mother, whose own joint stiffness was actually further advanced than that of her small friend, than it was to him. He would never again move like a two – year – old; none of us will.

It was my good fortune to be on duty that evening.

A steady stream of characters, dogs and humans, kept me busy and another grand day in practice was drifting to a close, and I could almost smell the lamb chops with mint sauce that is one of Theresa's specialities.

Chang and company were my last visitors and they listened patiently to the marvellous repertoire of feline screams originating from my consulting room. When I joined them Ms Rodgers peered at me from her chair in the waiting room then gave me one of her delicious smiles. Her first offering was delivered with her usual cheeky attitude, "Now then, vet, what an awful noise! Were you trying to kill that cat?"

"Ms R, that cat was actually trying to kill me!"

Ms R showed some initial interest in that feral cat.

Her concern for Chang caused her smile to change to a frown of sadness. The wrinkles on her cheeks were normally disguised by her permanent smiles, but when the smiles went; she looked even more like Chang, whose face was permanently creased in the normal Peke manner. The couple brought a stamp of approval to the suggestion that owners often resemble their dogs!

Ms R pointed a long finger at our friend and said, "He has me really worried this time."

When Chang, who had been sitting at her feet, recognised me, he rose, wagged his odd little tail, and wobbled towards me. I grimaced on seeing how badly he was moving, and said, "That does not look good. Come inside Chang and tell me what is wrong." I ushered them into the consulting room and watched the little chap hobble across the floor in front of me. I turned to his mother and said, "Now Ms Rodgers, this is odd."

She plunked herself down on the white plastic chair beside the examination table and I noticed how she shook her head from side to side and her eyes filled with tears. I put my arm round her, gave her shoulders a quick squeeze, and tried to comfort her, "Now then my special friend this looks bad, but I am sure it will not be as bad as you think."

"Well, you already make me feel better by saying that, and I trust you."

"That's it, that's more like you. Let's get on and find what the problem is."

"You are smiling, but Chang can hardly walk. Are you sure he is not that bad?"

"Hold on now friend, let's have a look at him first. Already, I feel it is not as bad as you think it might be."

"Why? What makes you say that?"

"He has a happy face. When they are smiling, the problem is never as bad as the owner thinks it might be. Look at him walking around the room, and, although his movement is odd he does not appear to be uncomfortable."

"I see what you mean, and, as you often say, he is reading the newspapers left by previous visitors."

"Excellent! Good girl." Chang was indeed enjoying the fabulous stories previous patients had left behind and I was again envious of the fabulous sense of smell animals have.

Ms Rodgers was in the pink.

In a striking, flamboyant frock in organza, she was dressed even smarter than usual; Patricia later informed me of the material, and, although the focus was on Chang my good manners allowed me to compliment the lady, "I must say, Ms R, you are looking very flashy today." I thought it odd she never acknowledged my compliment, and knelt on the floor to talk to the little fellow, "Now, Chang, this is different, tell me what has happened."

The lady coughed and the sharp noise she made caused me to turn and look at her, and her amazing spectacles again caught my eye. They could only be described as looking like the bottom of a milk bottle, as they were the thickest, heaviest glasses I had ever seen. She was totally blind without them, and, in all honesty, not too great with them.

"Well Alex, Chang and I have both been so pleased with our legs. Our latest round of medication and exercise is helping and I have even lost a few pounds," The old sparkle revealed itself as she continued, "In fact the local *Weight Watchers* club is feeling the pinch."

I had encouraged them to take regular walks, and it was during their afternoon stroll that Chang suddenly went lame. The manner in which she leaned into me when she spoke was quite touching, and I felt her pain as she said, "I have had a good feel for something like chewing gum in his pads and can find nothing, but you know my eyes are not too good so please check him out for me."

Chang was moving oddly.

As the waiting room was empty I opened the consulting room door and encouraged him to wander around and although the small chap's awkward looking stroll was distinctly unusual he did not appear to be in pain. We watched him for a few moments before I approached him and said, "Come along Chang, it is time for me to examine you," He was happy for me to pick him up off the floor and I continued talking to him as I placed him on the examination table, "So, my little friend, let me have a good look at you." He enjoyed the good scratching I gave his ears and rewarded me with one of his lovely smiles. The intensive drenching of saliva he bestowed on me was not quite as welcome; Pekes will be Pekes!

"Isn't it funny he walks so badly and yet does not seem uncomfortable?" Ms Rodgers vocalised my own thoughts.

"Yes, it is unusual, but also good, I prefer that to him being in pain."

A once - in - a - lifetime opportunity presented itself when Chang's problem turned out to be one of the strangest lameness cases I ever saw. It also proved one of the easiest to diagnose and repair. Chang was, as always, the model patient, and when the source of his mother's distress was found I enjoyed a silent little chuckle. I stood back for a moment, and wondered; what is going to be the best way for me to make some mileage out of this situation?

I was in practice in Drofter.

It is a lovely market town on the border of Lincolnshire, Nottinghamshire, and South Yorkshire, and is one of the loveliest areas I have ever known. The town boasts many good amenities of which the lovely gardens in Kings Park are worth a visit; it is a popular recreational spot, a well - maintained area that is a major attraction for the local people. It is inevitable that even such a pristine environment will inadvertently collect some waste. During their walk Chang's hairy little body managed to pick up what we used to call a Kojak lollipop; a sweet with a round, sticky head. Some youngster must have carelessly discarded the partially eaten lollipop, and the rejected sweet had become an integral part of Chang's anatomy.

The small object was firmly attached to the long hairs in front of his scrotum. The lollipop was an inch longer than his little legs and every time he tried to take a step his newly acquired part came into play. That caused his action to be completely abnormal with a most peculiar series of leg - lollipop - leg, hops.

My diagnosis was brilliant.

It was time to present it to the distressed owner and my mind was still calculating; how am I going to make the best of this opportunity? How am I going to turn this into a bit of fun, a chance to make the old lady laugh? Should it be explained along the lines that any male with three balls is entitled to move with difficulty? I rejected such an approach as being too risqué.

My verdict could not be delayed any longer and I allowed my voice to take on the tone of a learned professor, "Bit surprised, Ms R, that a woman of the world, such as you, was unable to identify his problem," I paused, nodded wisely a few times for effect, and continued, "From your many cheeky stories I would have thought that the problem, involving," and here I put even more emphasis into the words, "as it does, *his masculinity*, would have been right up your street."

Ms R did not follow me, "His masculinity!" She peered at me and said, "Well! I can see you are smiling and that must be good news, but what is happening?"

I made a big circle in the air with my hand and then allowed a finger to point deliberately at the area of interest. As she still had difficulty seeing the problem I continued, "Now then, Ms R, as you have not spotted the problem, allow me to take you on an interesting anatomical tour."

Only when I guided her fingers directly onto the spot did the penny drop, and her bright laughter echoed merrily throughout the clinic, "Well Alex, you really got that one over me for a change," She slapped me on the shoulder, stood back and continued, "Shall you remove it, or, should I take him to the parlour for the ladies to enjoy the moment?"

I puffed out my chest and suggested, "Ms R, you have to make a decision, either, I cut the lollipop off the dog or, I cut the dog off the lollipop?"

By then Ms Rodgers was back to her cheery self, "I suggest that in this case, it would be most appropriate if you would cut the third ball away from the two permanent ones."

A snip or two with scissors affected the cure.

Ms Rodgers paused for a moment, and, from the manner in which she stared at me through her fancy rimmed glasses, I guessed something fascinating was coming. I was not disappointed and her next comment made me laugh, "Do you think we should have his extra ball framed?"

We were both still chortling when she and Chang, who was immediately back to his original stride, walked proudly out of the clinic and his mother, who was displaying more than a touch of her usual swagger, even rolled her Rs.

Some cases have ended badly. Others have even been described as being a real balls up.

A ball off saved that day.

CHAPTER 2

EARLY DAYS

"THAT BIRD MUST go! It must go *now*!"

My mum was a touch upset.

Upset! I had seldom heard her use that tone, and following a deep breath she became even angrier and more followed, "Under no circumstances will I tolerate its presence in this house for a moment longer. It must go, and, it must go, *now*. What are you going to do with your life; always up to your eyes in animals I suppose you will have to be a vet one day."

Our mother was cross, very cross, and I tried to placate her, "But mum I had no choice, the bird was in trouble . . ."

"In trouble, in trouble you say. If it's trouble you are looking for it will not be hard to find. This is your last warning, that eagle, or whatever it is, must go." She stormed out of the bedroom.

I had never seen her so angry and I collapsed onto my bed, and thought; I don't suppose I should complain, there was obviously going to be a problem, but I had no choice.

My late brother Jackie; may the Good Lord hold him in the palm of his hand, was in the hallway listening to Mum and when he saw the door begin to open he shot off in the manner of a rabbit with a Lurcher on its tail. He hid away until it was safe, then sneaked back and peaked nervously into the bedroom and there was no sympathy in his voice, "You have really done it this time. Thank God mum is mad at you for a change, it's usually me and Joe who are in trouble."

"Thanks for the support! Go back to playing with your dolls." I threw a book at him.

Josephine Kelly was special.

Her legendary warmth and compassion were only some of the wonderful things that made her our mum. She was the mother of nine children, of whom I was the eldest. Both of mum's parents were Dublin born Irish, and I remember them for always being there when we needed help. Granda Kelly was a highly intelligent, well-read man with more than a hint of being personally affected by the troubles his native land suffered.

The West of Scotland was not for sissies as the hardships of raising a large family in the tough, post war era of a depressed Clydeside kept mum's feet on the ground. She was a simple down to earth person who always found time to act as the family agony aunt; I can see her in our daughter.
Our mum was also a dreamer and there were occasions when her head was so high in the clouds she must have heard the angels talking. When given half a chance she was an entertainer whom someone described as the hostess with the mostest; it stuck. She loved people, and, in return was loved by everyone, and we fondly remember how, with the odd glass of Babycham in her hand, and the gramophone playing, she could organise a party in a teacup.

Granda Niven was also a Dublin man.

Sandy was a carter, mainly of coal and his drinking escapades caused his horse to be a local legend for its amazing homing ability. After a hard day humping heavy bags of the black stuff, the man was known to take a drink or two then climb onto his cart where sleep would claim him. The horse would take him safely home and if there was a law in those days about drinking when in charge of a horse it never applied to Sandy.

Granny Niven was a real Scot of the Clan Stewart heritage; an accident of birth that allows me to wear the famous Royal.

As all four of Theresa's grandparents were Dublin Irish perhaps our zest for life and songs and stories stems from us being under the influence of those seven Irish grandparents! Our children still do not fully realise, or appreciate, the fact that genetically they are seven eighths Irish and wouldn't half the world give their right arm to be able to make such a fortunate claim?

Mum was a wonderful character, but there was a particular area of concern that caused her Irishness to reveal itself; she did not appreciate our bedroom shenanigans. Now hold on there, I do not mean that kind of activity, we were good Irish Catholic children. Well . . . most of us! Yes brother, remember the scantily clad girl in the wardrobe?

How we housed our pets was the problem.

It was the constant collection of animals, dead and alive, in every nook and cranny of our backyard that disturbed her. Worse still, when necessity demanded they lived in our bedroom that caused a marked reaction, especially if my pets caused a bit of, let's call it general untidiness.

Guilty as charged!

Our bedroom could get into a bit of a state when its frequent visitors failed to comply with mum's laws on general hygiene. Our Mum was more than adamant on the subject of cleanliness and one of her common phrases was, "Cleanliness is next to Godliness."

CHAPTER 3

THE SEAGULL

THE BIRD JOINED our family for one night.

That was enough!

One night convinced mum that my constant involvement with the odds and ends of the animal world would never change.

The bird needed help and I had no choice! We; my friend Brandy and I, saved him from the cruel sea that threatened to drown him when his rescue took place one afternoon as we walked the Clyde shore.

A bitterly cold spell had kept us inside and I was re-reading Black Beauty, for the third or fourth time, but the book failed to hold me. When the temperature began to lift I looked at the small dog lying on the carpet with her head resting on my feet and I made a swift grab at her that startled her for one second, until she realised there was the prospect of some fun. I said, "Hey Brandy, it's getting warmer, can you feel it? I am bored, shall we risk a bit of a walk along the shore?"

She gave one of her happy yaps.

It was associated with a funny, springbok-like pronking that only she perfected. I teased her by holding her firmly with both hands latched onto her silky collar of white, flowing hairs, "You don't seem too excited about the prospect, are you sure you want to come with me?" I tried to keep a straight face and pretend I was serious; no chance, she read me like a book.

Our Brandy was a beautiful mixture of Pomeranian, and whatever, with a long silky coat that gave her a touch of class. Even Mum, who told us regularly she had inherited a dislike of dogs from her own mother, secretly adored her.

"Yow, yow, yow!" She spoke to me using the little delicious noises only she could make then turned tail and left me to plonk her bum down by the back door.

We headed for Lover's Lane.

We made the short trip alongside the tar road and Dumbarton, our town, slipped behind us and then we crossed the Cardross Road, bypassed the Westcliff bus stop and turned left down Lover's Lane. It was still very cold particularly where the track went downwards in deep shadow and we marched on with a brisk step to generate the warmth we needed. We carefully crossed the railway and a further five minutes took us on through the fields until my great friend the Clyde welcomed us onto her beach where the wide, clean, and very flat sand, provided excellent footing for our adventure. There was even a hint of ice at the edge of the brackish river.

The seaweed covered rocks were surrounded by small permanent pools, and even in winter we enjoyed searching them for the many interesting creatures that rewarded our efforts. The many small boys who regularly explored the beaches must have been reminiscent of wading sea birds, and our to and fro motion as we turned over rocks and seaweed must have made us seem competitors to our feathered friends.

The small bitch was enjoying herself and once again I marvelled at how well dogs handle the cold, "Have you had enough? Do you think it's time to go home are your feet and toes as cold as mine?"

The lady smiled at me and when she gave one of her characteristic skips to tell me she was still enjoying herself it was easy to echo her smile and agree, "OK little one we will stick it out for another fifteen minutes." There were times when it was easy to nod with mum's thoughts that Brandy understand every word we said.

"This looks different."

As the slowly trotting Brandy wandered backwards and forwards over the beach the little one found something interesting and her attitude suddenly changed, and her alert, pointer-like stance caught my attention and dragged me away from my latest find; a decent sized crab that scuttled to freedom under a clump of seaweed.

The movement that captivated Brandy was obviously birdlike and I asked her what she thought, "Well my favourite little lady, what have you found, is it something different?"

Brandy was keen to investigate yet reluctant to approach it. She wasn't the bravest in the world, and when the thing moved she ran back to my side and snuggled up close to my legs. From that more secure refuge she uttered a low growl at the creature and I said, "Now then Brandy, you are a cheeky thing, and cannot make me think you are a big brave Alsatian," I fondled her ears gently to comfort her, or both of us, "Must we be careful of this?"

I paused for a moment.

I needed time to consider how best to proceed and Brandy surprised me by finding the confidence to leave my side and walk, rather stiff legged, five yards closer to whatever it was. Her growling became stronger and she raised her hackles to make her appear bigger, hoping to intimidate the thing. When it moved she was back at my feet faster than she could swallow a piece of cheese.

I gasped at that movement and felt my pulse race, "Gosh! It is alive, this is exciting," It was crying out to be investigated, "Jings! There's a clever little lady, what have you found?" It was about thirty yards from us, and, as it began moving I started running towards it, fearful it would get away from us, "Come on little girl, let's catch it."

Brandy's find became obvious and I shared her excitement, "Goodness me Brandy, it's a bird, it's a seagull." We were close enough to see the bird had a problem, "It's a Herring Gull and the poor creature is in a bit of a fix, look what has happened." A discarded toilet bag had filled with water, and, following a hard night exposed on the sand, the water had turned into a lump of ice. The strings that normally closed the bag were entangled round the bird's legs preventing it from making any other than the most basic of movements. The large black and white character was so exhausted it could hardly drag itself away from us.

Brandy was a real lady who loved her walks.

Rooting around on the beach was something she enjoyed, but hunting was not her forte and the gull had no fears from her in that regard. A few years later, had that find been made by my favourite character of all time; my best friend Shaun, the outcome would have been different.

The bird, the dog and the boy looked at each other, and Brandy was the first to comment with another excited, "Yow, yow, yow," indicating something had to be done. Her habit of turning her head slightly to the left suggested she was talking to me.

I was also excited, although my own mounting sense of insecurity made me cautious, "Yes Brandy, I agree that something will have to be done, but, it's a huge, fierce looking bird and I don't know . . ."

Brandy was behind me and she pushed her nose against my leg and prodded me onward making it obvious the next move was up to me. I inched my way forward to within two yards of the bird until it moved, and then it screamed at me and raised its wings and stretched them out wide on each side to intimidate me. It succeeded, and made me spring back, "Gosh Brandy did you see that? The thing is huge, what are we going to do?"

Brandy was hiding behind my legs, and, as I again inched closer to the bird she herded me in the manner of my first dog, Lance; a Border collie with a notion for working sheep, or anything. As soon as I was within two yards of it the bird stretched its wings up and out again, and it was enormous and anxiety again made me cry out, "Gosh Brandy, we must be careful, that is a scary thing."

Her reply was a weak squeak.

I realised the gull could not escape.

The bag wrapped around the bird's legs effectively anchored it to the spot, "At least it looks to be stuck in one place." I circled the creature cautiously with Brandy who was like a shadow stuck to my heels; she would have been in my pocket if she were small enough. I spoke to her, "If it cannot move we might be able to catch it, what do you think?"

Nothing happened for a few minutes and that inactivity gave Brandy the confidence to sneak up to within a foot of the bird when it suddenly lunged forward and attempted to spear her with its dagger-like beak. The small dog surprised me by not running away and I congratulated her, "I am impressed," I reached down and fondled her ears, "Clever girl, you have already worked out she cannot reach you, very clever!"

Brandy had established boundaries by then and responded to my encouragement by skipping round the creature, whose eyes constantly followed her. I raised my arms, stretched them out in front of the bird and when it responded to me in a similar fashion I said, "Jings bird, your arms are wider than mine." I moved from side to side and flapped my arms up and down as the bird mirrored my movements and made me laugh, "Look at us Brandy, don't you think we would make a good dancing team?"

Her growl grew deeper and took on a more assured note.

I removed my anorak, and held it outstretched in front of me.

I looked at the bird and the jacket and said, "Yes, this should shield it from us." Its scream was the loudest yet and I saw its tongue vibrating inside a huge, wide open beak. I noticed its breathing was heavy, and, on realising it was becoming obviously weaker, my confidence grew. I knew the bird could not reach me and steeled myself to stop worrying about the noise it made. I spoke to Brandy or myself or both, "Come now Alex it is only a big pigeon and you have caught hundreds of them."

My anorak became a Matador's cape and I flicked it from side to side in the hope of distracting the bird. My first attempt at capture was a failure as my throw was off and the anorak missed the target, and, as the bird swerved to the side it caught me on the chest with its left wing. It was a powerful blow that surprised me and caused me to stumble back and I lost my balance, and landed on my bum on the wet sand.

The brave little dog flew to my rescue and stunned all three of us by attacking the bird and earning a mouthful of feathers. She was the most surprised of all of us, and sprung back from the bird with a look of amazement on her face. I was still sitting on the sand when Brandy snuggled up to me and I felt so proud of her and gave her a long hug, one that was probably meant to reassure me more than her, "I am so pleased you are here with me, that bird tried to eat me and you rescued me from it."

"Sorry birdie, I have had enough of this!"

It was time to get the job done; I could see by the way the bird was holding its mouth wide open it was tiring rapidly, "Look at the poor thing, we have to do something, we are stressing it too much." I tackled it again, and, as it lunged at me my anorak dropped nicely over its head and body. I threw my arms around it and hugged its body close to mine and it went limp which allowed me to manoeuver the anorak and secure it. The bird again fought me and we struggled back and forward until it finally surrendered. It became so soft in my arms I feared I had caused some damage and I almost released it and said to Brandy, "No! That would be daft, I must hang on until I figure out what to do next." Although severely distressed it was obviously alive, "Got you bird, now let me get you out of this snare."

I released the struggling creature from the string, a process that took me more than a few minutes. The knot was not a difficult one, but the belligerent bird made my attempt difficult and caused me to mumble along in my usual manner, "Now then you stupid bird! I am actually trying to help you?" The struggle taught me just how hard a Herring Gull can stab with its heavy bill.

"Jings Brandy! Did you see that? Don't come any closer, this thing is a savage wild creature and it might do you a proper injury." If it is true that every experience moulds ones character, it was that serious pecking, and another much later from Monica's cheeky budgie, that left me with a cautious approach to birds. The blood flowed freely where he got me on the fine skin on the inside of my arm.

I am fiercely proud of my Irish roots.

However, there are a number of snags associated with Irish blood; one of which reveals the gypsy part inside me, the one that makes me a collector. I was always prepared for the fascinating episodes walking along my much loved Clyde shore brought as the daily flotsam and jetsam of the tides often turned up some fascinating, even useful objects. My pocket held the heavy, brown paper bag that was my constant companion, in the hope that something worth collecting would turn up, and, it was only when the bird was well wrapped in that bag and my anorak it ceased struggling. The fact of its being securely restrained allowed me to consider my next move, "Got you, but is that a good thing?"

I looked to my friend for advice, but Brandy didn't understand my problem and when she remained silent, I said, "I reckon we must take it home." That was obvious as such an exhausted creature was not in a fit state to be released into another bitterly cold night and I reflected on the situation, "If I take you home that will cause a problem." I stared at the bird, but kept my head turned away from it at a safe distance, as its bill was long and its' huge, pale yellow eyes bored into me and intimidated me.

Brandy yelped encouragement and advice, but I didn't quite catch her thoughts.

"This could really put the wind up our mother if we take it home."

Brandy refused to comment at a time when I needed some moral support, and there was only the two of us disturbing the huge, pristine beach. I tried again by asking my fascinated companion what our next move should be, "So Brandy, now that we have released it from the grip of that bag what should we do with it?"

She loved it when I talked seriously to her and the manner in which she earnestly looked at me made me wonder what was going on in her fascinating brain. She paused a moment longer then tilted her lovely face to the left, as though giving our problem serious thought, and then Brandy gave another of her excited little skips, and trotted for home.

"So little one, are you sure?"

She continued and her answer was a positive, "Yow, yow, yow."

That response gave me a clear answer, "Yes I suppose you are right, we must risk mum's wrath and take the bird home."

I took Brandy's advice.

I prayed earnestly that mum would be sympathetic, our plan had after all been made by the combined brain power of the two of us, and I reminded Brandy of her role in the problem, "Do you think if I blame this on you, and tell mum it was your decision, she will not get cross?" Our thirty minute walk with the increasingly heavy bird was an anxious one, and again I confided in her, "Brandy I have to tell you I am nervous about what mum is going to say."

She gave a single and less confident, "Yow."

"Mum is going to have one of her cadenzas if she sees this thing." My constant thoughts made it easy to forget the cold; this heavy bird is making me feel warm, but the reception we get from mum might be even warmer.

Knowing our guest would have to be concealed from her for as long as possible, caused my anxiety to heighten with every step that took us closer to home. We were lucky to find the house empty as Mum had popped round to talk to one of the neighbours.

CHAPTER 4

HOME

T HE FIRST PART of our adventure went well.

"That was lucky, and, as there is no sign of Mum we can plan our next move."

I again asked Brandy for support, "Here we are little girl, finally home and now where are we going to keep this thing?"

She looked at me, and then the bird, said nothing, and wandered off to the kitchen for a drink of water, which made me think; that's a good idea, I could do with a drink myself, but I will first have to make a plan with this bird. The gull obviously needed a temporary home and I thought; I have no choice, I do not like the idea, yet I have no choice. The most logical place to house the creature was the bedroom.

I was perched on a chair in the hallway.

My arms were around the peaceful bird that was either taking some rest or preparing itself for phase two when my partner in crime re-joined me and looked at me, and then the bird, without wagging her tail or talking. In the hope she might support me I poked my toes under her tummy and rubbed her special spot, "So! What is your problem now, have you changed your mind about this thing?"

She offered me the merest of half-hearted beats of her bushy tail and only the faintest of smiles, and her; *yow, yow, yow* was soft.

I looked at her bland face and said, "Are you going to be a fine weathered friend and desert me, and leave me to face the future by myself?"

The bird interrupted us by making a sudden croaking sound and struggled enough to push me on with my plan and I looked into the things big eyes and said, "You are right, it is time I released you from this straight jacket."

The bedroom was directly off the hall.

I pushed open the door and turned to warn Brandy, "I am afraid our plans must change." She refused to look at me, a trick she employed when upset, but I shook my head and said, "Sorry Brandy, I dare not have you in the same space as this bird when I release it." I was concerned the huge bird would attack her, and shuddered at the thought of that huge beak digging into her eyes so I excluded the unhappy little one from the bedroom and closed the door. Brandy was miffed at being locked out, and her whining took on an unusual note that chilled me.

It was the moment of the bird's release and my heart bounced as I knelt on the floor beside it and slipped it free from the paper bag and, as I stepped away from it I pleaded, "Now then you savage beast, please do not go dilly on me."

I feared the worst, and was pleased when his release went better than I dreamt it might. The gull shook itself in the manner of any bird rearranging its feathers then hopped calmly onto the end of the bed. It stared at me in a manner that, while still scary, expressed some contentment with the situation it found itself in, and then it brought up a long pink leg and scratched the feathers of its neck and stretched its massive wings. The gull gave itself an enormous shake and yawned and I took that huge gaping bill as a signal that was easy to interpret, "I think I understand you, are you hungry?"

The gull screamed.

It made a noise that must have awakened any sleeping infants in our neighbourhood; it was a call that boomed round and round the room, and encouraged Brandy, who had been constantly whining and scratching at the door to join in. Her yelping was at a higher pitch than I ever remembered and made me call out, "Jings crivens, what's this about?" I spoke sharply to both of them until they went quiet, "Now let's lay down some rules here," I rambled on in a manner that relaxed most animals, "That is much better, if you are going to stay here tonight you must be quiet."

Many newly rescued animals need time to adjust to captivity and the process is often a difficult one, particularly if they go on hunger strike. Not that fellow, he responded to our home as though raised with us.

There was only the leanest of suitable food material in the kitchen as our own ever hungry brood rarely left any scraps. I needed help, and hoped some would be found at one of our neighbour's houses and I popped round and explained the situation to my best friend, "Hi Ted, I am so glad to see you, I've, got a bit of a problem."

Before I could explain the situation he interrupted, "No! Please don't tell me you have been up to your usual stupid tricks, and you need me to share the blame?"

I guessed he was thinking about the time we got caught pinching apples from the orchard down the Lee Brae, or was it the time the farmer caught us collecting a few potatoes from the field along the Clyde shore. I was happy to explain my interesting situation, "No man it's nothing like that, I have rescued a huge seagull and I need some food for it."

"Wow! That is a different story. Come let's go, let me see it." The decent guy followed me home.

I opened the door carefully.

Ted's jaw dropped when he saw the size of the bird and his eyes widened even more when they fell on the disarray it had caused, "Bloody hell Alex! Look at the size of the creature! How are we ever going to cope with this? How are we ever going to feed it? And! How are we," He shook his head vigorously at that point and continued, "How are *you* going to keep it a secret from your mother?"

"I am sure we have to keep it here away from the weather for just tonight. He needs that to get his strength back and then he can fly off tomorrow morning. Please help me find some scraps, of anything, for it to eat."

The desperation in my voice convinced him, "I am not sure about this, but, I don't suppose I have any choice." He joined me in the search for food.

It could have won a gold medal at eating.

The bird's enormous appetite for everything Ted and I gleaned improved its condition. There was a downside to the equation, as everything that went down its enormous throat resulted in an opposite reaction and I and my room were amply rewarded for our generosity by the bird producing a magnificent amount of poo! It produced the most evil smelling waste products imaginable.

Ted panicked, "You must be mad. Your mother is going to play the riot act when she sees this mess, the stink is awful," He looked hard at me as his fingers pulled at a lock of his dark hair, "I am not going to take any of the blame this time." My best two-legged friend fled the room.

I had to leave the gull alone for two hours, and when I returned he confirmed our earlier suspicions and proved correct our theory that gulls are the champion poo producers. I looked from the badly soiled carpets directly into his huge eyes, "Look at this mess, have you produced all of this by yourself?" The smell was unbelievable, and apart from a dignified stare it ignored me, which left me wondering; how am I going to get myself out of this mess?

Mum came into our room unexpectedly.

Early the following morning she surprised us when I had hoped for time to prepare her for the problem. It was the spectacular mess his lack of toilet training produced that brought the ultimatum from mum, "What the ... heck, is going on here?"

It was the only time I had ever heard Mum utter anything remotely like a swear word. Ted was right! In fact, Ted was very right! Mum nearly had a heart attack, and if she hadn't been afraid to come into the room with that huge and very agitated bird, she would have half killed me.

Its company afforded me a fascinating insight into the rawness of nature. It had to be released and in truth I was glad to see it go as a single night's stay my room cured me of any thoughts I may have had of a career in the rehabilitation of seabirds. I nodded at mum, "Ok mum I will let it go, can you help me release it?"

She made a beeline for the door, "I am afraid of the thing. Please be careful and don't let it go until I close the door."

"Now then birdie, it's time for you to go." It yawned then flicked one of his its massive wings at me and caught me an unexpectedly sharp blow on the arm that made me cry out, "What is your trouble this morning? Can you not appreciate I am going to release you?" For some reason it appreciated being sharply spoken to and instantly became calm and respectful which allowed me to continue, "It is time for you to go, but, give me a minute to think, I am unsure how to manage the problem."

My first idea was to catch it, then take it onto the lawn via the front door.

I picked up a badly soiled blanket, and approached it in the hope I could trap it under the blanket. The bird was much stronger than when we had caught it on the beach, and he opened his huge beak and screamed constantly at me while using his wings aggressively to batter me. Again I remonstrated, "You really are a stupid bird, I am trying to release you," I backed away from it towards the door, "You are a big scary thing and we need another plan." I scratched my head and thought; there is no way I can catch it, what will happen if I open the window and stand back?

As I sneaked to the window I begged for peace, "Please be reasonable," The latch opened with its usual grating sound and as the glass swung wide I offered it freedom, "There, the window is open so please pop through it?"

The bird studied me. looked at the window and then hopped onto the windowsill, and, suddenly he was no longer our guest.

My brother Gerry; of happy memory, who had been returning home, got quite a shock. As he walked along the path the bird launched itself through the window and nearly scared him to death and his plaintive call touched my heartstrings, "Help! What's happening?"

"Sorry brother I never saw you there." I could see Gerry by then and noticed how as he too watched the bird, he lifted a hand towards it and waved goodbye.

If I was young, he was much younger and Gerry was still shaking and I felt the tremor in his voice, "I am glad he has gone, but you could have warned me, I thought I was being attacked by an eagle."

The bird's steady wing beats allowed it to climb gracefully into the cold grey sky. The ease of his flight thrilled me and made me confident his recovery would be complete, "Would you look at that, doesn't he look special up there?" My anxiety was replaced with a feeling of great joy as we craned our necks to watch it circle the immediate neighbourhood from a considerable height. We took its sharp, raucous calls to indicate it was enjoying the freedom of the sky and I thought it was expressing its thanks to Brandy and me for having saved its life and I said, "Go friend. The sky is where you belong and I am glad we were able to help you."

There is much to be gained from the act of releasing a wild animal back into its natural habitat. It was only one bird and we felt proud to have made a difference.

The devastation remaining behind was the worst I ever experienced.

Brandy refused to join me, and, as she sat by the doorway she issued soft squeals that indicated her thoughts on the subject. Gerry, who had been out of the room for most of the morning, agreed with the dog, "Over to you mate, there is no way I am sleeping in there tonight, nor am I going to help you with the cleaning."

The whole world was against me and I expressed my displeasure to the picture of Dumbarton FC that had pride of place on the wall above my bed, "Now here's a fine mess, you would think the bird might have shown its appreciation by helping me clean up my smelly bedroom."

I convinced myself the Sons of the Rock nodded in agreement. The actual mopping up operation only lasted about fifty minutes.

But the smell!

CHAPTER 5

PONY IN A WELL

"**O**UR PONY HAS fallen into a well."

The speaker was almost hysterical.

She sobbed, "The fire brigade is here, but she is fighting and we need you, desperately, urgently, to sedate her."

"I am on my way." I put the phone down and dived for my shoes.

Theresa, sensing some drama unfolding, had snuggled up to me to hear the conversation and she said, "Please wait for me, I must come with you." It was a most unusual case and easy to guess Theresa would join me. A call summoned our neighbour June to baby-sit our already sleeping angels.

We needed supplies and raced for the hospital to pick up some Immobilon; it is a powerful tranquiliser that the law demanded we kept stored under lock and key. It is a dangerous drug and when it found its way into the wrong hands; let's leave that chilling thought for now!

Less than fifteen minutes later we entered the yard.

Steve Thompson was a general builder who operated from a smallholding four miles East of Drofter out on the Wheatley road. The clock was nearing the hour of seven and the light was slowly and gently beginning to fail, but still sufficient to clearly light up the scene that resembled something from a disaster movie. There were two big fire brigade machines whose flashing lights dominated the yard and my wife could hardly contain herself, "What a sight! I wonder if the BBC is here, wouldn't that be fun? I can imagine the headlines; HERO VET SAVES PONY and we might end up as film stars in a big movie." Excitement pushed my normally reserved wife over the top.

"This does look interesting." My own mind whirred, considering the challenges we were about to face as we went to greet the six smartly uniformed men who were obviously happy to see us arrive; they looked professional and ready for anything.

The superintendent introduced himself as Wilfred Dickson; a tall, slim and youngish fellow with a commanding attitude who quickly briefed us, "Thanks for coming we have an interesting scenario that demands your professional expertise."

The owner had returned from a quiet ride along the country lanes.

Chloe had dismounted at the gate to the rear yard, and had been walking her pony back to its stable when she heard a loud crack, accompanied by a tearing sound. It was the sudden, hard pull on the reins which dragged her round to face the scene and she saw a large, gaping hole appear in the concrete driveway. She was lucky to avoid being captured by it, but Apache; her pony, had not been so lucky and had disappeared before her eyes. Her desire to save her friend had caused her to remain holding onto the reins and that had produced a marked scald reaction on the gloveless palm of her left hand.

The girl had screamed, urgent cries for help that summoned the rest of the family. They were shocked, yes, but common sense prevailed and as unusual problems demand special attention they summoned the fire brigade. The lads were having a quiet evening and responded with delight to an interesting challenge.

Ted; one of their members, knew horses.

By talking quietly to the partially submerged and frightened pony, he had managed to place a thick, soft rope round her neck. That and her existing bridle gave them a measure of control, and then somehow they had encircled her chest and abdomen in a piece of thick webbing; a makeshift sling that was already attached by heavy ropes rigged to an impressive support system. From there it ran up to an overhead pulley that was suspended from a crane-like projection that extended from one of the engines.

That system was more than adequate to perform the task of lifting Apache out of the hole, but flesh and blood requires more than brute force and she struggled, and fought against them when they attempted to hoist her. The jagged edges of the concrete threatened to rip her skin to shreds and that initial attempt was abandoned.

Superintendent Dickson directed us to the scene.

As we neared the pit our anticipation mounted, and Theresa gasped when she saw the hole that measured about four yards by two yards. Only when I peered down the drop of about another yard into the hole did I understand the full extent of the problem. The skewbald pony was half lying on her side and my first glimpse caused me to whisper, "You poor creature, how are we ever going to get you out?"

Dickson must have read my thoughts, "We have an idea, although it will be challenging, difficult even," The superintendent looked earnestly at me, "We must get her out, and soon."

As I congratulated them on their excellent effort thus far, my mind raced with thoughts of how her rescue might be attempted, "Well done chaps, the water is deep and you have saved her life by preventing her from drowning; she could easily have been swept away under the concrete."

The owner took me aside and gave me some useful information on his daughter and her pony. Apache, so named from her distinctive colouring, was a mixed breed with a fine personality. The much loved; about fourteen hands tall pony was on the chunky side. He said, "Apache has been with the family for about eight years and she carried Chloe's sister before she took over," He paused and touched the sleeve of my jacket and I noticed how his heavily lined face was pale with anxiety, "If anything bad happens to Apache my daughters will take it badly, and we thank you for coming, please do your best."

I studied the small man carefully; he had a girth that almost matched his height and his massive cardigan caught my eye; it was in a heavy Aran knit type of wool knitted with a distinctive stitch and its unusual nature was added to by a single, large and odd coloured, button. It strained under the effort of holding the garment closed over his large naval, and made him look warm when everyone else sported the minimum of clothing. An old, torn cloth cap protected his almost bald head and his rosy cheeks could have been those of a Madame from the Follies. I had never met him before and had some difficulty understanding his soft West Country tongue.

I listened carefully then returned to the officers.

My conclusion was that any rescue attempt would prove fruitless if the animal continued to struggle, "The situation is difficult and my plan is dangerous, but I have no choice," Not since I had given a talk to Andrew's class at school did I have such an earnest audience, as to a man they ceased breathing, "I will have to inject her intravenously with Immobilon, the drug will tranquilise her deeply and that will give us the opportunity you need to hoist her out."

They all nodded and Dickson agreed, "That is what we thought, because when we tried to move her she panicked and kicked out badly, and looked as though serious injury might result from her being jarred against the concrete edges of the hole."

I nodded in agreement, "I agree and please join me; we must speak to the owners again."

I outlined my rescue plan as the family held their breath.

They were deeply shocked and I did my best to handle the matter professionally, and sympathetically, "I have no choice other than to heavily tranquillise Apache," I highlighted the procedure we would have to follow and described the possible complications, "I cannot rule out the likelihood she may already have severe limb or internal damage; she may have inhaled water which could easily set up pneumonia, and indeed the shock of the rescue itself may overwhelm her," I concluded by informing them that in my opinion we had no choice and any delay was likely to lead to greater difficulties, "In a case such as this I have to be governed by your formal opinion, will you give me permission to proceed, knowing the risks as I have outlined them for you?"

The owner; a very practical man, appreciated the difficulties, "I agree we have no choice and you must attempt to rescue her," He motioned me to walk with him to a spot some yards from everyone, "My daughter is a sensitive child and this pony is her world. I have never met you before, but there is something about you that gives me confidence," He turned, stood directly in front of me and looked me straight in the eyes, "I am sure you will do your best, yes, it is over to you now."

His hopes hit home hard and made me think; nothing like a bit of additional pressure to keep me on my toes.

"OK superintendent, as you have witnessed we have the owner's permission to proceed. Let's do this."

It was time for the rescue to begin.

It struck Theresa that one problem had not been sufficiently addressed, one intimately connected to the Niven family and she expressed her concern, "Alex what is the plan, how are you going to reach the pony?" She stood directly in front of me and continued, "Immobilon is a nasty, dangerous drug, how are you going to administer it to this, sad distressed creature?" Theresa knew that drug and felt we were in a desperate situation.

She followed me to the car and I chose that relatively private spot to explain my thinking, "Tess this is a real mess and I agree it is dangerous, but you know I have no choice," I put my arm around her shoulders, kissed her lightly on the forehead and said, "I need your complete support, and, I need you to be strong."

I gave Theresa a hug and was very serious, "You will have to handle the antidote for me, and, if there is a problem you must stab me with it."

CHAPTER 6

THE RESCUE

THE MADAM MUST have her say. My heart skipped beat after beat. In the first place Alex only calls me Tess when we are in trouble and, secondly, I knew the position he was in and well, much as I disliked the idea there was nothing to be said or done that would change his mind. It was a tense situation and I promised my support, "We do not have time to call for backup and the thought scares me to death, but, we have no choice."

The firemen prepared Alex for the rescue.

They attended to him in a manner that, while it oozed efficiency and professionalism, only heightened my anxiety as they fitted him into a harness, a cradle of thick belting that supported him around his chest and between his legs. I shook my head and asked God to protect him as a crane lifted him into the air for a few yards then lowered him back to earth. They practiced this a few times until everyone was confident the belt was secure, fitted snugly, and would not prevent the freedom of movement his arms needed.

The superintendent was satisfied, "That's it lads all is in order."

Then the reality of the rescue attempt became fact as the crane swung Alex up and then over the gap in the concrete and they began lowering him into the pit. He had previously removed most of his clothes, leaving him adorned in a pair of tight fitting shorts, and, in spite of my tension I thought;

thank the Lord I have at last got him to wear decent underwear, and, his bum looks good, his hard training schedule for marathon running is giving him tight buns.

Ted held the pony by a lead rope attached to her heavy head collar.

Alex had managed to reach in and replace her work bridle with a heavy head collar and Apache had surprised and encouraged him with the welcome she gave him. I could hear him talking quietly to her in that soothing, almost magical voice he somehow finds from deep down. I suspected he was the prime target, but there is no doubt that he has an uncanny ability to work with frightened animals.

There were about twenty people quietly engrossed in the scene; the inspector had warned us to keep quiet. I found a comforting arm linking mine as Chloe, noting my concern, and, with unspoken words felt we could comfort each other. I squeezed her arm and when I looked into her eyes the depth of her own distress was palpable, and our ancient sisterhood bonded us together. Something made me run my fingers through her long, gorgeous red hair and she when snuggled up to me I saw how her rather plain, round face was spoiled by a severe bout of juvenile acne that concentrated its effects on the left side of her mouth and cheek.

Alex quietly, almost gracefully, slipped into the hole that glowered at me; it was an intimidating space surrounded by jagged edges of naked concrete and I felt Chloe wince as my fingers dug into her arm.

The tension on Theresa's face made me wince.

The rescue plan had been easy to formulate and, as the final buckle of my harness tightened, a touch of nerves reached me and the enormity of the act made my pulse run, and, as I looked around at the faces of the anxious spectators their concern was obvious. At a distance of a few yards Theresa's big brown eyes held mine as she silently mouthed; please be careful and I imagined a rosary asking Our Lady to protect me was already underway.

Reality touched me as my feet hit the water and indicated it to be running with a strong current directed towards the pony. I drifted directly into her, and, as my legs contacted the solid wall of her chest, I continued talking, probably babbling on to her in a meaningless mumbo-jumbo, "There's a good little girl, my name is Alex. You mustn't worry about me. I am a friend who is here to help you." I deliberately avoided any of the direct eye contact that many horses consider a threat, and tried to make each statement short, soft and rhythmical.

The firemen heard every word of our conversation and Ted later told me my ramblings included me talking about cowboys, that John Wayne featured extensively, and that Apaches were famous Red Indians. At one point I explained to the pony there was no longer any fighting between Native Americans and the European soldiers and farmers who had colonised their land. He wished the conversation had been recorded; I didn't; people have been locked up in the funny farm for much less!

The first touch of a frightened animal is important.

Initial contact with an injured animal yields valuable information; it offers an insight into the animal's attitude to its predicament, and often suggests how it is likely to react to treatment. The news was good, as Apache, as with most frightened horses, appreciated firm body contact and I gave the signal to lower me deeper, and at the same time I used my left hand to give the mare's withers a positive scratch. It was my intention to further reassure her that I was a friend, a sympathetic partner in her distress. My chat to her went something along these lines, "There's a brave little Indian pony. I am sorry to find you in this mess. Let's hope we will soon have you in a nice warm stable." I continued scratching her on the neck and withers, an area that friendly horses scratch for each other to bring relaxation.

She was anchored by the heavy girdle supporting her, and the bulk of her body remained in one spot. I could feel the force of her hindquarters gently paddling in a constant, perhaps automatic, attempt at swimming. My left hand continued to caress her neck as I slipped the fingers of my other hand under the right side of her jaw to search for the large artery I used to estimate the strength of her pulse. Throughout my career I have used the pulse as my main indicator of the health of an animal's circulation; I was able to give her, and everyone else who could hear me, the good news, "That's great girly, your pulse is still normal."

"So little one, how much tranquiliser will you need?"

I took note of the owners' description of Apache and added that to my own visual inspection, and a direct palpation of her torso, to help me estimate her weight. I gave the prearranged hand signal for the man operating the winch to raise me slightly, to get me closer to the edge of the concrete to support my arms on the edge of the hole.

The mare surprised me by whinnying, as though she felt I was abandoning her, and I attempted to reassure her, "Not to worry. I am not leaving you. I must get you some medicine. See! I have stopped now." I placed my bare feet firmly against her chest, and used my toes to massage her. She turned her head and rubbed her nose against my thigh, and only then did I risk looking into her eyes. She made a soft noise, a gentle nicker through her nostrils.

"That's my girly, so you think I can help you." I felt her responding to our contact, it was reassuring her. I gave an ear a good pull by applying my thumb on the inside and my index finger on the outside and then drew them firmly from the base up to the tip. She liked that, and, as she continued to relax, I was given an unexpected bonus as her strong body helped stabilise my position.

How much of the tranquiliser did she need?

I had used the drug many times in the past and gave myself a silent talking to; Alex you must relax and be confident in your ability to do this properly. Stop pussy footing around and get on with the job.

My initial estimation suggested she would need three mls of Immobilon then a little voice inside my head urged caution and made me chat to her, "How much medicine do you need? You must be feeling weak and tired and I don't want you to flake out completely. Do you have any idea?" There was no reply, but she snuggled up to me convincing me she was enjoying our chats. "I think we should go for a little bit less, what do you think?"

Apache made another soft nasal noise and I gave her ear another pull, and said, "So you agree with me? That's it then, we will go for two and three quarter mls." There was a risk that under dosing would cause her to struggle, but my gut feeling suggested I was right to reduce the dose, in view of her shocked condition.

Theresa brought me the drugs and she whispered, "Please be careful, I am not enjoying this."

I almost agreed with her, but controlled myself and said, "Not to worry my dear, we are going well thus far." I loaded the drugs into syringes; my arms supporting me on a thick piece of webbing that had been placed as a protective cushion around the jagged rim of the hole. Theresa passed me the tray on which the small green box containing the drugs, needles and syringes lay. I deliberately avoided any eye contact with her, afraid the emotions gripping her would cause me to lose focus. Although the upper part of my torso was sticking out of the hole, my feet constantly massaged Apache and I had to put out of my mind the fact that while I was cold all over my lower limbs were getting very and dangerously cold.

The smart green box flipped open.

The twin bottles of Immobilon and its antidote Revivon almost smiled at me as I carefully, oh so carefully, filled two small, clear five ml plastic syringes to the two and three quarter ml mark with the drugs. The Immobilon syringe was fitted with a yellow, eighteen gauge needle one and a half inches in length and the Revivon syringe was tipped with a tiny needle more appropriate for vaccinating dogs. There was a good reason for the dissimilarity in needles; in the event that an accident occurred which resulted in me inadvertently injecting myself, or even scratching my skin with the dangerous Immobilon, the small needle would be perfect for injecting a few drops of the antidote into my naked arm.

The tranquiliser is colloquially called *elephant juice* as it is more suited to the immobilisation of large wild animals. Its' dangerous effects on humans; where as little as a tenth of one ml can prove fatal, necessitated great care when handling it. The superintendent had been fully advised of the situation and had agreed that if Theresa had any problems he would inject me, and wasn't that a cheerful way to begin the rescue?

The syringes were soon filled.

I gave a hand signal for the firemen to lower me into the darkening well and Apache was encouraged by my re-joining her; we had begun building a bond, a strong one she always remembered and I greeted her, "Now then my china! Are you pleased to see me again? I told you I would be back."

She rubbed her head against my leg, and repeated that happy nasal whicker.

"That's it friend, I told you I was coming back," My fingers explored the ventral part of her neck as I searched for a vein, "That's it girly, I am searching for your jugular vein."

"Now then Apache I did not expect that! You have given me a bit of a problem." In the place where a strong flow of venous blood would normally have been palpable, there was a ridge of scar tissue stretching upwards towards the angle of the jaw and I was later advised this had been caused by a badly placed injection. I outlined my findings to Apache, loudly, in order the others would hear me and said, "The vein on this side is damaged. I hope I can reach some healthy circulation below it or, I might have to change my approach."

My fingers slipped further downwards, continuing to probe for healthy tissue. At the point where her neck met the water the lower part of her vein bulged with blood and it made me ponder; it is there, but this is becoming more and more difficult. I did not think it would be feasible for me to inject her so low down on her neck and thought for a few seconds about the possibility of injecting Apache intramuscularly. The drug does work when administered in that fashion, but is associated with an initial bout of excitement that can prove dangerous.

I issued a constant stream of fact and gibberish.

I had to explain the problem to the fascinated workers above me, "I am sorry Apache, but we have an unexpected difficulty. The vein on this side has been previously damaged. You will have to be calm when the nice men lift you, *on my command*, about six inches higher."

I gave her ear another firm pull and said, "We are going to lift you *now*!"

Gently, expertly, the fireman on the hoist attempted to do that and caused Apache to struggle, and part of her front right leg came clear of the water. That sudden movement caused her knee joint to catch me a blow on the arm, an unexpected jolt that upset my balance and caused the loaded syringe to jab dangerously towards my shoulder. Someone above me gasped, no prizes for guessing who.

The flashing needle was a weapon that could easily kill me and the dark contents of the syringe imprinted themselves vividly on my mind as my reflexes made me twist away to safety as the needle missed my arm, but, as the scene lurched back and forward, my acrobatic juggling almost caused me to drop the loaded syringe as my fingers were so cold my reactions were slowing down.

Theresa later told me how her heart almost stopped when the pony's struggles caused that problem although our positioning inside the hole had obscured from her the fact I had almost injected myself; had she seen that!

As my racing heart began to slow I reappraised the situation.

We were in luck as we had gained an important fraction and Apache had settled into a better position with the healthy part of her vein about an inch above the water. By some miracle of Divine intervention my cold hands were steady; they had to be, as my left thumb pressed firmly against the vein underneath the water. It was below my selected injection site and the angles were all wrong and I continued talking, "Good girly we are nearly ready. And now I need our friends to *drop me* about six inches deeper into the water." The crane operator was on automatic and in harmony with me by then and followed my instructions perfectly.

Apache relaxed, "Now little girl, that did not seem to worry you. This is looking better and we might manage to do the job this time." My armpits shivered to the touch of the cold stream and caused me to suddenly think of winter; imagine this was February? The reflex paddling of her hind limbs was now more obvious.

The vein distended nicely.

My persistent touch had the desired effect and, as my right hand brought the needle directly onto the skin over her neck I informed her of what was to come, "Ok little girl. Here we go and please do not move, it will only be a little prick."

The amazingly sharp metal slipped into the vein and although the mare hardly reacted, part of her neck, including the syringe and its attached needle, slipped under the water and I said, "You are an excellent patient, although you have made things difficult, I wonder what I should do next?"

It was impossible for me to operate my normal injection technique, which involved drawing back on the plunger of the syringe. When the needle is safely inside the vein any retraction on the plunger of the syringe allows the vet to check for the back flow of blood that indicates a bull's-eye. I could no longer see the business end of the syringe and the correct thing would have been to begin another attempt. That would have required us lifting her in order I might clearly see the needle and syringe and I was worried about taking such a risk.

I juggled the underwater syringe and it felt right.

There was none of the stickiness that may be felt when the needle is in the wall of the vein or in the subcutaneous tissue so I decided to proceed and tried to keep my voice calm, "I have no choice girly, so here goes."

I depressed the plunger of the syringe and was relieved to feel the liquid empty easily into her bloodstream. I withdrew the needle from the vein, and threw the empty syringe upwards and behind me and issued an instruction, "OK Tess, here it comes." I was confident that Theresa with her gloved hands knew exactly how to deal with its still highly dangerous contents as the remaining drops of bloody drug could easily kill a human. The fingers of my left hand slipped over the injection site and I pressed it firmly in an effort to stop the vein bleeding.

It was time for a serious talk to the patient creature, "Apache you are a brilliant patient. You hardly murmured when that big needle slipped into your vein. Are you feeling dizzy yet? It will only be a few seconds before the anaesthetic begins to work and then you will feel woozy and comfortable." I continued on in that manner while awaiting the first signs of the drug taking effect.

I waited patiently.

I continued to stroke her body and talk to her and prayed silently the injection had been a true one, then spoke aloud for the benefit of the firemen, "This is the bit I do not like. I am watching you very carefully and the next few seconds may seem to take a long time."

I was sure she was listening to me, as there was a soft, reassuring snuffle then her lips flashed at me. Forty seconds later the mare's attitude changed and I called out, "Yes! Magic! I have hit the target, get ready chaps."

Apache's paddling became stronger and all four legs began trotting as the drug began to take effect. Ted maintained his hold on her head rope and never took his eyes off me and I called to him, "Try to manoeuvre her head away from me, it is very heavy and her nose is threatening to drag me under."

It was time to escape and I primed the team, "That's it guys, nearly ready." Ten seconds later I gave them the hand signal and the winch had me up and out of the hole very quickly.

It felt good to be on dry land again and I took a quick gulp of some warm sweet tea that someone thrust at me and then jumped up and down to get my circulation going as someone else threw a heavy red towel over my shoulders.

• Seconds later the tranquilisation process was complete and clearly visible. When Apache's whole body slumped into the sling that was my cue to complete the rescue, "Right, it's time! Let's get her out of here."

They hoisted her out of the hole and she flew through the air as Pegasus, the flying horse. She rose from the dark hole that could easily have been her watery grave and her slumped body sailed through the air, with her long legs dangling, and her neck not far behind them.

She was swung round and onto the lawn.

Theresa continues.

It was amazing. Alex's arm described a backward arc and the empty syringe was tossed in my direction onto the concrete where I, wearing a pair of thick plastic gloves collected it carefully, and walked to the nearby water bucket. I had been well drilled on how to process the waste, but I confess the tension of the situation made me tremble. I immersed the entire syringe and attached needle under the water, and I pulled back on the plunger and the syringe filled with water and was then directed into a flower border. As I depressed the plunger it emptied with a long, noisy scoosh.

As the syringe was being flushed for the third time I was so happy to see Alex emerging from the hole and, as any danger of contamination from the Immobilon was now unlikely, I dropped the syringe into the bucket and was caught up in the drama and watched with fascination when a sudden, loud and very clear instruction from Alex instructed the pony be lifted clear.

There was almost complete silence from all of the others as the powerfully tranquilised pony appeared to us to be dead; she was suspended awkwardly from the sling with her heavy head dragging her long neck earthward and Chloe called out, "Oh no my friend is dead."

I almost agreed, then a closer look revealed her to be breathing and she began trembling vigorously, "Look Chloe, look at her chest moving, she is alive."

Apache rose through the air and was swung through space for about ten yards until landing at our feet.

Vet and firemen were by her side.

We stripped her of leather and ropes and I said, "OK chaps I will bring her round, please stand back." I took up the syringe containing the Revivon, and removed the small just-in-case needle, and dropped it into the bucket containing the other syringe and advised my nurse, "Tess, please continue to keep an eye on that bucket." I fitted another of the big yellow needles to the syringe.

The mare was lying on her right side and I knelt on the ground beside, and behind her neck and when I touched her she trembled vigorously and flexed her neck. She continued paddling with her front legs and my voice became louder, "I am so sorry little girl, but with a bit of luck this will soon be over."

Her muscles were under such tension that injecting her was impossible without help and Theresa later remarked how my plea had a marked note of tiredness in it as I said, "Please Ted, take hold of the head collar, stretch her neck out for me."

Ted knelt beside me and only then did I notice the enormous strength in his short, hairless arms that ended in fingers that were each almost as thick as my weak wrists. His left hand embraced the leather of the head collar while his right cupped her muzzle and that afforded him the good grip required to straighten her heavy neck, "How's that vet? Can you see where to inject her?"

Theresa tells it better.

I had remained strong up to that point, but the situation was getting to me and soft tears streamed down my cheeks. The pony's owner recognised my distress, and once again comforted me when she snuggled up to me and linked her arm through mine. I pulled myself together and focused on the scene and was just in time to see Alex place the large needle into the blood vessel and I saw the dark blood flow back into the syringe and then he steadily injected the Revivon.

As he stood up I could see how the effort was getting to him, he had that rather stiff, almost clumsy action he gets when his back muscles are in spasm. A few steps took him over to the water bucket where, much faster than I had done, he also cleaned out that syringe and gave the earlier ones a final flush.

I could not resist sneaking to his side and wrapped my arms around him, "Well done my love, you have done your best."

He almost sunk into my embrace, but steadily gazed at the little wet body lying on the lawn, "It has gone well, better than I had hoped for and please God let us be successful?"

Apache's struggling increased markedly, then stopped completely.

When someone cried out, "Has she died?" Alex shook himself free from my grip and re-joined the mare. My hand went to my mouth, although the anxious gasp was from Chloe who also thought she had died.

Apache began moving again, and this time it was my turn to wince, as Chloe; her face a deathly pale colour, used her nails to return my earlier effort. I felt sorry for the girl who had been at my side throughout the entire process as a silent, hardly breathing partner.

The mare paddled faster and faster and struggled in a manner reminiscent of a sleeping dog chasing rabbits. I had to keep her down until the antidote worked, so I sat on her neck for about twenty seconds. The force generated by her recovery soon became too strong for me to hold my position and, as I slipped from her neck she attempted to rise, and fell again. From behind I heard a marked gasp from someone in the crowd, the only evidence that the stunned audience were still alive.

Apache rested for another ten seconds.

"Now then girly we are almost ready. I think you are looking good and you will get up at the next attempt," As she tried to rise I pulled her head forward and shouted at her, "Now then little girl this is your chance." She grunted heavily, rose to her feet and took a few staggering steps forward.

She raised her head and whinnied loudly and that broke the spell and was a dramatic finale that brought relief from the tense drama embracing all of us. The crowd spontaneously burst into cheering, handclapping, and lots of other noises; people were hugging each other.

The pony was shaken, but walked round the lawn and gave out a loud whinny and I called for Chloe, "Come now little mother, I need you to come and talk to Apache."

The pony recognised her immediately and greeted her by rubbing her very wet nose up and down Chloe's clothes and her attention was so rough the girl stumbled and almost fell over. She laughed, "Apache that was a bit rough, are you so pleased to see me again?"

As if on cue the mare gave another loud whinny.

Someone had organised dry cloths and towels and soon three pairs of hands were rubbing the pony dry, much to her obvious enjoyment.

When confident I could leave the scene I popped into the house.

I had a quick, very hot shower then donned the emergency trousers; commando-style, I always kept in the car, and my original shirt, socks and shoes. On my return the happy throng were enjoying liberal quantities of tea and Apache was dry and looked amazing, "So girly we made it."

She rubbed her face against my chest and snickered at me and I asked, "So, do you still recognise me?"

She gave her most powerful whinny yet and almost knocked me over with the force of the hug she tried to give me, horses do not really have the right anatomy for Alpha-type group hugs.

"Well done Alex, thank you so much for saving my friend." The hugs and kisses I got from Chloe conveyed the same message of thanks I received from Apache and they were more comfortable.

I began to revive after the large whisky, that appeared as if by magic, slipped down. I gave Apache a final examination and an encouraging bill of health whereupon she nipped my arm, her very personal way of saying thanks.

We took our leave of the happy scene.

Owners and fire brigade warmly congratulated me on my professionalism and dedication and I was in danger of a marked degree of head swelling until Theresa brought me back to reality, "So you think you are the cat's pyjamas?" She decided to drive me home, to rescue me from my band of adoring admirers.

I was proud of my husband.

He was already sleeping beside me well before we reached home. Although the dangers of the job, the long hours and the efforts required were considerable, there was no doubt the man fitted into that environment. If life could be difficult at least it was never boring.

My follow-up examination revealed Apache to be very well. She had some muscle soreness that returned to normal, until within a week she and Chloe were again exercising.

That was our second experience with the fire brigade.

It was one of the best, not the last.

CHAPTER 7

STUDENT LABOUR

I SUPPOSE I always wanted to be a vet. My much interrupted schooling posed problems.

Various situations happened at critical times and acted against me, and everyone except my mum, tried to convince me the exacting qualifications required were beyond me. Only she was able to stand up to the headmaster of our school at that time who; even after my name was on the honours board, still refused to acknowledge me.

There was a period in my later schooldays when the possibility of a vocation to the priesthood was of some attraction and I remember a fascinating interview with the great Fr Magauran who was the Parish Priest of St Michaels at the time. The great man patiently listened to me and I will never forget his advice, "A grand idea Alex and I think when you have lived your life in the real world you must come back and have another chat to me."

Animals proved to be the greater calling, although it is interesting that with maturity, ordination to the Permanent Deaconate called; the good Lord always knows what is best for us; we do not always listen.

I spent most of my schooldays dreaming of a career with animals.

My hopes became obsessive and the more people told me I was not clever enough for veterinary science, the more I developed a rigid and determined effort at study. I was never brilliant, but made up for it by working hard and eventually my efforts did earn a place at veterinary school. In those days the interviewers were keenly influenced by the likelihood a man had the necessary bedside manner to make a good vet; which is unlike the modern situation when academic performance is everything.

I did get the nod and will never forget the feeling of elation that followed the opening of the envelope holding my letter of acceptance to Glasgow University. I was at that time closely linked to the Navy when the summer holiday, which marked the end of my schooling, found me working as a labourer on the site of the Faslane Naval base. My dad; rightly suspecting the importance of the letter brought it out to me, "I know you have been waiting for this letter and I was coming this way anyway and, that's rubbish, your mum said she could not wait until tonight to know what it says."

The fact it was of a healthy size and clearly stamped with the University's seal suggested its contents were of a positive nature, as rejection slips are delivered in simple format. I remember saying, "Well here we go." I confess my hands were seriously shaking as the great missif was ripped to reveal its contents. The splendid news of my being offered a place at vet school ensured the evening was marked by a serious celebration.

Family finances were always weak.

Thus the holiday seasons for most of us were never in actual fact as they were intended to be, and all of my holidays from school and university from the tender age of thirteen were spent working as a labourer on building sites and for the Post Office.

The PO always used students during the hectic Christmas period.

I probably did a total of about twelve weeks with them and one embarrassing time found me taking telegrams out to the Burroughs Factory on a bicycle. There was something seriously wrong with the gearing on the bike and although I eventually delivered the telegram I could ride the bike no further and collapsed in a heap by the side of the road, whereupon a friendly and very kind lorry driver stopped, flung my bike onto his lorry and said, "Looks like you have had enough for today, I will drop you outside the depot." Phew! On my return the supervisor looked at me, frowned and said, "That is amazing. I don't know where you found that bike, but it should have been sent for overhaul ages ago. You must be a real athlete to have used the thing."

My reply was along the lines of, "Well I need the job and did my best."

"Great and again well done son, now come with me and we will fix you up with another machine."

"Well thanks but no thanks. I don't need the job that badly so can I please go on the rounds with a bag?"

There were also big problem with the foot patrols.

The adverse weather was often a factor and particularly memorable was one morning up at the top of Westcliff when the most disgusting high wind imaginable made standing even difficult. My round that should have taken me three hours only lasted thirty minutes when the wind dragged my bag up and away over the fence. When I attempted to catch it I found the bag trapped against the steel fence while its contents went blowing down towards the Clyde and on to Port Glasgow. I was devastated and when I reported it the supervisor said, "Yip. That does happen a few times every year, here is your next run." As I turned to leave he said, "And watch the dogs on that run, some of them are fierce."

I thought he was joking and after all I was a vet student, dogs were no problem for me. My route took me up Castlehill and it went like a dream; the weather was reasonable, the load was light and I made a few bob in tips. Until I got right up to the top and found the wolf pack; there were four of them and they were deliberately and knowingly lying in wait for the next postie, who happened to be me. They were a motley mixed size crew of mongrels and I said, "Good morning gentlemen I suppose your sense of smell is so good you appreciate that I am actually a student vet and not a real postie. So if you don't mind I will just pop up this close and get on with my business."

Although I ran fast one of them did tear my trousers although I think fear caused me to actually make more of a mess of them than the dog did. As I ran into the close one old lady happened to open her door and I pushed her back inside and slammed the door hard behind me right in their snarling faces.

I was shattered and also nervous that I might have frightened the elderly lady who shook her head at me and said, "Hang on son." She picked up a brush and dived back into the fray whereupon there was a huge scream from her and a painful squeal and within twenty seconds she came back in again, smiled and said, "Those bloody dogs and that's enough of that, but you'll be needing a cup of tea after that won't you."

The job at Faslane was a fascinating one.

It was there I developed expertise with the jack-hammer; a heavy duty drill that I used in the demolition of the old reinforced concrete jetties. The intensity of the hideous noise permanently affected my hearing; there was no suggestion of ear muffs being necessary in those days for mere, expendable labourers. Is it any wonder that the constant abuse of the shipyard worker encouraged that interest in socialism and even communism that earned the area its name of Red Clydeside?

One scary incident is worth repeating; it was a close shave that taught me and the other group of working students to be careful, particularly when around heavy machinery.

One of the other student labourers got it wrong; he could not resist the opportunity to test drive a dumper truck that had been parked close by. OK! I suppose we encouraged him and eventually he eagerly mounted the steed and found the command that made it go forward.

We cheered him on, "That's it Henry, go! You have mastered the beast." We were having a nice bit of fun until the humour of the situation changed and we became anxious. He panicked properly as the edge of the jetty loomed closer and we; the other student workers, gasped as the danger of the situation became startlingly apparent. Henry appeared to freeze in the seat and sat there immobile in a manner that made us think he might go over the edge of the jetty with the machine and even our massed alarm calls failed to drag him back from that state of dangerous, suspended immobility.

Brian ran alongside him and screamed into his ear, "Get off now Henry or you will be drowned." Only then he was able to rouse himself and he jumped off the life-like creature which went gently chugging along and we watched in fascination as it plodded up to the edge then plunged spectacularly, eagerly, into sixty feet of the dark blue sea water of the bay.

Henry ran off and we never saw him again, and he never even dared to contact the office for his back pay! To say the general foreman nearly had a heart attack would be a serious misstatement; even my mum never got that cross!

The machine was recovered two days later and I was lucky enough to be a minor part of the rescue mission. It was only a success due to the skill of two navy divers, who were able to secure it with some heavy chains, but it was the groaning noises that issued from those chains during the lifting process that illustrated how difficult the rescue was; the noise was quite human-like and it sounded as though they were complaining under the pressure of the pull exerted by the big powerful crane as it winched the dumper to safety.

I joined the hotel industry for a short time.

One Easter found me working on the restoration of the Grosvenor hotel in Glasgow; a project occasioned by its being severely damaged by fire. I spent days on end bashing down old ceilings; in former days eight inches of soot had been incorporated into those ceilings in an effort to reduce noise pollution and the very messy dust, when released from the site of its long imprisonment, poured directly on top of the workers. They always kept the best jobs for the students, but the money was good. It was amusing when much later in life the happy marriage of Alexis and Mark allowed us to revisit the site and to find it much cleaner that it had been in my time!

Sometimes it was easy to get myself into a hole.

At the age of fifteen I spent four weeks digging holes on a building site with a number of regular labourers. We were under the supervision of a tough general foreman who thought the company was not getting their pound of flesh out of skinny little me. That was hard, back breaking work, which found me sleeping solidly at night.

It was only at the end as he presented me with my final pay packet he realised his mistake as that final pay envelope was a transparent one to allow the foreman to verify its contents. The pay slip revealed that my salary of three shillings, ten pence and one farthing per hour was only one third of that of a regular labourer's salary. The usually tough and distant foreman softened his attitude, "Sorry laddie, If I had known that's all you were earning I would have given you a soft job, I would have used you as a tea boy and for carrying messages". That would have been nice.

October 1966; seems a million years ago and at last the day came when I enrolled for a five year course of study at Glasgow University. The work was hard but by the grace of God and a lot of hard effort I survived the experience.

CHAPTER 8

THE CALF AND THE FARMER

CATTLE ARE AMONG my favourite animals and my dad enjoyed telling a story about my earliest animal adventure.

My interest in animals is a genetic thing so it was inevitable his attraction for animals would be handed on. I have only a faint memory of it as I was three years of age at the time although it is one that because of its frequent retelling almost became urban legend.

Dumbarton had a farmer's market.

It was held on Tuesdays somewhere along College Street, and was a place my father and many others found fascinating. The reader must be aware that life was very different in the 1950's, a time well before technology appeared. Most small towns had a market that was an integral part of the fabric of society for the life it brought to the town and there was always a large turnout of spectators; something that rarely happens today.

Once upon a time, (I've always wanted to begin a story like that.) I was sitting proudly atop father's shoulder at the market and, even allowing for my dad being on the short side, I had a clear view of an unpleasant accident which occurred in front of us.

Small animals including sheep and calves were usually delivered to the market on the back of tractor driven trailers; this was a time before society considered animal welfare to be of great importance, and they were not always as well cared for as they might have been. One calf that was being delivered for sale fell from the cart transporting it, and, as the creature slipped from the trailer, one of its hind legs was trapped between the tailgate and one of the tractor's wheels.

It happened directly in front of us and I heard Father call out, "Look Alex the poor calf is in trouble."

His call was taken up by the many other interested spectators who witnessed the accident. There was a few moments of excitement and frantic activity until the calf was released. As the crowd settled down it was obvious the animal was severely injured as it could not rise from the ground.

I was very close and even at that tender age I wrapped myself up in its misery and was caught by its beautiful eyes that were full of sadness and pain and called out, pleading for help. Many calls offering advice rang out from the well-meaning public; a wave of concern that was broken by the powerful roar of the farmer whose attitude was a tad different to that of most of us, "This f***ing calf is useless, it has broken its f***ing leg."

The crowd backed away from the large, scary farmer who callously flung the poor beast back onto the trailer and went about his business.

It was suppertime that same evening.

The day's news was being discussed and Granda Kelly brought up the subject, "Tell me Alex did you have a good day at the market? Did you see lots of lovely cows?"

I shocked everyone when I repeated, word for word, the farmers distress call, "This f***ing calf is useless, it has broken its f***ing leg." I did this complete with an expert rendition of the swearing and that was surprising in another respect as my early attempts at talking were on the slow side, yet, in that instance, my speech was perfect.

My poor mother nearly had another cadenza!

My Uncle Gerry's attitude was quite different.

He took a different approach to my rough tongue and thought it hysterical and could not resist asking me the same question.

I gave the same answer, "This f***ing calf is useless, it has broken its f***ing leg."

That brought the house down and I became a star turn. As the rest of the family and any friends arrived I was asked to repeat my performance. It soon turned into a much repeated party act and I became a regular exhibit by being swung into the air by the plus six foot Gerry and then placed on a table where the visitors had a clear view of me.

The question was always the same one, "What did the farmer say when the calf broke its leg?"

It was only after half of the town had heard my youthful rendition of the farmer's cries that mum was able to bring the event to a close.

CHAPTER 9

DUCHESS

"ALEX WE HAVE a problem with one of the cats."

Eleanor's pretty face held that look, the one that always got my attention.

"I am worried about one of the cats we spayed this morning, can you examine her?"

It was nearing three in the afternoon and Eleanor's timing was perfect as my first appointment was still fifteen minutes away, although her expression alarmed me, "I don't like that look on your face."

She smiled at me, a weak, small smile, but one that gave me hope I was not about to court disaster. She tugged at her straggly brown hair as though re-enacting the daily morning battle she had controlling it, and said, "This is a funny one," She turned away from me and strode purposefully out of the office.

I reflected on the morning's work; I think I neutered about nine cats and three bitches and then there was a bitch that I did a complicated mammary tumour removal on. That surgical list had been pretty much a routine one for a Tuesday and nothing special had happened, that I could remember.

Eleanor's face always mirrored her emotions.

My attention drifted again to a wisp of her almost curly hair energetically attempting to make its escape from the thick rubber band entrapping its colleagues, but it was her powerful eyes, partly hidden under her very attractive dark eyebrows that caught me, and easily showed her concern and I said, "OK, let's have a look, what is the problem?"

Her tongue had free reign, "It's the Siamese female, her surgery and recovery were straightforward, but there is a definite problem, it looks as though the anaesthetic has affected her eyesight."

We entered the cattery.

The usual reassuring calls greeted us, and offered me some relief from the nurse's monologue. It was always a noisy place when invaded by human activity, as the patients called out for attention, and vied with each other for notice. As one would expect the only Siamese present was the most vocal. Duchess; a gorgeous seal point of about eight months of age was our most striking patient. Her beauty was absolute and would have been sufficient for most cats, yet there was something else about her that made her special; she exuded that degree of superiority typical of her breed, that something special that ensured she was a real queen. In spite of being in unfamiliar surroundings with its many strange, and perhaps threatening smells, her need for company, and desire to be with people had made her this morning's favourite.

Eleanor was a brilliant nurse and also a great cat lover and she had brought Duchess through early as the first patient, more I suspected to enjoy playing with her, rather than a need for us to rush into the mornings work. My focus had been on scrubbing up for the actual surgery.

The pre-anaesthetic checks and anaesthesia had been performed by Craig. When lots of cats were in for minor ops we had developed an efficient, production line system which, by using two vets, streamlined the process.

"I cannot remember anything unusual either."

My mind whirred away in the background, but could not bring to my attention anything untoward, "No! I cannot think of anything that might be responsible for a post anaesthetic problem."

Duchess was meowing fiercely, emitting the constant, high pitched calling which is typical of her breed as she moved to and fro vigorously along the front of the large cage, and arched her spine and carried her strong and very flexible tail straight up over her back.

"Now then Duchess, you look well to me. When you carry your tail up so high it makes me think of a television aerial."

Eleanor nodded in agreement, but still did not smile, and that heightened my senses and forced me to concentrate and I turned my attention back to the cat, "Well my pretty one, you do seem to have forgotten about your little op very quickly." My voice encouraged her and she began marking strongly against the steel wire of her cage, by rubbing it vigorously with the glands on her face. It was as though she felt if she had to be incarcerated, her hospital bed might as well be personalised and everything about her manner suggested the normal feline activity expected from a prime example of her species.

"She looks fine to me, but . . ."

Eleanor interrupted me, nothing unusual there, "I thought you would say that, but I am not happy with her."

"What I was about to say, before you jumped at me, was that you are usually right," I tried to reassure her by saying, "I do appreciate your help and I rely on your support. You never miss anything so . . . Yes! Bring her into the consulting room and I will examine her."

Eleanor was a bonny lass, a true star, and my working relationship with her had been a catalogue of success over the previous six years. Her strong, open Yorkshire personality, had allowed her to fit easily in with our hard working philosophy; Yorkshire people are honorary Scots anyway! If Eleanor thought there was a problem her opinion had to be taken seriously. Our attitude to medicine was governed by an unspoken principle that declared us all part of the same team and we worked together in an atmosphere of respect that contributed to a harmonious environment. We had no time for Prima Donnas, excepting such fascinating characters as Duchess of course!

I saw the problem immediately.

As Duchess was placed on the table the cause for Eleanor's summons was clear. Duchess had a very obvious problem as she was cross-eyed, and not just slightly so, she was a World Champion in that regard. Her eyes pointed in such a wayward direction her vision had to be severely affected and I blurted out, "Goodness me, now I see what you are worried about, I have never seen one as bad as that before, she can probably see round corners."

"The problem is that she was not like that before surgery. I have asked Craig and Patricia if they had noticed anything and they both say no."

"That's right, they worked with me this morning, and you say they never noticed anything?"

"Craig did the pre-clinical check and he could never have checked out her mucous membranes and missed this."

"That is strange, I wonder what is wrong?"

"That is why I called you. You are the vet, and had better come up with some answers, I will fetch an ophthalmoscope?" Her hands were on her hips.

"Yes, that's a good place to start."

I examined her in detail.

My normal technique for a detailed neurological examination swung into gear and it progressed well and failed to reveal any abnormalities, other than the amazingly severe crossed-eyes. There was no obvious evidence of the other problems, including balance defects or the delayed recovery we occasionally found following an anaesthetic. It was only the weird anatomical positioning of the globes of her eyes that were out of the ordinary; they were set obviously out of character in that striking face. Her vision, although mechanically impaired by the unusual placement of those eyeballs, appeared normal.

The retinae; often described as being windows to the brain, when examined by the ophthalmoscope demonstrated a wonderfully clear picture of various colours inlaid with the normal pattern of blood vessels. The tapetum, an especially bright area packed full of receptor nerve cells that give felines their special aptitude for seeing in the dark, was a shining picture of health.

I scratched her ears and said, "What beautiful retinae you have my little one, they look perfectly healthy to me." The pale blue irises responded normally to light, by contracting when a torch was shone directly onto them, and, soon dilated again when the light source was removed. "This puzzles me, she is absolutely perfect except for those eyes." I chewed the inside of my cheeks; a dead give-away I was unsure and puzzled, and my mind searched its data base for related information, and, finding no answers I sought a second opinion.

Craig was working in the adjoining consulting room.

He had already begun the afternoon's appointments and I waited for a few moments until he finished with a basketful of puppies. The routine health check for the little ones is an important time in their lives. He completed their first inoculations; the first of the routine vaccinations against distemper, hepatitis and leptospirosis. It would only be a few months down the line that parvovirus would change our modus operandi in such a dramatic and aggressive fashion.

When he joined me I brought him up to speed on the problem, "That Siamese from this morning, Eleanor tells me her eyes were normal before the op, are you totally sure you detected nothing unusual about her eyes when you carried out the health check?"

His answer being confidently in the negative only heightened my worries. Our routine health check included an inspection of the vital signs in an effort to reveal any latent or unknown problems that might increase the risk of anaesthetic reactions. Our normal procedure involved taking the temperature, listening to the chest with a stethoscope and palpating the pulse and we also checked the colour and moistness of the mucous membranes of the eyes and mouth.

"Obviously I remember her, she is such a striking individual and I could not have missed such a pair of eyes." Shaking his head vigorously he stepped away from her for a moment, "Sorry Alex I have no idea what is going on here." He was already en route to regain his position in the consulting room.

Craig's opinion confirmed mine.

I shook my head at Eleanor, "Well! This is an odd problem and I better pass on the news." There was nothing for it as my duty as a partner indicated it was my responsibility to convey any difficulties directly to the owners and I said, "Well Eleanor, I do not know what is going on here. Please get me the owner on the phone I better give them the bad news before they arrive to collect her."

Cat spays were usually discharged in the late afternoon of the same day they had been operated on. On the odd occasion where surgery had presented us with a problem we preferred to hospitalise the animals until I felt comfortable to release them.

"We seem to have a slight problem." My explanation to the owner who was unknown to me, was simply that Duchess had not reacted well to the anaesthetic, "So if you do not mind I would prefer to keep her hospitalised in order to monitor the situation," I tried to make my approach a sympathetic and confident one, and in the absence of any other clinical abnormalities, I was convinced there was no cause for alarm, "It is a routine plan . . ."

The interruption from the cat's concerned mother was expressed with not just a little anxiety, "Is she going to die?"

That outburst threw me for a moment then I blurted out, "No! She is not going to die," I continued with a description of the effects of anaesthesia, "We use a modern anaesthetic called Saffan which is extremely safe, and very rarely associated with side effects," I tried to sound calm and confident, "Duchess is not yet one hundred per cent and I would feel more comfortable if she remained with us and we continued to monitor her condition."

Joan Briggs the owner was soon at ease and relatively easy to deal with. She gave me the impression she was not the normal Siamese cat owner who would have been hysterical by that stage and informed me it would be possible for her to collect Duchess the following morning, and, unless advised by us to the contrary, she would visit the hospital at nine am.

The afternoon and evening drifted on.

Duties passed without anything of note happening and my schedule was the normal heavy one that kept me fully occupied.

Craig rang the manufacturers of the anaesthetic in an effort to glean any relevant information, and he later informed me this problem had not been previously reported, "Their vet was fascinated and said he would like to be fully informed of any developments."

Duchess enjoyed a small meal and was regularly examined. All of our five man vet squad inspected her and the girls enjoyed playing with her and, apart from the markedly crossed-eyes she appeared normal and this was confirmed by her extraordinary range of vocal repertoire. Many people feel there are cats, and then there are Siamese; they can be very vocal; the calling female is said to be able to waken the dead, and their general attitude to life certainly suggests them to be quite special, and makes them popular. It was only with the introduction of the Maine Coon variety many years later I found another cat that was more interesting; they are big generous creatures with a beautiful long coat, and the most extraordinary face. Their stunning looks, coupled with an almost dog like attitude to life, make them easily my favourite breed.

The following morning hospital rounds confirmed the status quo.

Duchess appeared completely normal and further head scratching about the possible explanation for her condition failed to reveal an obvious explanation and I decided she should be discharged from hospital, and, prepared myself to be confronted by her owner, "We have no choice other than to discharge her to Mrs Briggs, although, I dread how she is going to react when she sees what we have done to this special creature."

Eleanor's face again took on that sad look, then, after a sudden thought, she said, "Well if she talks about getting rid of her I will take her home with me."

"Let's cross that bridge if we come to it, surely she would not even think about such a possibility . . . would she?"

"There is no accounting for people! What about that man last month who wanted us to euthanase his Black Labrador puppy because it had a white chest? What about his attitude?"

"Please relax girl, slow down a bit, I am sure we won't get to that."

Eleanor carried on with her duties and her observation left me with food for thought.

The appointed hour arrived.

Duchess and owner were reunited in my consulting room and their meeting was immersed in tenderness, "There you are my beautiful girl, are you pleased to see me, did you think I had run away and left you?" That question was hardly required as Duchess was very excited at their reunion and made so much noise the neighbours must have thought the fire brigade were coming.

As they fussed with each other I was happy to stand back and enjoy the happy scene. When the lady was able to extricate herself from the overjoyed

Duchess she looked at me and said, "Mr Vet she looks so well to me so what was all the fuss about?"

"I agree she does look well. She is a stunning creature and we all have enjoyed having her here as our guest, but," I paused and held Duchess' head in my hands, "This is what we are concerned about," I pointed her very active head towards the lights of the consulting room in an effort to make the problem an obvious one, "It's her eyes."

Joan tried to look directly into the cats face.

Duchess made that difficult by her exuberant squirming and calling out and it took a few patient moments before I was able to direct the owner to the problem. At last the cat paused for the few seconds the owner needed to study those eyes, and she said, "Let me have a better look at you darling," The lady turned towards me and flashed a smile then offered me a response, a most unexpected one, "So that's what you are concerned about!" She turned to the cat picked her up and gave her another warm, and very snugly cuddle that made me think; that looks so nice, I feel more than a tad jealous.

Only then did she turn back to me and being unable to wait any longer for a response, I suggested, "That's a relief, at least you are not panicking about the problem."

"The problem!"

The next huge smile she gave revealed the most gorgeous set of strong, even teeth that were framed by a face that, by being suddenly illuminated, revealed its previously hidden attractiveness. She had a very pale complexion set off by a mane of luxuriantly thick black hair which she swung for effect, and said, "That's not a problem. I thought you were going to tell me she was going to be an invalid or something awful." The lady's lively personality continued to flow and was matched by that of Duchess whose ecstatic greetings were heard by Patricia in the upstairs office.

This was yet another time when the match of owner and animal appeared to perfectly complement each other and Penny, who was in the next consulting room, later offered an interesting opinion," That pair is so well matched, if she picked that cat for herself she did it in the exact manner a lady normally applies when selecting a set of matching shoes, handbag and dress."

Hmm! I thought; has the age of the designer cat arrived?

The lady played with me.

She had me hooked and delayed her final comment on those eyes, "That's not a problem," She held the cat right up against my face and continued, "Come Duchess, let the nice vet take a good look at your gorgeous face."

I was by then also relaxed, content the situation was under control when Joan repeated, "That's not a problem," She reached a hand over to me and tenderly stroked my arm and another flash of that wonderful smile followed, and then she dropped the bombshell, "I was not really a cat person, but my friend who bred Duchess persuaded me to take her, as . . . as her eyes made her unsuitable for sale."

The penny dropped.
It clanged to the floor and my jaw sagged, and made me stammer, "You mean . . . you mean that . . ."

"Yes you dear, silly man, Duchess was born with those crossed eyes."

CHAPTER 10

CRAIG . . . AGAIN!

I WAS LOST for words, but the owner was happy!

The contented owner left the clinic.

Joan's cat Duchess was complaining loudly; like most Siamese cats she was strenuously objecting to being confined to the basket. I was initially relieved that the problem with the cross-eyed cat had been solved, and then I became angry; my obvious relief that Duchess had experienced no physical problem from her operation was considerable, then very soon it gave way to a sense of disappointment and slowly changed to one of mounting anger.

It was obvious our practice had failed as our normal pre anaesthetic protocol had not identified an obvious abnormality when Craig, who had, or was supposed to have, conducted a pre-clinical examination on Duchess had missed the cat's crossed-eyed deformity? The cold, clinical answer to the problem was clear; Craig had not conducted that examination correctly and it was the second time in two weeks he had failed, he had again let the practice and himself down by his sloppy, unprofessional attitude.

Craig was a super chap; an attractive, easy going lad from Newcastle, he had only been with us for a few months straight from Liverpool University, and we made the usual allowances for inexperience. He was a likeable lad, and was quickly becoming a favourite with staff, and clients alike, and, while his rough edges were obvious, there was, however, nothing we could not cope with, or indeed had not experienced before.

But this second error was inexcusable and, as it came hard on the heels of his first real bit of negligence, it really made me cross.

Is this cat a male or a female?

Two weeks prior to the episode with Duchess we had one of those days when the surgery list for the morning was swamped with cats. Seven or eight females had been booked in for spaying and a similar number for castration. Craig was responsible for the pre-clinical examinations and anaesthesia, and when the preliminaries were complete, Eleanor passed them into the theatre, where the swift removal of their bits and pieces, soon ensured them to be of the sports model variety!

The penultimate case was a nuisance; my usual incision through the flank opened up the abdomen and I slipped the spay hook inside and fished it upwards and away from the bladder to pick up the uterus. It missed, twice, which necessitated my probing gently with a finger in the hope I could find it and I muttered, "Come on now little womb where are you?"

Andrea who was assisting me enjoyed the degree of humour I injected into that search and laughed, "That's it Alex, you have such a way with words and this lady is bound to yield to your advances."

My return smile flickered for a moment and then I said, "Damn it! I still cannot feel this thing and I will have to enlarge the incision to allow me a better look at what is going on."

"Now then Mr Vet perhaps you are getting tired after doing so many this morning?"

"No lass! That's not the answer, I am on top form."

By that stage my sense of humour had been completely replaced by a sense of frustration and my voice held more than a tone of irritation as I barked at my nurse, "Andrea! This cat has been spayed before." That did happen occasionally when a new owner of a young cat automatically booked it in for neutering without even thinking it might already have been fixed.

Then something made me hesitate.

I felt myself grow cold as another possibility nagged at me and made me slap the spay hook onto the tray and say, "Or?"

At that point all conversation ceased as I was in a black space and slipped into a hard silence as an almost unthinkable solution to my problem begged to be heard. Had we made a mistake, did we have the sex of the cat wrong and were we in fact dealing with a male cat?

The patient was enclosed in drapes with the entire body; apart from the operation site, was covered in a green, sterile sheet of cotton. My nurse grimaced and said, "I had better take a look," Andrea lifted the cloth where it covered pussy's nether region and, as the green linen drifted away, my nurse saw them clearly and in full view and her eyes widened and her eyebrows lifted up into her scalp, "My, my, my, would you just look at the size of his equipment? There can be no doubt that this she is definitely a he!"

"Damn! Damn! Damn!" I also had a look and a large pair of pom-poms decorated the car exactly where one would expect to find them.

"Craig!" My angry voice rang out, "*Craig, come here now!*"

Andrea later told Penny how my cry bounced of the tiled walls.

The errant veterinary surgeon obviously suspected a problem, and appeared almost immediately by my side and said, "What's wrong, do you need some help?"

I chose to say nothing and watched Andrea struggle with her emotions. She knew it was not a laughing matter, and worked hard to control herself. She beckoned Craig closer with a hook of her finger, and pointed first at the flank incision, then rather theatrically lifted the drape and pointed at the rear of the cat with a long finger.

As she lifted the green cloth the young man saw the problem and whispered, "Oh no!" The immediate embarrassment he felt was reflected by a bright red blush that covered his normally very pale complexion. He could hardly speak and continued to stare at the cats balls as though they were getting bigger and bigger the longer he stared at them.

I had an anaesthetized patient on the table and, irrespective of how badly my feelings were about the present situation that is where my focus had to be and I dismissed him, "We will talk about this later"

I closed off the flank incision.

The unlucky ginger cat's second operation immediately followed. The fluff over the testicles was plucked off then the hairless area was disinfected. Each side of the scrotum was sliced in turn with a sharp scalpel; a cut that dug easily through the skin and into the firm flesh of the testicle itself. Each organ was then pulled free of the scrotum with a twisting movement which allowed it to come free of the body and then the cord collapsed back into the abdomen sealing itself free from any danger of postoperative bleeding. Had he been an older creature the cord would have been tied off with catgut. He was soon some two stone lighter.

The cat recovered well and following Craig's explanation to the actually, quite amused owners, nothing further developed on that case, he was lucky in that respect.

I conducted a post mortem.

Sorry! Bad choice of words! Rather, my post-surgical investigation of the problem with Craig allowed him the opportunity to explain himself and he was unable to offer me any explanation as to how he had misread the sex of the cat. Although I was no longer angry I was still disappointed, "The fact that it was a ginger cat should have suggested it was likely to be male, I cannot understand why you never sexed it correctly."

Craig; his rather short, slim body smartly dressed as normal, sat opposite me. He had his lower lip between his teeth and moved it from side to side; a mannerism of his when stressed, and his hands were underneath the desk and I heard the noise his nails made as he scratched them along the underside of the wood.

We had a long chat about the mistake and his disappointment with himself was clear, "I cannot understand how I managed to make such a basic error. I can only apologise again and promise I will concentrate much better in the future."

From his attitude I hoped he would pull up his socks and do better in the future.

And now!

Scarcely two weeks later and Craig and Duchess had caused me another headache. Only two weeks after that problem with the Siamese we were faced with another discussion on his lack of professional conduct, and again Craig had no explanation for missing the fact that Duchess had the most amazing set of crossed-eyes; his apology was again profuse and his embarrassment profound.

My concern was clearly expressed, as was my disappointment that so soon following the previous incident he had again let the Practice down. The gravity of the situation was clearly and calmly laid out before him, and he was given a stern warning that should another case of neglect become apparent in the immediate future his employment with us would be in some jeopardy.

We held our scheduled partners meeting.

It so happened that my partner Seamus, and I, were scheduled to have a business meeting that evening. We held them monthly and they were an important opportunity for us to discuss all aspects of the running of the hospital. The meeting followed the usual agenda; business was going as planned, and our stocks of drugs which had been climbing, had been satisfactorily tightened up.

The final item was a review of staff performance with only Craig's performance on the agenda and when I outlined his two problems, Seamus commented, "I like the lad, he does have real potential, but, you must have noticed the problem, he simply cannot work in the same space as Eleanor."

I was taken aback at his comment, "That's a surprise as I thought they were getting on well together."

"Yes! He does like her," Seamus paused for effect, shook his head, and, with that great, generous grin on his face said, "Have you not noticed he likes her, too much?"

It transpired that Seamus had also noticed a couple of minor deficiencies with Craig, but, being the worldly chap that he was, he had put it down to an infatuation with Eleanor, "Have you not noticed that he moons about after her all the time, he is like some new born calf looking for its mother? The poor lad's hormones go haywire when she is around."

"Ah, so that's what is happening." That was a very logical explanation for his problems, a very human explanation that will no doubt have many readers nodding in agreement.

The following morning highlighted my concerns.

I had a quiet word with the sensible Andrea, "Tell me, Seamus says that Craig has got the hots for Eleanor and that it is affecting his work, how do you see the situation?"

She smiled and threw another couple of questions back at me, "Really Alex, in all honesty have you not noticed how bad he is with her? Why is it that you are always the last to notice these things?" She was smiling and shaking her head at the same time, and I loved the twinkle she had in her eyes, and could not help following her lead and began to relax. She continued, "I am trying to rearrange the duty schedules to keep them apart. Eleanor is happy with her boyfriend, but you know what she is like," She rolled her eyes at me and continued, "The flirty thing is actually encouraging him."

Is it an animal or a people problem?

There is a fascinating aspect to veterinary practice that has clearly established that many of our problems are more likely to be associated with people than animals. The beauty of normal human interactions that Desmond Morris so clearly expressed in his book; *The Naked Ape* came so obviously to the fore again.

"Well, well, well, so you and Seamus are thinking along similar lines."

"Yes! And it is a problem, and what are you going to do about it?" Andrea switched back to her business-like attitude.

"I am not sure yet, perhaps we should put him exclusively out on farm practice for a month or so?" I thought that would give him a chance to clear his head.

"Our problem there of course, is that we are not yet confident he is ready to face most of our farmers." She shook her head slowly from side to side.

"I agree with you. He is too soft and they will eat him for breakfast," There is a huge difference in attitude between farmers and those who own small animals; they are much more knowledgeable and do not easily cope with inexperience. My final thought for the day offered us some breathing space, "I will chew it over carefully this coming weekend."

The weekend flew past.

Monday morning found my mind still unsure as to how best to deal with the situation. I liked the lad, and was confident he did have a long term future with us and was aware that any insensitivity on my part might scare him away.

There have been many times in practice when events have suddenly changed in a manner for the better, when sometimes we have been plain lucky. The Craig problem went away after he spent his long weekend back in Newcastle where, at a family Christening, he met a stunning girl who did the trick for us; she not only took his mind off Eleanor, she married him and became the mother of his children.

It is not only in the television soapies that love conquers all.

CHAPTER 11

LAMBS

"**A**ND NOW I understand your confusion."

"So it's not as bad as I thought?"

Farmer Oliver was relieved, but I held my breath, closed my eyes and concentrated on the deft manipulation my fingers were involved in, and then said, "You were correct in saying you have two hind legs, but . . ."

He interrupted me, "Got it now, the two legs are from different lambs, its twins that are causing the problem, isn't it?"

"That's exactly what the problem is." I turned away from the ewe to smile at the excited farmer; the twin Suffolk lambs were presented in the breach position; backwards, and the farmer, who had recognised that two hind legs were indeed trying to squeeze through the vulva, was unable to understand why he could not deliver them and had summoned my assistance.

"Twins are actually simple when you have delivered many sets of them, experience helps with everything, although I admit that in my earliest days, when I first started delving into the inside of a sheep, when the legs were mixed up," I paused to concentrate on a tricky bit and grunted, "That's it!"

"Well done Alex you have done this before."

Oliver's sons were captivated by what was going on and yet they stood back respectfully, and in complete silence and gave us the space we needed until I invited them forward and said, "Now boys watch how quickly things will happen."

I pushed the lamb's legs back into the ewe's uterus.

The case was fresh and well lubricated and she was a big ewe with a roomy pelvis and I said, "It's as though they sometimes get stuck in the queue and cannot decide who should come first." There is something about my odd mind that makes me think of nonsense at times such as that, and that was why it was easy for me to imagine the lambs talking to each other; a conversation that might have gone something like:

"That does feel better does it not?"

"Sure does sister, so why don't you pop into the world first?"

"That's very kind of you brother, but probably best if you go first . . ."

"Thanks sister, but really you should be the first . . ."

Sheep are sheep because they are sheep and, if left to their own devices they would have taken another twenty minutes or so to be delivered, and that would have been a dangerously long delay.

I quickly repositioned the lambs.

The ewe would probably have managed the situation from this point by herself, but time was getting on and I again intervened by giving a gentle pull on the first lamb's legs and it dived into the world. I passed it to Oliver who began the normal midwifery routine by firstly cleaning mucous out of it's mouth and then he suspended the lamb by its hind limbs and gave it a couple of gentle swings to get its circulation going; an act that looks odd, but it often helps weak lambs to establish a normal breathing pattern.

As Oliver was attending to the first lamb I slipped a hand back inside the ewe, repeated the process and very quickly both of the twins were lying restless on the straw of the lambing pen. The ewe had taken the birthing very well and almost immediately jumped up and began licking her babies and pushing them around in the normal sheep fashion.

I turned to talk to the boys, "That was quick, oh! They have already gone back to their football."

Oliver laughed and said, "They are always keen to watch you working but they have been hands on with the lambing for so long it takes a lot to hold their interest."

"It's a grand job when it goes well."

The farmer stretched his fit looking frame to the sky as though untying a knot in his back and rubbed his hands together and I thought it odd I had never previously noticed where the ring finger on his right hand had been shortened by some accident. He echoed my constant thoughts on veterinary practice, "Your job is the same as mine in some fashion. It is the best job in the world when it is going well, but it can be a hard, depressing effort when things go wrong."

"You are right there Oliver, very right," I loved attending lambing cases and continued, "I must also say it is such a pleasure to be doing this job on a bright sunny spring morning such as this, rather than at two o'clock on a cold foggy night."

He liked that and looked around then said, "It was this exceptionally mild, early spring that made me leave the ewes outside in this field, rather than housing them permanently inside."

"Yes that was a good idea, lambings always go better in the cleaner environment such a beautiful, dry meadow as this offers," I waved my still bloody hand expansively round the thirty acre field which, with its mature trees and permanent pasture was a beautiful place; indeed for Theresa it would have been the perfect picnic place, and continued, "I suppose this is how nature intended them to do the job."

The ewes were left to themselves in the field until they went into labour or actually lambed, and then they were isolated in one of the dozen or so temporary lambing pens that had been constructed with straw bales and standard wooden pallets. These were strategically placed adjacent to the south facing wall of the large barn where they would receive the maximum protection from the elements should the weather deteriorate.

Their lambing caravan was close by.

I pointed at it and said, "So your wife Rose will be up in the house now having a bit of a rest?"

"Indeed she is and it is a well-deserved rest! She uses the caravan every night for the whole of the six weeks our lambing lasts, and every single night she patrols the ewes and doesn't miss a beat."

"The conscientious shepherd wins the prizes every time, that's for sure." Most ewes manage the whole process of lambing by themselves, but the minority that do need help are the ones that make the difference in profitability; healthy lambs earn money, while dead lambs are of no value to anyone.

We rambled on for a bit, my morning had gone well and although I had a decent run of farm visits planned for the day my life was under control; not for long!

"The kids are enjoying the weather."

Oliver smiled at the sight of his sons kicking a ball alongside the burn at the bottom of the meadow without disturbing the many sheep in the area. We smiled our own thoughts for a moment until Oliver said, 'The burn is actually flowing very high, there must have been a lot of rain in the hills, but they are very careful."

"Well, Rose is the mother hen of all hens and I would imagine she has warned them, hang on, one of them has just disappeared."

Oliver was at least twenty yards in front of me and Graham; the younger of the twins was screaming for help, "James is in the water he has fallen into the burn."

I sprinted hard and reached the edge of the burn a few seconds after Oliver who had already jumped off the bank into the burn that was only about five yards wide, but about two feet deep and flowing fast. I lay on my tummy and stretched out a hand to Oliver who already had a good hold of James and my voice was full of the emotion of the moment, "Thank God you guys look all right, here, take my hand and I will give you a pull up."

"Wait a bit," It was the ten year old James' voice that brought us to a halt. He was in that excited state where his laughter at his own carelessness threatened to minimise the danger of the incident, "Look dad, look over there," He pointed downstream to where the burn opened up into a much wider and deeper pool, "There dad! On the ledge can you see her?"

There was a ewe stuck on a small ledge.

She was about one yard from the top of the bank and some six inches above the water although her back end was partially submerged and she was in a thoroughly bedraggled state, soaking wet and very dirty, but there was something else about her that alerted me to another problem, and made me say, "And look at her I think she is sick?"

"That was lucky," Graham voiced our thoughts and repeated them, "It was lucky that James fell in or we might never have found her."

There was another almighty splash and Oliver's entry to the burn caught us by surprise. It was only much later we were able to congratulate him on his method of entry; it was the belly flop of all belly flops! Yet he was in the pool and beside the ewe before I could even blink. She was on the same side as us and I moved the ten yards or so towards them and again lay on my tummy and stretched my hand out towards them, and with Oliver pushing her towards me I got a fair grip on a front leg. I was leaning over and down the bank which was about two foot above the water and as I pulled at the ewe the bank started giving way and I felt myself sliding towards them. I shouted, "Quickly boys grab my legs and pull me."

"That's it Mr Vet we have you now." The strong lads were able to pull me and the ewe back about a foot or so and then with the better purchase I had on the harder earth we soon had the sheep to safety.

"Come dad take our hands." Oliver half climbed and was half-pulled onto the bank and we were soon grouped around the ewe.

She was lying flat out.

When I noticed her abdomen was tight with bloat I explained the situation, "I think she has a touch of milk fever and that is probably why she fell in," I left them with the ewe and called over my shoulder, "Back in a minute!" I loped off the eighty metres or so to the Saab and collected some calcium, needles and syringes.

On my return I commanded, "Right chaps keep her upright."

"Yes we have her and the gas is already coming up," James wrinkled his nose and continued, "But the smell of it!"

"Dad! Do you recognise her? It is Doris, number 147." I think it was Graham and although I picked up the interesting tone to his voice I concentrated on treating the ewe.

"Doris! Are you sure this is Doris, number 147, Doris?" Oliver sounded alarmed.

"Hold her head up and to the side for me," Oliver presented her neck correctly to me and as I parted the thick, wet wool and pressed my left thumb into the jugular furrow the large vein stood up, "Great, that's it and . . . here we go." The sharp needle felt no resistance and life giving calcium steadily flowed into her bloodstream, "That's it, give me about five minutes for this, I mustn't rush or it might upset her."

The magic of calcium.

"Look at that dad, look at how quickly she is improving." Although he was still shivering from the effects of the cold burn James had forgotten about his misadventure and was thrilled to see the ewe looking better.

"Every time I do this, and I have done it hundreds of time, the magic of calcium never fails to fascinate me."

"Why does it work as well as this, why don't all drugs work as fast as this, why . . ."

Boys will be boys and the questions flowed and I had to leave their questions unanswered as the ewe went suddenly into a hard labour which made me say, "Gosh, but she needed that calcium, her womb was also paralysed from the milk fever," I repositioned her to make her more comfortable and said, "The lambs are coming, let's get them out."

Within five minutes we had a healthy pair of twin female lambs and I stood and stretched my back and watched carefully as the now normal looking ewe began mothering her babies. The two boys guarded her protectively to prevent her slipping back into the burn as their father who had gone to fetch the Landi, headed back towards us.

As Oliver joined us he spoke to James, "Number 147 you say, but are you sure?"

"Yes Dad. I am sure it is her. I remember Mum talking about her yesterday and how she had lost her ear tag."

"What a lucky day."

We put the ewe and her babies in the Landi.

She was soon safely in a lambing pen and Oliver pulled the boys away from her, "No boys! Let her mother her lambs for a half hour or so, and then we will get her cleaned up. She and they need a bit of time together."

That was good thinking on his part and with a period of relative calmness surrounding us I asked the obvious question, "So tell me about this number 147?"

Graham said, "She is only the most valuable animal on the place, it was her lambs that made all the money at the sale last year."

It was that ewe.

In this flock of highly pedigreed and very valuable sheep she was the most important Suffolk ewe in the whole county and possibly in the whole country.

Our good day got better and better.

CHAPTER 12

DOGS AND CARS

D OGS AND CARS are a bad combination because,
They and machines are not designed to be bosom buddies.

The dog's unpredictability, its relatively small size, and its tendency to move erratically can cause problems and often the first thing the driver is aware of is a blur, a suspicion that something solid is close; often it is a completely unexpected noise, perhaps a soft thwack followed by the fear and anxiety adrenaline release brings. On the occasions I was the driver the shock always made me call out, "No! I have hit something? Is it a rock, or, is it . . .?"

Have you experienced that sinking feeling? The heart-in-your-mouth one where you realise that knock was you hitting flesh and blood? My occupation as a country vet caused me to spend upwards of thirty thousand miles annually on all types of road conditions, and, inevitably I was personally involved in a number of accidents. Dogs, cats, cattle, rabbits, hares, foxes, horses and many birds were some of my unwilling partners, and the few people who attracted my attention in that respect always did so due to carelessness on their part; it is difficult to apportion such blame to animals.

Drofter had a high incidence of accidents involving animals and cars, and indeed they were almost a daily occurrence.

All RTA's are a problem!

Or are they? I remember the case of a colleague who admitted a dangerous dog for euthanasia as he; the dog that is, was regularly biting people, and, when admitted to my friends' clinic, proved difficult to deal with. He actually escaped from the clinic, and raced off into the town with the speed of the Flying Scotsman until, when he ran across the main road it was his last journey as he met a car and instantly graduated to the next life. His break for freedom at least afforded him a final thrill of excitement, and the fact he was killed directly outside the clinic saved the vet many blushes; can you imagine the implications had he bitten again?

The many RTA's in Drofter caused sleepless nights.

A number of clinical cases always fill me with nervous anticipation, and give me a hollow feeling in the pit of my stomach with colic, laminitis and RTA cases being particularly stressful. RTA's are unpleasant and distressing, as animals and people are emotionally disturbed, the family members are distraught; worse still when they themselves have actually driven over their own dog. I thank God human medicine was never my chosen career, as the thought of talking to parents who have run over their children, or indeed lost them from drowning in their own swimming pool . . .!

Animals are our lives and we share the owner's emotions, and an emergency consultation is tricky as it is conducted in the midst of a highly charged atmosphere. The injured animal needs immediate attention and this may be complicated by the realisation the humans present also need emotional support. Their cries for help have to be set aside as my priority is the animal, and I am aware my professionalism may be interpreted as callousness by irrational, shocked owners. The situation is heightened if the accident takes place at a time when the support of the complete team of professionals is unavailable, and the traumatised owners have to act as my assistant in the care of a much loved pet.

I have to obtain an accurate history by asking questions:

> Did you see the accident happen?
> Did a wheel go over the dog; internal organs may be crushed.
> Was the dog smacked on the side and forced away from the car?
> This more common when larger individuals are involved.
> Was he instantly, and obviously, in severe distress?
> Did she gradually deteriorate, could there be any internal bleeding or brain injury?
> Did he walk away from the scene of the accident?
> Is there an obvious lameness or a fracture?
> Has his breathing deteriorated since the accident took place?

My primary focus is damage to vital organs and I cannot waste time palpating a fractured limb, or suturing superficial cuts, until I am satisfied of the condition of the brain, heart and the liver. I estimate the levels of shock and haemorrhage; including internal structures such as the spleen.

This may take only five minutes, and, then priority treatment is initiated and only then may I have the time to speak to owners.

The following example of an actual case will help to understand the process.

CHAPTER 13

MAX

IT WAS SIX pm on a Friday evening in June.

The Standerton family were having a picnic supper.

They were enjoying the clear daylight which Britain enjoys during balmy summer evenings and nearby Clumber Park; a magnificent National Trust property about eight miles from Drofter, was their destination.

Max; their 2-y-o part bred Labrador, accompanied them, and the combination of weather, environment, children, and energetic dog ensured a fun filled evening. A tennis ball demonstrated Max's excellent ability to retrieve, and their two daughters enjoyed running and laughing in the freedom the vast open spaces Clumber offers. Mrs Standerton later stated how her thoughts were along the lines of how peacefully everyone would get off to sleep after expending so much energy.

The children were in full view of their parents when their evening of carefree leisure was suddenly transformed when Max met a car. While chasing his ball into some long grass, Max startled a resting hare that ran south, away from the main house and lake and the normally well trained Max set off in hot pursuit. There is no need to blame the creature as even the best trained individuals react in that instinctive manner.

Well! By now I am sure the reader has guessed what happened? The driver was not at fault as his slowly moving car had no chance of avoiding the collision as the animals were moving very fast and his visibility was reduced by the massive rhododendron bushes that are a feature of the park.

Max ran full tilt into the nearside front wheel.

The impact caused him to somersault into the air, and his twirling body slumped onto the tar. The car screeched to a halt, the children screamed, and the relieved hare; which had almost been run over, disappeared from view. Max was in trouble, although his initial excitement allowed him to regain his feet and he attempted to regain the comfort of his much loved family; a journey that lasted no more than ten feet before the reality of the situation found its mark and he fell in a heap by the roadside.

Max's breathing was labored and he was in great pain and his left back leg was lying at an absurd angle and was obviously fractured. Bob Standerton hastily improvised their picnic blanket as a stretcher, and placed its carefully beside his wife Celia on the back seat of the car, and then raced to our clinic.

Their anxious journey can be imagined.

The family arrived at the clinic at seven thirty; we normally ended around seven, but that Friday evening was one when half of Drofter consulted us! My partner Seamus and I were members of Drofter Round Table and had planned on attending a formal dinner and had joined forces in the hope of an early finish and were already dressed in penguin suits; our consulting jackets covering everything except our black bowties.

I was at reception when the family arrived, and, as the situation was an obvious emergency, our trauma protocol swung into action, "Hi Bob, follow me straight through to the treatment room." I knew the family well as Max had been introduced to me as a puppy owing to him being badly affected by travel sickness, in actual fact he was an Olympic champion in the vomiting stakes. The family proved an excellent example of what can be achieved when vet and owners work together as we cured him completely through behaviour management and homoeopathy; a system that is outstandingly successful in such cases.

The look on the children's faces spoke volumes for their emotional trauma.

The fracture was obvious and my investigation and examination were conducted as previously described.

Max was in severe pain.

He was not unduly shocked and there were no other obvious injuries. The family were present, and sensibly did not hamper us and, when satisfied with my preliminary examination, I turned my attention directly to the children and smiled, "The news is generally good," The family collectively let out a single breath and I continued, "Apart from the obviously fractured leg, he seems to have escaped any other problems."

One of the anxious, tearful girls, piped in, "Can you save him what can you do?"

I looked at her, gave her a quick hug and said, "I am sure we can help Max and I will begin by giving him something to make him feel better," I looked into the eyes of Linda, the younger daughter, "Do you think that would be a good idea, do you think he would like some medicines to help him relax?"

The whole family replied, "Yes please."

I injected Max against pain and shock.

Following his initial therapy all of us began to relax, and then was an appropriate time to discuss the case in more detail, and to reassure them, "Now children, this is what I am going to do. I will keep Max here this evening in a comfortable kennel and the injections I gave will help him sleep, and take away his pain," I gave the dog's ears a reassuring stroke, and continued, "In the morning when he is feeling better I will take some X-Rays and they will show how much bone damage there is."

I looked at Bob who was trying to wrap his arms around all three of his ladies at the same time, a task easier for him than me, as his long, lean shape made him fit them easier than mine could. He disengaged himself, gently rubbed Max on one ear, and turned the greenest of green eyes towards me, and said, "You are the man, we must be guided by you."

"Splendid!" I reached out to the girls, and brought their long, slim hands together between mine, as though we were having a prayer session, squeezed them and said, "Can you visit me tomorrow morning at nine o'clock? I will show you the pictures and we can put a plan together?"

One of the children asked a reasonable, pertinent question, "Will he be lonely here will someone talk to him?"

I explained that one of our vets lived on the property, and, he would regularly monitor Max and then Bob took charge of the situation and marshalled his family, "Thanks vet, I agree with you and that is a sensible plan," He put his left arm around his wife, and both children snuggled up between them, as he said, "Ok guys let's leave the professionals to look after Max."

All of them gave the sleepy Max a gentle little pat and left.

Seamus and I eventually got off to dinner.

I would love to tell you it was unusual for our social plans to be disrupted by accidents, and emergencies, but they were, however, a regular part of daily life, and we accepted them as part and parcel of the profession. Meals were so often missed I developed an almost canine attitude to my food that is with me to this day; I still gobble my meals down for fear the telephone will go, and my food will sit untouched on the table as I run off to save a life. Theresa still complains about my eating habits although I think she has almost come to accept them.

Max had a reasonable night.

I was pleased to find him looking as well as I could have hoped for. He managed to stand on three legs and hobbled outside, his tail wagging slightly, and performed his morning toilet and his urine stream was strong, clear, and revealed no blood when dipped into a simple test strip. I talked to him, "So Max that was a bit of a shock you got yesterday."

He gave me a faint smile although the obvious pain in his glazed eyes indicated how he felt, and I said, "Not to worry friend we will soon help you." I gave his ears a rub and took him through to the prep room, where my second examination confirmed that only the hind leg was damaged.

Andrea said, "He looks good to me, and, I have already prepared the theatre. I suppose you will have to pin it this morning." She turned on her heels and left me admiring how well trained she was.

I met the entire family again.

We chatted about Max and I invited them to see him through the window, rather than allowing them to meet, and initially that seemed harsh to the girls until I reasoned with them, "It is my experience that too much contact with an injured animal pre-surgery upsets them, it raises their hopes of going home, and by increasing anxiety levels it generally makes them more difficult patients."

That is not the case with seriously ill animals where carefully selected owners are very important and I have no hesitation in sending them home, as many animals; particularly cats, are better nursed at home by doting parents than in some veterinary hospitals.

As our discussions unfolded I switched on the X-ray viewer and the lights flashed onto the screen and highlighted the problem; the white of the bones stood out against the black background of the radiograph, and were highlighted by the bright light source.

The films brought an instant gasp, and comment from Jenny, who at eleven was the elder of the two sisters, "Wow! Look at that I can see the broken bone."

The discussion developed when I showed the family radiographs of a normal femur for comparison, and explained how the fracture would be repaired. I demonstrated the surgical technique by showing them actual radiographs of a similar case and the type of pin that would connect the broken pieces together. Children love to see and feel these things, it gives them confidence, and makes them feel part of the healing process.

I discussed the procedure with the family in detail, including Max's likely stay in hospital, the aftercare required, the expected duration of healing and the financial implications. The family immediately decided to proceed with treatment, and completed the necessary paperwork at reception then left me to get on with the job.

Jenny had the last word, "We will pray that God will help him."
I agreed, "You can't beat a bit of Divine Intervention."

CHAPTER 14

A WELL PINNED FEMUR

D OG MEETING CAR is distasteful! True, but it does have a very positive aspect to it.

The injuries offer vets an opportunity to practice sophisticated surgery. Andrea; the duty nurse for the day, had tranquilised Max who looked pretty woozy; the instruments, drapes, gloves and everything else were in place.

We placed the sedated Max on the table in the preparation room, adjacent to the theatre. Andrea was on his left side with her left arm under and around his neck, and from there it went on round his body until her palm supported his right shoulder. Her right arm ran over his back and formed the other half of a comforting embrace and Max was totally secured in the correct position when her right hand held up his right front leg at the elbow.

She cuddled his black body firmly, gently, in an embrace that was effective and practical. Andrea's neck and face were close to the dog's mouth, and only rarely did she feel threatened by such a caress; had he been a difficult dog the process would have been made safer by fitting a muzzle over his mouth.

The hair over the vein, for a space of about two inches, had been removed with an electric clipper and washed with surgical spirits. The thumb of Andrea's right hand compressed the vein running along the dorsal aspect of his arm until it distended and she said, "OK Alex I am ready."

Andrea's control was perfect.

Max hardly felt me insert a small, sharp catheter into the engorged vein and then I connected that catheter by six inches of clear plastic tubing to a syringe containing thiopentone. The backflow of his dark red, venous blood into the catheter indicated the needle to be in place. General anaesthesia was required, and began when half of the measured dose of thiopentone was injected quickly into the vein and Max slumped into Andrea's arms, and then she allowed him to gently slip onto the table as went into a deep sleep.

His dark brown eyes stood out in sharp contrast to the large white stripe covering much of his black face and the globes of his eyes took on a glassy sheen as their normal sharpness disappeared. I checked his reflexes by tapping the corner of his eyes and found the plane of anaesthesia to be as I desired and no further thiopentone was required, which made me say, "Got you my fine friend, you are off to the land of nod."

"Another one bites the dust." Andrea was full of it.

"Jings, but you are in fine form this morning."

"Well it is Saturday morning after all, and my husband is taking me for a long ride on his new bike."

"I should join you one day, can you see me on a bright red Harley? Perhaps I would look the part if I let my hair grow into a bushy ponytail?"

She shook her head.

"Then a few tattoos, to finish off my new image?"

"Stop talking rubbish Alex."

"I agree, on with the business."

"I will secure the catheter."

The coils of the plastic catheter were taped firmly onto the limb, and Andrea continued, "Perfect! I will connect the drip." A saline infusion was part of our standard practice during surgery as the fluids helped prevent dehydration, and, in the event of an emergency, any drugs required could be quickly added.

Max was sleeping contentedly, so comfortably he reminded me of the happy state into which a well exercised puppy sinks following a meal. With him lying on his right side Andrea opened his mouth to expose his throat for me by holding his upper jaw in her left hand, and pulling his long pink tongue forward with her right hand and she said, "There you are, I am sure that tube will fit, or should I give you the next size up?"

I had a good view of his larynx in the back of his throat, "I think you have got the right size, you are rarely wrong," I inserted the red, rubber, cuffed tube through his larynx, and on into his trachea where it fitted snugly, "That looks dead right." I made it airtight by pumping a few cc of air into the cuff via an attached plastic syringe and I said, "Ok gas girl, give him some happy juice."

Andrea connected the tube to the anaesthetic machine via some black rubber tubing. The gas flow system was designed to allow liquid fluothane, the main anaesthetic, to be vaporised into the oxygen that fed in from large black cylinders.

We worked well together.

With the first part of the process safely underway, and the skilled Andrea monitoring Max's reactions, I was able to shoot and develop more detailed X-rays. I returned after about five minutes and found the couple as I had left them, "Nothing unexpected, we can operate as planned."

"Excellent! I have done a complete instrument check."

The hair over the upper side of the damaged limb had already been close clipped and shaved, and the skin covering the surgical site had been thoroughly washed and sterilised by Andrea, using a combination of an iodine and disinfectant solution to kill off any bacteria that might be lurking there. Less than fifteen minutes had elapsed since the needle first pricked him.

My head was covered with a green and white checked, closely fitting skullcap to completely cover my short brown hair and a snug gauze mask covered my mouth. My hands and arms were thoroughly washed in the same mixture that had prepared the patients skin and I controlled the water using my elbows to operate modern, long limbed tap levers.

Andrea opened the first sterile pack and I picked out a green surgical gown, inserted my arms into it then shook my hips to make the gown fall into place. Andrea then picked up the long cotton ties that were attached to the gown and tied them behind my back and to prevent contamination she took great care not to touch any other part of the gown. Sterile drapes were placed over most of Max' body, and, when clipped together they left only the shaved area over his thigh open. A pair of tightly fitting, size seven and a half, surgical gloves were the final act in the process and we were confident my potentially unclean body was completely closed off from the operating site.

Only then did we move him into our spotlessly clean operating theatre.

"Spot on Alex, at least you look like a surgeon."

"Hmm!" Andrea took up her position on a chair by Max's head, from where she would monitor the anaesthesia and I stood to attention with my hands raised to the level of my head and asked, "OK sister I am ready, can I cut?"

She tested his reflexes again then commanded, "Under control, let's go".

I reached for a scalpel blade; a shining number twenty-two blade had already been released from its packaging and cried out to be clipped onto a holder. It was soon directed at the patient, and the first incision dragged a straight weeping red line of approximately four inches down the centre of his thigh. The cut was directly through the naked skin and followed the line of the femur and the large blade was so sharp I scarcely felt the pressure of steel on flesh. A few small blood vessels bled and were sealed by twisting them with a fine pair of artery forceps. The operation continued by exposing the femur with an incision through the fascia; a silk-like sheet of tissue that connects the two main muscle groups in that area.

The fracture was obvious.

As the radiographs had suggested it was a clean one with two small bone chips still attached to the periosteum; a thick tissue that adheres to and covers the surface of the bone. I was satisfied and said, "I know it sounds daft, but it always reassures me when I have opened up, and see that the fracture is the same as per the radiographs."

"Anaesthetic is perfect!" Andrea continued, "I know what you mean, do you remember when that assistant we had years ago, got things a bit mixed up, his films were not good quality and the fracture was worse than he thought?"

"I don't remember that, who and when?"

"It was that Aussie lad, George, don't you remember the panic phone call you got from me to come and take over?"

"Now I do remember, I think I used rush pins on that one, I suppose it must have gone well, or I would not have forgotten it and," I paused for a moment, "It's bloodier than I thought." The collision had caused a significant amount of local haemorrhage and although the fluid component of the blood would be reabsorbed I was unhappy about leaving a number of large blood clots, and swabbed them away. There was the expected degree of muscle bruising and no significant tearing, "It always surprises me, how a dog can get whacked so solidly by a car, and yet be so little affected by muscle damage."

Andrea stretched her legs and peered into the wound, "I see what you mean," She immediately returned to her machine and reported, "Anaesthetic perfect, twenty minutes gone."

Fractures are a common part of veterinary surgery.

They are repaired as a carpenter might connect two pieces of damaged furniture by bringing the two pieces of bone together and fixing them in the correct position. Carpenters and surgeons both use screws or nails, but I had a wonderful advantage as my surgical repair technique was based on a system of connections that only had to hold for a short term. My connections enjoy the power of nature; it does not matter how beautifully the cabinet maker creates his joints, they will never heal into a new and permanent connection. They can look fantastic, and be associated with the most extraordinary skill that only an expert may detect, but, remove the connectors in two hundred years and the repair will fall apart. Not so the body, as the repair I was about to initiate had natural healing as its agent. And yet surgeons earn much more than even the most skilled carpenters!

His bone needed pinning.

The best method to repair Max's fracture was to perform a procedure called intra-medullary pinning. The femur is a long, thin and hollow bone that can sometimes be splinted non-invasively from the outside of the leg, using a complicated system of pins and supports. In the present case, Max needed open surgery directly onto the bone, and my plan was to insert a stainless steel pin resembling a heavy knitting needle, inside the bone where it would form an internal support. My exposure of the damaged area was excellent and the fracture was obvious, "Looking good from my side, are you ready for me to begin the interesting part?"

"I am still under control, and ready to increase the gas if he reacts to your efforts."

"Great, so here we go." A one quarter inch diameter pin, its two ends sharply pointed, was trapped in a standard, but sterile hand drill and inserted into the uppermost fractured end of the femur. I advanced the pin, using a circular, screwing motion of my wrist, up the inside of the bone towards the hip joint and it slipped fairly easily along for the first two inches, until the point engaged the solid bone at the top of the femur and I said, "That's it Andrea we have reached some good bone, how is he taking it?"

"He is telling me what you are doing as his pulse has climbed."

"They always react at this point, are you comfortable, or should we up the gas?"

"I think you should keep working for a few minutes, I will tell you if the pulse goes any higher."

I maintained a steady pressure on the pin.

The shining steel disappeared as it gradually pushed through the solid bone, until the pressure suddenly decreased when the sharp point bit through the end of the bone and I said, "Excellent, I am through the heavy bone." I continued pushing slowly until I felt the point underneath the skin at the top of the hip. I made a small incision through the skin at that point and rambled on in my usual manner, "Come my little darling, come to daddy." I caught the gleaming metal in strong forceps and pulled out the first two inches.

The length of pin still inside the wound was too long, and I pulled more of it up and through the femur until only one inch of its distal end projected from the bone inside the wound. I removed the drill from the end nearest to the fracture site and reconnected it to the long piece protruding through the skin at the top of the leg.

I reversed the process by slipping the tip of the pin inside the wound and then directed it into the lower piece of bone, and already I smiled at how eagerly the two parts of the fracture appeared eager to re-join each other. They fitted well together, but were still loose and would only become firm when the lower end was anchored into the healthy bone around the knee joint. I encouraged it to commence its homeward journey by using some firm pressure on the drill and pushed the pin downwards.

At that point I twisted pin and bone until satisfied the two pieces fitted snugly together and a surprising amount of pressure was required to push the pin deeper into the hard bone round the stifle, which made me say, "I am surprised at how tough this bone is."

"That is a good sign as healing should be perfect."

I nodded at Andrea, "You are right, good girl."

I again twisted and pulled at the fracture to test its stability until I was happy and said, "We are looking good Andrea, it's as solid as Dumbarton Rock."

"My end is also going well."

I paused and stretched my stiff back.

"I will now remove the excess pin." Three inches of the pin was sticking out from the top of the leg, and I removed that by using a small hacksaw to cut it off close to the skin which left about half an inch of steel still remaining and I explained my thinking, "I am confident he can keep this pin forever, so I will tap it deeper into the bone," I remember again thinking how hard his bone was, as it needed a firm tap or three before it was well anchored, "Gosh, but his bone structure is very good."

The small skin opening at the top of the leg was closed with one horizontal mattress suture. The main wound was rinsed with sterile saline and then the fascia closed with thin interrupted catgut sutures, and I finished by closing the skin with more nylon sutures. The surgeon had a satisfied smile on his face, and happily addressed his excellent assistant, "OK Andrea that was fun and it has gone well, now I will help you tidy up."

She began stripping the drapes from Max and called out, "Let the weekend begin."

My anaesthetist was happy.

I counted and sorted the instruments and as Andrea began clearing up she said, "Now then Alex are you sure nothing is left inside?"

"Perfect." We would never forget a Border collie presented to us as a second opinion and the complicated surgery that was required to remove a large piece of his bowel that had been chronically damaged, as a result of a six inch pair of artery forceps being left in the abdomen following a routine spay.

My musings were interrupted when Andrea laughed the loudest laugh ever and I chuckled at the happy soul who was obviously looking forward to her weekend, and she laughed on and on, and on, and, if anything her laughter got louder. She was looking at the dog and then, when she glanced at me it was her facial expression that, proving to be irresistible, brought me back to the operating table when she explained the source of her mirth, "Alex we have a problem," She was still laughing hard, "Please pick Max up for me?"

I was also laughing.

Andrea's chortling was always highly infectious, and when I slipped my hands under his trembling body nothing happened! Max refused to leave the table; he did not wish to go! We had a problem and his anaesthetised state assured us that Max's reason for not leaving the operating theatre was an involuntary one.

His stubbornness was easy understood; I had actually pinned his leg directly into the table, which explained why the bone had seemed so firm. For the only time in my life during such an operation I had gone too far, my efforts had allowed the lower end of the pin to emerge from his femur, through the side of his knee, and into the table.

Well! What a laugh and then I thought; how embarrassing!

We had three choices; either Max could stay in the hospital for the rest of his life permanently attached to the table, or, by a bit of careful modification, and with much manoeuvring, that same attachment could be permanently managed after he was conveyed home, or we could detach him from the table.

Max voted for freedom. We all did and the additional treatment required was soon performed. It took a matter of a few moments to disinfect the protruding pin and remove it with a few firm strokes of the hacksaw. The operation was finally, and most definitely, over, the anaesthetic gas was out of his system and, and, as Max began recovering, he was placed in a warm kennel where Andrea continued to monitor his vital signs until he came round. By the time we tidied up the theatre, he was again back to normal, sitting up and looking remarkably well.

I reflected.

My initial amusement yielded to worry; ever my biggest critic and worst enemy, my conscience caused me to chew over possible problems as my hunger for excellence drove the following questions.

The WHAT-IFS began!

> What if infection had entered the bone when the tip of the pin came through?
> What if that additional effort had reduced the stability at the fracture site?
> What if the fracture failed to heal?
> What if the operation had to be repeated?
> What if?

Surgery usually goes well, not always.

It has been a constant source of amazement to me that problems usually develop when they are unexpected and that some procedures that seem to have little chance of success often go well. Simple operations that have proceeded to everyone's satisfaction may be the ones that; as Billy Connolly would say; *bite your bum!*

Max's leg healed perfectly and by six weeks post operatively he was walking well on the leg.

The vet!

I often thought about that incident and the staff often laughed about it. The vet sometimes wakened in the middle of the night as though from a nightmare, thinking of the great WHAT-IFS.

I was in luck.

Thank you God, that's another one I owe you!

CHAPTER 15

A HUNGRY HORSE

JAMES WOOD'S HUNTERS were in poor condition and
The Big Boss gave me more priceless advice.

We were discussing the poor condition of James Wood's hunters and thin horses in general. I had been investigating the matter, and as yet had been unable to come up with any kind of workable theory to explain the problem.

The boss shook his head and outlined the likely reason for the horses being thin in his own indefatigable manner, "James is an idiot, he works his horses to death and forgets the most important aspect to feeding is to open the bloody feed bags; he is simply a miserable fart who doesn't feed his horses enough."

That down to earth exposé in animal husbandry offered a simple answer.

The following day my mentor's advice still rang in my ears.

I was able to establish how easily what appeared a difficult case, was soon solved. I timed my next visit to the Wood stables for feeding time to watch the process; observing animals feeding has always been one of my favourite pastimes. The horses were obviously hungry and eagerly gobbled up their rations which prompted me to ask the groom, "Your horses eat well, do you often get leavings?"

The groom surprised me with her comment; a rather unguarded one which slipped out of her plain rather flat face, "These horses never have leavings, I think they could do with more food." That was already a gold star for the boss' thinking.

I looked at the clear chart dominating one wall of the spotless feed room; it rather garishly, due to the proud blue and green writing thereon, stated clearly by weight what each horse was supposed to be fed, so I nodded and said, "That looks efficient and orderly and sounds about right for working horses," I then asked the groom how she weighed out the food, "All looks as it should be, what plan do you follow when weighing out the cubes? It can be easy to get it…"

Cynthia stopped me in my tracks, "I always do the measuring myself and here is the scoop I use, and I am very careful to ensure the measures are exactly as Mr Wood instructs me." She presented the stainless steel scoop to me as though it were a family heirloom, and her haughty attitude instantly reminded me of the name of a beautiful chestnut mare by Crepello called *Indignant Lady*!

I softened my attitude and gently asked her to help me.

"No one is suggesting you are doing anything wrong and please work with me on this. I would like to do a little experiment so please fetch me a kitchen scale and weigh the contents of the scoop."

Cynthia's eyes instantly brightened at my request, "Do you think it is possible the scoop might not weigh the two pounds it is supposed to weigh?"

I explained my thinking, "Scoops are an accurate measure of volume, but you must realise the different types of grains often actually weigh less than we think they do and that got Cynthia quite excited, "Well! That could be the answer."

She was back from the house in a flash and her bright red face was serious as she set up the scales. "Ok let me do this now," she popped a scoopful of feed into the bowl, stood back and carefully studied the pointer and then she clapped her hands sharply together, "Gosh, would you look at that?"

I moved closer to get a better look and the girl continued, "You are such a clever man, the scoop only weighs out at one pound and eight ounces," I remained quiet and she continued, "Spot on there Mr Veterinary, there is no problem with disease here, these horses are simply hungry."

The scales did the trick for us by establishing clearly the horses were being underfed. The answer to the problem was as the Boss suggested and when we measured the amount of cubes they were being fed by weight, rather than by volume, Woods was genuinely astonished to find he was underfeeding by a factor of almost a quarter. He smiled when it sank in that the answer to his problem was a simple one, and when he changed his pattern of feeding the grateful animals soon got back to normal.

I tried that technique on another consultation.

The problem horse was being fed almost twelve Kgs of cubes daily; an impossibly large quantity of food for the hunter who was looking thin; in fact he was very thin. This was my third visit to examine and ponder on the condition of the animal; I was well and truly puzzled by the case and was getting nowhere close to finding an explanation for his leanness.

His owner was Claudia de Montefort and she was not to be trifled with. Her family was an ancient one whose finances had taken a turn for the better when, in the dim and very distant past, an ancestor had rescued some King or other, from death under the flashing hooves of a stampeding battle horse. It is no mean feat to rescue any individual who is in such trouble, but if that act can be carried out for the most important man in the kingdom it brings rewards.

The estate he gained for such valour originally encompassed much of the hamlets of Tuxford and Markham Moor and most of the fertile land between. Yes, there was no doubting the fact of the matter; Claudia de Montefort was probably at least half the lady she thought she was, and there was still a lot of money in the family, although most of the land had long since found its way into other hands. There was a bit of scandal that suggested how one of her later ancestors had mistakenly sided with the wrong brother in another of those Royal family squabbles that fill the books of history.

They had a beautiful home in Tuxford.

They resided on a rather special parcel of land close to the large dairy farm of the Cobb lads who were themselves farmers and landowners of note. The remaining de Montefort land amounted to about fifty acres and was dedicated to the care of half a dozen hunters. Both Claudia and Guy her husband were members of the local hunt and also frequent guests at the big and very important Belvoir meets. Unusually for such fanatic horse people their only equine pursuit was that of riding to hounds, and they took a long and complete break from riding during the off season that embraced most of the summer and a bit more. That they loved their hunters and lavished on them only the best available hardly needs saying.

The autumn season had only just begun when Claudia consulted me on a hunter that was thin. Grey Lord; their ten year old super star, was not working well, and I was called in because their usual vet; a specialist from Lincoln, had taken a three week sabbatical. I did know them having had the dubious pleasure of attending a number of routine problems in the past; young budding horse vets get to become proper horse vets by initially picking up any crumbs that fall their way.

Tuxford is a fascinating village.

It has a long and distinguished history in the annals of the legends and facts of the county of Nottinghamshire; the lack of coal in the immediate vicinity saved the region from the rush into urbanisation of much of the county. The sensible attitude of the locals to farming and the many conservation minded people in the area, allowed some of the chalky meadows to thrive as they had done since before the Doomsday Survey. Wood anemone, Giant Bell-flower and Butterfly Orchid are some of the pretties that may be spotted if one cares to look for them.

My first visit to Grey Lord brought out something unexpected; it was highlighted by the numbers of Autumnal Gentian flowers blooming on the roadside outside their entrance. I actually left my car for a better look at them and within a few minutes a loud *view halloo* brought the lady of the Manor to my attention as her powerful voice echoed off the walls of the stables, "Are you all right there is there something wrong with your car?"

I shook my head, gave her a big wave and climbed back into the Saab and finished my journey, whereupon her next question thoroughly surprised me, "Were you looking at my *Gentiana amarella* plants, I hope you didn't pick any of them?"

It does not matter how long I have been in practice, people always retain the ability to surprise me; I would never have guessed that such a strong minded woman would have been so knowledgeable about plants. Her enthusiasm, coupled with the fact she appreciated my interest in such matters, had an amazing effect on my relationship with the family, and my association with them immediately raised a couple of rungs on the ladder and I became their usual stable vet.

We took a late afternoon walk through the stables.

Before my already good day came to an end I again examined their handsome big grey hunter, who's long and rather plain Irish head spoke volumes for his inherent kindness. I checked him out thoroughly from top to tail sighed and said, "I simply cannot find the slightest thing wrong with him, apart from a slightly higher pulse rate than normal and his general weakness. His stable doesn't have the powerful urine smell of an individual with kidney disease, but he is thin and he doesn't look like one of your horses."

While Claudia and I were discussing him one of the grooms; a Yorkshire lass called Margaret, asked if she might feed him, "Sorry Mam! Would it be convenient if I give him his supper now, or should I leave it until the vet has gone?"

Claudia looked at me and when I nodded at the girl a large basin of food was dumped into the horse's manger. I remember thinking that the manger being placed on the back wall of the stable was in an unusual position. The horse immediately and very positively attacked his food with an alacrity that suggested the possibility of a medical reason for his weight loss was unlikely and Claudia exclaimed, "That does not look like any of the usual problems to me. He just does not look like a sick horse and I wonder if we are dealing with an unusual liver or tumour problem?"

Her words clearly expressed my own thoughts and I nodded again, while my restless mind whirred away even when asking the usual questions, "I suppose you still deworm and have their teeth done in the usual manner?"

Our discussion continued as we watched the horse wolf down his food; a pause that gave me time to consider my next move, "I am coming past this way first thing in the morning. Please exercise him as usual, but do not give him any breakfast. I will collect some samples from him and we can ask the lab to check out the usual parameters.

I was soon on my way home.

My journey was made somewhat more pleasant by the sudden and dramatic lifting of the low stratus clouds that had hidden the sun for most of the day, although my mind was still turning over rapidly; there must be an answer to this problem, there has to be a logical explanation for the horse being in this condition. My mind stopped whispering and I talked to the Saab or myself, "This is no good Alex, you must try some lateral thinking in this case, it is not a medical problem nor is he simply being overworked."

The problem made me restless during most of the evening, and the morning found me keen to check the fella over again. On arrival at the farm I collected the multi-coloured vials of blood for the lab, made slightly more difficult as Grey Lord was more agitated than normal; in a stable with very set ways the lateness of his much needed breakfast was beginning to pee him off. I spoke to him, "Now then big man, please relax. I must put a note on the lab request to the effect that your blood report will have to be considered in view of your being excited." It is a fact that blood counts; in particular haemoglobin, pcv and sedimentation rates are affected by an increased heart rate and we took these into consideration when looking at the results.

I popped up to the Manor house.

It was my intention to advise Claudia the bloods had been taken; coffee was also possible. I took a less direct route than normal to enjoy more of their magnificent garden when I saw the old dovecotes; there were four of them, massive structures that although partly buried under an exuberant growth of ivy were still imposing.

The lady of the house happened to be coming in my direction and, on noticing my interest in the dovecotes, she again surprised me, "Morning Alex, are you interested in pigeons?"

My reply along the lines that racing birds had also been a family hobby encouraged the lady to delve into that subject at a length which surprised me, "Tuxford is famous for its pigeons," She continued by telling me there was at one time a huge market locally where birds for the table were sold in enormous numbers, "One well recorded event that took place around eighteen eighty confirms that a single higler (a dealer in pigeons) from Huntingdonshire, actually bought no less than seven hundred dozen birds from one market here on one day."

Pigeon squabs were valuable sources of protein.

That was true all over the world and partly explains why they regularly crop up (nice pun there) in Biblical times. Most houses encouraged pigeons to nest in their roofs as the birds flew out to gather their own food and the squabs were regularly harvested two, even three times annually as free meat.

As our discussion flowed along those lines, I saw this lady in a different light and I was wrapped up in her presence and, although perhaps about fifteen years older than me her attractiveness suddenly struck me; perhaps I had never seen her smile before! She was at that beautiful stage in a woman's life; that stage when they know who they are, and are confident and comfortable with themselves.

We rattled on a bit more about pigeons and then I remembered my partner Seamus' father was an expert on such matters, and had an impressive collection of photographs of dovecotes throughout the land; she was fascinated!

I took my leave of the farm.

The blood samples were carefully packed off for processing. The results were telephoned through to us the next day and apart from a mild degree of anaemia; as evidenced by poorer than normal haemoglobin and red cell figures, the horse should have been in perfect health. None of the enzyme parameters that might have suggested cancer or other significant organ problems revealed any abnormalities.

Although the blood results were actually good news they were still disappointing as it is often more difficult to satisfy owners with negative results, rather than confuse them with healthy results in an otherwise abnormal animal.

Claudia's reaction was exactly as I expected, "I suppose it is good news that nothing unpleasant has been detected, yet I am still confused; what is wrong with the poor creature?" That's how she reacted to my detailed report on the telephone. At the same time she also asked if I could pop in again, as another of the hunters had gone lame behind after a long run that morning through the ploughed fields near Newark.

I was uncomfortable and puzzled.

It was with some consternation I returned to the farm, and, it was again late afternoon when shortly after my arrival, another groom Celeste, brought out Jameson, a huge chestnut thoroughbred who rather unusually had no white markings on his legs. The only attractive thing about the rather plain creature was the perfect diamond of a star that shone out clearly on a flat forehead before it climbed onto a long Roman nose.

The farrier had already removed his shoes in an effort to find bruising or a small abscess under his steels; always check out the common things first.

Jameson was well known to me; his size at 17 hands was big for a thoroughbred and his conformation was not good due to a long sloping back and rather weak quarters which led down to the straight hocks that are often the source of problems in hunters. He was not a particularly pleasant horse to deal with and a kick was always possible, and I had learned he would not tolerate any *namby pamby* approaches; it was important to be confident with him or he would push his luck and be a nuisance.

The big chestnut stood square on the cobbled yard. When he turned his head to look at me it was easy to imagine his mind working out what was going to happen next. I walked boldly up to his shoulder and slapped him rather more generously than normal on his nearside wither, than I would have done with most horses, and at the same time I introduced myself, "Now then you great big lump of mellow Irish whiskey, you must not forget who you are dealing with today. You know I will not stand for any of your shenanigans." He almost smiled at me, and produced a great sigh to indicate he recognised me and that he would behave himself.

My examination followed the usual pattern.

There was a touch of tension and sensitivity of the hamstring muscles above the stifle joint on the off side, and, although he walked fairly well, he nodded a bit when trotted in the confined yard. I needed some more information and asked Celeste, "I need you to take him into the paddock and trot him out for me, it looks like a slight strain on the hamstring tendon and I wonder if he might loosen up with some work."

The rather dour groom was unusually noisy; she never stopped chattering as she fitted him with a bridle and we set off towards the paddock at the rear of the stables. That was different as we usually worked in their schooling arena, so I asked what her intentions were, "Why are we not going into the arena with him?"

Her reply satisfied me, "We harrowed that deeply this morning and it might still be on the soft side."

I followed horse and girl to the paddock, and, as we left the yard, another groom started feeding the horses. As I passed Grey Lord's stable I halted for a moment to again watch the big fella's attitude to his food; the manner of his munching away with his characteristic speed and enthusiasm made me bite my lip.

Celeste soon had the chestnut into his stride and on the lunge he wasn't moving that badly; in fact he was almost back to his normal stride. His gait never followed the usually fluent pattern that makes the moving horse such a thing of beauty; his conformation ensured him to be a hunter rather than a show horse.

I absentmindedly drifted away from him and watched their little flock of pretty bantams.

It was easy to enjoy the little birds.

They were gathered at the back of one of the stables and from their excitement it was obvious they were feeding; they squabbled and scratched as chickens usually do and something caught my interest and urged me to stride over to them. Only then did I notice something of an unusual nature was taking place. The birds were feeding on a mixed grain ration that appeared to be slipping out between a gap in the bricks that formed the back of one of the stables. As the paddock was set at about two feet lower than the stables it was not difficult to identify where the grains were flowing from. Each of the four stables in the line had a single window space opened at their rear for ventilation and it appeared to be the second stable from the right that was causing the excitement.

I almost shouted, "Why that must be Grey Lord's box that the . . ." My opinion was confirmed when the long plain nose of the big grey peeked out of the window and it made me slap my hand hard against my thigh and called out, "That's it I've got it now!"

I had solved the horse's problem.

With the aid of a batch of happy little chickens; Grey Lord had an expression on his face clearly telling the chickens to stop eating his food, the reason for his almost canine hunger and poor condition was clear. I was so excited I forgot completely about Celeste and her chestnut as I almost ran round to the other side of the stables and, on entering Grey Lord's stable I immediately went to his manger. It was beautifully lined in hard plaster and was spotlessly clean and more to the point it was completely empty of food and yet the manger itself appeared superficially at any rate to be in an excellent state of repair and I was fascinated.

I explored the manger with my fingers and only then did the reason for the leak become apparent; there was a gap between two of the outside bricks where the mortar had fallen out. It was a space of about half an inch deep by three inches long and was concealed from anything other than a detailed inspection, by the fact that the upper brick was set just a shade prouder than the others and perfectly concealed the hole in the wall.

It was easy to piece together the final answer and I talked to him, "No wonder you are thin, you are plain hungry." As the fella was being fed his muzzle pushed most of his meal out through the hole in the wall. None of the grooms had noticed the problem, although twice daily they would routinely have checked for any leavings and the fact his manger was always spotlessly clean ensured there was no further need for the grooms to examine it carefully. My smile was a huge one as I turned to the horse and continued, "Great news my friend we have found the problem and I am now going to organise you another feed."

I closed the stable door firmly behind me and called to the other groom, "Come Margaret and see something very exciting, but please bring me another full feed for Grey Lord and put it into a basin." We soon had the food in the box with him and he at first gobbled it down in his normal manner until, probably realising this feed was not going to disappear, he settled down into a very contented rhythm of normal munching.

At that point I remembered Celeste and the chestnut.

The dutiful girl was still energetically working the horse and as I approached them it was clear he was again working well. There was no way I could begin to talk about the chestnut until the happy tale of the grey and the chickens had been thoroughly explained. Credit to the girls, they were disappointed none of them had noticed the problem until the anatomy of the damaged area was clearly pointed out, when they agreed it was not an easy spot to find.

I turned my attention to the chestnut that was becoming increasingly agitated and no doubt worried he was going to miss a feed. We brought him back into the yard and again I had him standing square on the cobbles and thought; definitely a bit of a tweak on the hamstrings, but why?

Prof Weipers, the brilliant Dean of the Faculty at Glasgow always said; "The answer to most horse's problems are in the feet, and, if you do not find anything wrong there then the answer is clear," I remember how he paused for effect at that point and continued, "Go back to basics and study the feet again."

Right, I thought; if it was good enough for the Dean! In all fairness Jameson was not the most perfect of specimens as far as conformation went, and therefor he was one of those odd characters where the base line to work from was disjointed. I wondered; if it is his feet the toes on his hind feet are a touch longer than they should be, so I asked the groom, "Tell me Margaret have you just changed farriers?"

She responded that Mr Channing; their farrier of many years, had been out of action for three months due to sustaining a nasty fracture to his femur as a result of a bad kick, and that one of his young chaps; and here she almost swooned, "He is the most gorgeous thing you have ever seen and when he bends over and shows off his . . ."

"So Margaret I get the message but what about the feet?"

"Gosh I am so sorry, I . . ."

"The feet Margaret, I need to know about the feet."

"Yes. Edward is excellent although he did remark last week that Jameson's feet have gone up in size."

"Ok that is interesting, I must talk to Channing."

I called him from the stables.

"Now then Farrier Channing how are you, is that leg of yours coming back into action?"

His reply was typical of a man from the depths of Lincolnshire and his lovely soft accent held just a touch of humour in it, "I should have consulted you right at the beginning. The doctor said at one point that they did not know whether or not to fix it or to chop it off, and I told them they must either fix it or shoot me. It's still very stiff but if I do not get back into action soon my wife will kill me."

We continued on in the normal banter that exists between most vets; not all, and farriers, and then I explained the problem in some detail, "I need your help with one of the de Montefort horses, the big ugly chestnut . . ."

"That can only be Jameson you're talking about, he is no oil painting is he?"

"That's the one although they do say he is a fabulous hunter, don't they?"

"And as the actress said to the Bishop; that's the name of the game."

I did not quite get the intended message from that last statement, and we got down to business with Channing telling me he would be back in the saddle next week and, as much as he did like Edward and had high hopes for him he did have a bit of a problem focusing when he was in yards where the girls were pretty, "He spends so much time chatting the lassies up that he loses concentration, and, where I have noticed the problem is that he is getting a bit lazy with the hind feet."

"Bingo, that's what I hoped for."

Channing finished off by saying, "It's obvious the young fellow is shoeing some of the hunters as though they were in training and, in an effort to give them a longer stride he is allowing the toes to sneak away from the feet a bit."

"That's an interesting thought."

"Leave it with me and I will make it my priority to sort him out next week."

I was happy the farrier had agreed with my opinion, but, at no time had I actually told him what I thought was wrong, at no time had I suggested what should be done to fix the horse, and at no time had I actually given Channing my opinion.

I had followed my standard practical approach when talking to a farrier. I told him how and where the horse was not functioning properly and then allowed him to come up with a solution. The art of talking to a farrier; of getting him to carry out the necessary corrective trimming, is to wait patiently until he suggests what you would like him to do and then to congratulate him. In that way the farrier thinks it is his good idea rather than me straying into his territory and upsetting him by telling him what to do!

I do not have any chips on my shoulders, but what I do have is an excellent rapport with a number of farriers and at the end of the day it is the horse that wins.

Jameson's feet were duly and correctly trimmed the following Monday.

We put the horse back into work and he hunted again a week later and was sound for the rest of the season.

I am convinced that Grey Lord knew I had solved his problem as he always seemed happy to see me.

But! I think the chickens hated me!

CHAPTER 16

IT'S A WASTE OF TIME

THE UPLANDS TO the east are challenging, and the hills of Dumfries were calling me.

It is a region where only specialists, animal and man, can survive and even thrive. Andrew Cummings was such a man, a man designed for such an existence; a man whose family had farmed there for so long only an oak casket would drag him off the hill.

He caught me watching a mountain hare one day, smiled and said, "I see you enjoy my hills, I confess I always have to watch the hares myself, they seem so superior to most other creatures."

I resisted the temptation to respond and was glad I did, as his next comment still clings to me many years later, "When I see a hare running up the hill I feel their freedom and they make me think of what a joy heaven must be." We were kindred spirits as we watched the hare jog up and over the hill.

When he was thinking Andrew would take his hat off his head and rub it across his forehead, and when he did it again the pause that followed encouraged me to consider him in more detail. The tall, heavy man must have played in the second row at some time, and, although his spine was now well past such activity, his frame hinted at the powerful shape that had blessed his youth. His face, particularly the ears; large stick out ears that were always sunburned and dominated the sides of his face, bore the marks of the many hectic encounters his youth had encouraged. He had a strong rugged face that lorded over a chiselled chin that when thrust forward gave him an air of substance, and made him a man worth listening to.

1972 was a time of traditional attitudes.

Farmers had a different relationship with their animals and the land, and this was typified by Andrew's cow Rachael who as the house cow was a more valuable part of the homestead than their sixty or so beef cows. When regulations came into force concerning the identification of cattle, the house cow was often missed; the mandatory insertion of numbered steel tags through their ears did not really apply to them, did it? It's always seemed odd to me that cows wear earrings; mind you, when I think of what young ladies get up to nowadays, but that is another story. Bulls; however, look very masculine at the best of times, and a large copper nose ring even enhances that look.

Theresa, who says my attitude to ladies getting dolled-up is also primitive, once forcibly commented to some of our friends, "Alex can at times act like a cave man, he believes the vast majority of women look better without makeup and his special dislike is face paint with, what he calls, 'that thick Christmas style of bright red lipstick.'"

When Theresa again brought up the subject my defensive comment threw her, "I cannot even imagine what you would look like wearing such rubbish."

I thought the conversation was closed, not a chance; the end game arrived a few minutes later when she said, "Silly me! I should take the fact you prefer me wearing very little makeup as a compliment to my own exceptional skin."

"There you are my dear, how can makeup improve on perfection?" Sometimes I think rather well on my feet.

Our lives in veterinary practice were brim full of excitement.

That morning's visit was another adventure, one that began with a four forty am telephone call, from an obviously excited, and out of breath Janet, "Mister Vet please visit us at Balgowan; its Rachael, she's trying to have her calf, but things are not looking good. She is lying flat out on her side and beginning to blow up, Andrew thinks she has milk fever, and she is not good."

"Gosh Janet, that does sound bad, I am on my way so please open some of the gates for me."

Theresa's natural sleep patterns do not allow her to awaken as quickly as mine do, so there must have been something in my serious response that roused her, as, for some obscure reason she was also awake and said, "I am coming with you."

"Are you sure my dear, it is still very early."

Her reply was a gruff, "I said I am coming".

"OK my dear, but get a move on, Janet is excited and quite out of breath as her cow sounds bad."

We flew along the empty country roads and ten minutes passed before Theresa realised what she had done, "I must be mad, here I am out in the pitch black, on my way to see a smelly cow, when I should be snugly tucked up in my warm bed, I must be mad."

She was actually talking to herself, but I responded, "Now my love that is not a nice attitude to take! Why not think of this as a time for us to do a bit of bonding?" She's a good woman and I was looking forward to her help with the gates so I squeezed her thigh gently, she almost smiled.

Balgowan is on a large country estate.

The farm is situated some four miles off the tar road and is reached by a stop-go process during which seven sets of gates have to be negotiated. I never dared leaving gates open for fear of the sheep who always watched me closely, always looking for an opportunity to indulge in their favourite hobby of seeking greener pastures, even in the middle of the night.

A sheep's second hobby is dying; they drown in water buckets, they bloat up when they lay on their backs for too long, and they get one infection after another. I often wished I could listen to their rambling conversations as some of those woolly chats would have been interesting and probably along these lines, "It really is getting boring in this field so let's have a bit of fun? Maybe one or two of us should do a bit of dying, that usually livens up the situation." It has been said, by those who know a thing or two about sheep, that they are so stupid they can actually pull the wool over each other's eyes!

The morning was untroubled by any daylight.

I was grateful for my wife's company as I watched her stoically open and close the last of the farm gates. As the car screeched to a halt outside the small byre I said, "Please bring the calcium while I take a look." I jogged into the barn and went straight to the cow.

Andrew's cow was in trouble and as I knelt beside her and felt her pulse I knew for a fact his cow was in big trouble, "Awful, simply awful."

"Here is the needle."

My hand automatically took the needle from Theresa's hand, and plunged it into the cow's jugular vein and then set up the calcium drip she passed me and I cried out, "No!" I breathed deeply before continuing, "Please don't die on me! No, please don't die!"

I held the brown glass bottle high in the air hoping the medicine would flow into the cow as fast as my own heart rate was racing and the desperate tone in my voice clearly indicated my opinion to the others, "We are too late, we are losing her and there is nothing I can do." I shook my head from side to side and said, "No! No! No! Look at the colour of her blood." Some of it was oozing back into the syringe and it was dark, much too dark.

My concerned wife offered to help, "What can I do, can we help?"

"Sorry dear this is a disaster."

Theresa agreed with me, "I have never seen blood this colour before, is she, really going, to die on us?" I didn't know what to say and merely nodded my head.

Rachael was in big trouble.

Theresa later remarked there had been a haunting note of despair in my voice, "I am sorry Andrew we are losing her." The drip, which on so many occasions had almost miraculously brought life to dying cows, rushed into her blood stream and I pleaded with her to hold on and give the calcium the few minutes it needed to work, "No! Please don't die on me," I could not stop pleading with the cow or myself and sadly, no one was listening!

Sometimes I hate being right!

Rachael gave a great sigh, stretched out her neck, opened her mouth and made her final noise. She exhaled a loud rush of bubbling air, a characteristic noise that as it heralds the end of things, is termed the death rattle; she was unconscious and at least her end was not painful.

It was a sad scene and also an irritating one, "Damn it, but she has just died on us!"

My outburst began to release the tension that gripped us and Theresa said nothing, although the grip of her fingers on my arm clearly indicated the pain she felt and one of her nails actually drew blood.

CHAPTER 17

CAN WE SAVE THE CALF?

R ACHAEL'S CELEBRATION OF life had closed, but we had to continue. In the practical world of farming the chapter that had been Rachael's life ended and I did not have time to wallow in self-pity, nor was I able to indulge myself in depression, I had to focus my attention on the wet, pathetic looking, little creature trying to squeeze its way into the world, and said, "Come on guys, let's help this wee thing." The fragile bag of skin and bones we faced had been unable to drag itself into the world as the Milk Fever that caused Rachael's fatal paralysis also delayed her calf's birth.

Janet issued a grim prognosis, "I am afraid the calf is also dead."

My opinion was similar, but until it was actually born I could not be certain, "You are probably right," I grabbed its front legs and said, "Hang on there, did you see that?" Her tiny tongue moved slightly, "We have a chance to save this calf."

Janet waved her head sharply from side to side and her almost white short pony tail reminded me of a Shetland pony in full flight as she too confirmed that movement, "I also saw it move, can I do something to help?"

"Hang on a moment." With my hands gripped firmly on each of the small front legs I was already pulling the calf from its mother.

Another calf was born.

After nine months of being pampered in the comfort of her dam's uterus, the real world called her and, because the calf had taken too long to be born it was deprived of oxygen and we had to act quickly. Theresa was slipping into shock, standing there and not reacting and a swift glance towards her made me aware of how horrible the experience was for her. It was her first taste of death and she was at a loss for words, and unable to act and continued to look blankly at the pathetic calf, as the rest of us moved quickly with the new found energy emergency situations bring.

As she came closer to me Theresa was in an odd numb place and she looked blankly at the calf and stuttered out a few words, "I, must, help."

I was abrupt with her and tried to change her attitude and focus by almost shouting at her, in what was a dramatic and insensitive manner, "Come Tess waken up and help me do something to help this poor, motherless creature."

As her reactions began to improve she picked up my sense of urgency and began to respond, while the calf's incomplete respiratory efforts made me shake my head and cry out, "Tess, look at the poor creature. Can you see how badly she is breathing?"

That brought a gasping reply from Janet, "She already looks a goner, have we any chance of saving her?"

I shook my wife gently on the shoulder and replied, "She doesn't look good, but maybe with Theresa's help we can save her."

My wife looked at me.

Her wide, gorgeous eyes that were full of sadness began focusing better. The calf was breathing although the infrequent, shallow rise and fall of her chest gave us little hope. Andrew noticed the mucous membranes in her cold, wet mouth were the wrong colour of red and said, "I don't like that colour it is much too dark."

Janet echoed his doubts, "I do not like that tongue she is going to die." The tongue held the same colour as the rest of the mouth, a deep, dark, and definitely unhealthy looking purple and her heart rate was much too fast, while its associated pulse was weak.

The sense of urgency in my voice kept everyone motivated, "Quickly Andrew and Janet! Hold her up by the back legs and help me drain fluid out of her lungs." The slip of a calf weighed only fifty pounds and they soon had her swinging upside down in the air, her tongue lolling aimlessly from her mouth while I used a towel to clean a cupful of mucous out of her nostrils, mouth and throat and then issued my next sharp command, "OK, that should do, let her down and I will give her a blow," I enlisted Theresa's assistance, "OK Tess, now the real work must begin and you know what I need you to do."

By that time my young wife was almost back to normal and she knelt in the straw beside me and said, "Yes . . . I can do this."

I breathed into the calf's nostrils to initiate CPR.

I gave the calf what might have appeared to the casual observer a long, romantic kiss. My lips completely embraced the soft skin of her muzzle and, as my exhaled air became her intake supply, it caused the skinny chest wall to expand. Only a few seconds had passed since we dragged the calf free from her mum and as Theresa had recovered we began operating as an efficient team, and I continued to encourage her, "That's it Tess you have the right rhythm."

"Good, it also feels right to me," Her own hurried breathing caused her speech to sound distorted as she compressed the weak, frail chest of the calf with the flat of her hands, and counted, "Right! Here goes . . . one . . . two . . . three . . ." She marked time by counting out at intervals of two seconds, each time she depressed the ribs.

CPR is a combination of two physical efforts.

The first phase involves the operator breathing for the animal and the second is a compression of the chest, a squeeze that is designed to encourage blood to flow from the heart into the circulation and lungs. As Theresa counted out the sixth squeeze she paused, and I again blew into the calf's nostrils and then as the chest inflated Theresa continued her six squeeze routine. It was Theresa's turn to encourage me, "That's it Alex, if this baby is going to have any chance we have to keep going," At the end of her next cycle of chest pumping she continued, "Yes, we must keep going, I think we have a chance."

My wife showed remarkable resilience by swinging from being a total zombie to being in control and I again admired the manner in which she can summon up such energy, and how she can be so determined and so enthusiastic. I lost count of the many times she said, "We must keep going, please keep trying for another few minutes."

When first acquainted with CPR her reaction was interesting.

Theresa's initial reaction was to wrinkle her cute little nose in displeasure as it seemed such an unpleasant activity, yet her first effort had met with thrilling success. She had been excited with saving that calf's life, and impulsively kissed her vet as a reward for his efforts and the taste of my mouth, still wet from the products of conception, surprised her and made her blurt out, "My, but that was a really sloppy kiss, the taste of your lips is quite, different."

Our friends often asked her about kissing near dead calves and she always remarked how surprisingly sweet the smell and taste of the fresh birth fluids are, and then admitted that CPR was never likely to feature in the Guinness Book of Records.

The little one proved difficult.

There was no response and I became frustrated at the thought of another failure, "Dear God it is bad enough losing one patient, please do not let me lose two at the same time." I was exasperated, I hate losing patients!

Matronly Janet's thinking was expressed in a manner that suggested we would be unsuccessful, "There is no point wasting any more effort, you two have done your best," We had never worked on a calf for such a long period and the patience of the matronly, sixty something lady was slipping away and she said, "Mister Vet it doesn't look good, I don't think she is going to make it."

I glanced at everyone to assess the general feeling and I could not help feeling she was probably right, but before I could comment Theresa joined the conversation, "No! Please don't give up! I know we can do this, please!" Her earnest appeal encouraged us to continue.

I spluttered out my intentions, "Yes it is bad, but not yet hopeless, we must keep trying for a few more minutes."

I felt Andrew's heavy hand on my shoulder, "It's no use Alex, you have done your best, and you should stop now."

His paternal voice, coupled with the tiredness that threatened to engulf me, almost convinced me to give up and then the look on Theresa's face forced me onwards, "Not yet Andrew! Come on team, cheer up, we will give it a few more minutes."

Our rigid application of CPR was rewarded and we won!

Theresa had just finished more than fifty cycles at CPR, when the lump of wet, cold, immobile meat, that was the calf, suddenly surprised us when it let out a gasp, produced a huge yawn and started to breathe by itself. The tired Theresa was suddenly rejuvenated and released an excited Alleluia; one that was as powerful as any she would ever utter during the highlight of the Easter celebrations, "Alleluia! She is coming round, have we saved her life?"

The calf was alive, and the colour of the mucous membranes lining the inside of her mouth began to lose their hellish darkness and rapidly began the transition to a healthier shade. First they lightened to a softer red then hurried on to a much richer pinkness and her heart rate slowed to near normal levels, and her breathing began to be less hectic. Her little body began to move as oxygen rich blood flowing into the muscles of her limbs and neck, kick-started her life.

If the calf's first gasps had been a surprise they were well echoed by Theresa's further, and even more excited comments, "Well look at that, she is breathing, we have done it."

Our calf was indeed alive and quickly developed a restless trembling over her head and shoulders that extended until it embraced her entire body. It was followed by a marked contraction and extension of her limbs that made her become obviously, and increasingly so, alive. Her slender neck bent in an effort to raise a sorry looking head and an incongruously long pair of wet ears flopped wearily from her high, domed forehead. Even then the eyes were special; a pair of huge, dark brown and very beautiful eyes stared at me, and had me day dreaming, imagining they were thanking me for saving her life.

I stood up.

That move, although it was designed to ease the aching pain in my lower back, caused a change in personnel as it must have been construed as my giving Janet the chance to take her place in the drama. She joyfully leapt into the scene in a manner that suggested she had been waiting on the side lines to become useful, and she spoke to the calf, "Now little one, my pretty little girl, this is my chance to do something."

Although I thought she was actually talking to herself, I enjoyed the efficiency of her treatment, and encouraged her, "That's it Janet, give her a good towelling, I bet you have never done this before?"

She jumped to the bait, "No! You are wrong I have done this many . . ." She paused for a few seconds to steal a glimpse at my smiling face, and said, "Why Mister Vet, you have got me again, you are always teasing me."

The farmer's wife continued towelling and every part of the calf's chest and abdomen was subjected to her massage, with a degree of energy that would have seemed harsh to an outsider. She must have witnessed birthing problems many times in her long, stock filled life, yet there was still more than just a touch of excitement in her voice, "Now then little one, this good rubbing will soon help you breathe better."

Theresa linked her arm in mine.

We watched Janet rub the calf's body in a circular motion that helped replace the generous licking she should have received from her mother. Theresa left my side and joined Janet on her knees in the straw and said, "Is there anything I can do?" She was ready to repeat CPR if the calf stopped breathing. She fondled the calf's head and said, "It's amazing! Her ears that were so slippery and cold are changing and I can feel her body beginning to warm up," She paused and looked at me for a moment and her smile was a huge one, "Is it because her improving circulation is pumping blood through her little body?"

"Spot on my lovely wife, as her circulation improves she will warm up." I stroked Theresa's shoulder and somehow the dirty wet mark I left there was unimportant. I was, however, still cautious, although I was excited and beginning to share everyone else's optimism I had been disappointed before, I had seen them improve, only to fade away.

It took a further ten minutes before our calf began to look like a real animal and begin to resemble a fellow creature who had decided the world might be a place worth sharing and then my perceptive wife also picked up on the eyes I had first noticed, "Alex, look at her eyes she is going to be a real beauty."

"I also noticed them, why her eyes are nearly as lovely as your own." My wife enjoyed being buttered up, and she deserved some reward for the part she played in the rescue.

Andrew had been a quiet, almost unnoticed bystander.

It was he who brought the scene to its climax, "Now doesn't that look better than it did a few minutes ago?" He shook his head, and attempted to dig a thick index finger into one of his large ears and took a short pause before delivering his next comment, "Well done team, I am amazed at how determined you both were to save her life," His next comment was typical of a man who had spent much of his daily life wrestling with the hills, "Yes, indeed this little one deserves to play its part in this life and thanks to you Alex and Theresa for working so hard when I was convinced you were wasting your time."

It was, however, typical of that understated man, that he, Cummings, the hard working farmer at Balgowan was the first to change the scene and he turned to me, patted me softly on the shoulder and said, "Now I suppose we should get on with our lives," He scratched his forehead again and said, "And not one of us has even had the time to say good morning!"

That morning on Balgowan was an enriching experience.

Throughout my career such incidents have affected me and yet they have allowed the balance between the good times and the bad times to swing in a positive direction. The question I am often asked is, "Would I change my life if the opportunity arose, would I still be a vet?" The question does not even throw up any imponderable barriers, "Yes! I would do it all over again."

We lost Rachael.

We saved her daughter and such incidents involving life and death, are lessons in the University of Life, and were instrumental in moulding vet and farmer alike to become the men they are. Andrew was a man well past maturity and I suddenly noticed the look of age about him, his face, that was always deeply creased around his mouth, seemed older, more tired and he yawned deeply, exposing the yellowing enamel on his front teeth and, with a little smile observed, "Well Janet, at least it's a heifer so we might get another house cow out of this mess."

Theresa tugged at my sleeve, pulled me to the side then whispered, "What does Andrew mean by a house cow?"

I smiled and replied, "On many farms, particularly the more isolated communities, they keep a very special tame cow to produce milk for the household, and for the rearing of orphan calves and lambs."

"Oh! So losing Rachael is an even bigger loss to them than I thought."

I simply nodded and we followed Janet to the house.

Normality was quickly restored and the household swung back into action and the farmer's wife became her usual cheery self, "That's good news because she has only thrown bull calves for the last three years. I'll put on the kettle and we must have breakfast".

Andrew agreed, "Yes my dear. We will leave the little one to rest for a bit, and then she can have some colostrum."

During breakfast the atmosphere was reasonable.

We discussed only our success with the calf as closure to death comes quickly in farming practice. Our business at the kitchen table was soon complete; the meal had been attended to at a faster rate than usual as my anxious wife constantly pleaded, "Do you think we are leaving her too long by herself? It must be time for us to check her again? Are you sure we should be taking so long over our breakfast, don't you . . ."

"Enough whining woman, will you stop worrying over that calf?" Although my response had been tongue in cheek it bit hard, and Theresa's eyes took on that pre-tear shedding look, the one that melts all defences and made me concede, "OK. Let us go and look at her now." Although I attempted to make my attitude a confident blasé one, I too was anxious.

Janet was the first to leave the table.

She busied herself preparing breakfast for the two Border Collies that were the resident sheepdogs. Their meal was a collection of yesterday's scraps and a couple of slices of burnt toast that had also been casualties that morning; lost due to the excitement of the day. She led the way, carrying the basin of food and was surprised on finding a single dog by the door, "That's odd where is Chance this morning?"

She was one of the strangest Border Collies I had ever seen, as half of her face was pure white with a vertical split between the two sides running straight down the front of the head. The white half also contained the palest of pale wall eyes and that was lucky in a way as it softened the effect of what would have been by itself a remarkably chilling sight. The farmer on the next farm had been about to drown the puppy due to its odd looks and it had been rescued by Janet who had asked she be given the chance; hence his name, of doing something with it. Indeed as things turned out she was not only an exceptional worker she was also extremely intelligent and friendly without developing the irritating habits of the spoiled lapdog.

Andrew agreed with Janet that he was surprised at the dog's absence and with some irritation in his voice he then said, "Leave their food for the moment until we check out the calf."

Our revisit was tinged with regret.

Those feelings heightened as we regained the scene and deliberately ignored the prone body of the cow that might have dominated us.

It was the sight of Chance that made Theresa gasp as the dog was snuggled up hard against the calf and was obviously doing her best to mother it and she said, "I have never seen that before, what a clever dog you are, you know this poor calf has lost its mother and are trying to help." Chance came to greet Theresa, gave her the softest of soft little whines and licked her fingers and then returned to her new baby.

Janet said, "This is the most remarkable creature and it is as though she does everything she can to go out of her way to thank us for saving her life."

Although she had not yet managed to find her feet, it was clear the calf was stronger and her body had already dried, allowing her to take on a sleek and softly hairy look. Theresa had to have the last word; that will come as no surprise to our many friends, "Oh I am so happy I came with you this morning," She snuggled up to me, and gave me one of her special hugs, "I feel the time we saved by my opening the gates may have been important, had we been a few minutes later my calf would have died."

Note she said; *my calf would have died*. I was already learning that much of the secret of marriage was to agree with my wife and I said, "You are right, although your energy during the CPR kept me going, when I was tempted to give up."

We headed for home.

Although nearing the end of March it was a comfortable morning with the weak reluctant dawn beginning to struggle from its resting place in the East. Perhaps it was our tummies, generously filled with a fine Scottish farmhouse breakfast that made the return trip a comfortable one.

The cycle of gate openings on the return journey did not feel too much of a nuisance and at the final one the loud, almost musical, bubbling sound of a whaup (curlew) came up to greet us. The large plover-like bird soared into flight from the bog away to our left with his regular call bubbling over the hill and heralding another working day. Theresa called out, "Isn't there something haunting, magical even, about the cry of the whaup?"

There are a few bird calls that easily signal ones position; the cry of the African Fish eagle is definitely one of them and the first cuckoo announcing the coming spring is another. The plaintive note of a whaup over a hill moor in the dawn is a perfect example.

The final gate clashed to a close.

It banged sharply behind Theresa whose mind still mused on the morning's events. There was time for a final, reflective look up the hill towards Balgowan where the farm was snugly embraced in a sea of grass and heather. It would forever be imprinted on the celluloid of our memories by its association with Rachael's death.

The plaintiff call of all whaups afterwards brought back memories of what had been for us a morning that summed up the highs and lows of veterinary practice.

CHAPTER 18

TESSA

W HEN WE RETURNED six weeks later Janet took Theresa by the hand.

She led us into the room beside the kitchen, and, as she opened the door Janet turned, looked gently into Theresa's eyes and her voice was soft, "Have a look at the result of your successful morning's work."

Rachael's calf was already a much different creature and she, and Chance her constant companion, made it obvious they were happy to see us.

"Jings look at you, who would ever believe such a gorgeous creature is the one we struggled with that night?" Theresa's eyes lit up like the lights on a Christmas tree.

"We are so pleased with her, she is perfect and a very lucky little girl," Janet stepped over to my side and gave the sleeve of my jacket a soft tug and smiled a very special smile before turning towards Theresa again, "It is all down to you and we have named her Tessa, after you."

Theresa was speechless, we both were and for a moment I thought she was going to cry, then a look of pride made her face take on an almost heavenly glow, making her as beautiful as I ever remembered her, "Wow! What an honour and that has never happened to me before, it makes me feel as though I am her mum. I am so thrilled to be linked by name to such a gorgeous creature, thank you so much." As she expressed her thoughts, her actions reflected that pride and she knelt and gave her calf a big hug. Tessa also showed her appreciation by giving one of those long gentle *moos* we heard so often in the future. Chance joined in with another version of her soft gentle whines and such a happy scene gave all of us a lump in our throats.

Tessa was more than special.

As the calf had been named in Theresa's honour she became even more important than we could have imagined and Theresa talked about Tessa so much in the future we felt she was part of our family.

"Well Alex, how do you think she is coming along?" Andrew was anxious to see what I thought about the calf; he also had a great grin on his face, one that suggested there was more to come.

In the midst of that happy moment there was something interesting about the calf that caught my attention. I saw the beginnings in her of a different specimen to her late mother and I studied the calf, Theresa, and then the calf again, "Ah! I think I've got it Andrew!" I quizzed my wife on the subject, "Now Theresa, can you notice something unusual about your namesake?"

Theresa stood and took a step back from Tessa and it was clear from her reply she had not noticed anything unusual about the calf's appearance, "I can see you are looking puzzled," She studied Tessa for a further few moments then said, "To me she is simply gorgeous and I don't see anything unusual going on."

"Stop mooning over the thing for a few minutes and concentrate. You have seen lots of Jersey calves by now so what is there about Tessa that makes her quite different?"

Theresa again looked carefully at Tessa as the calf relished the good scratching her ears received, "She doesn't appear to have any white colouring on her body, and, she is also much stronger looking than most Jerseys, is it something like that you are thinking about?"

I was impressed as my wife, after a shaky beginning to her life in farming, was getting the hang of the thing, and I was also pleased my patient teaching was reaping its due benefits, "Now there's a clever girl, that is part of the answer," I linked my arm in hers, and gave it a squeeze before continuing, "What is it about her shape that catches your eye?"

Theresa looked at me then disengaged herself from my arm. She stood back from the calf and took her time before replying, "She is chunky when most of the Jersey calves I have seen are fine, refined things."

"Now you really impress me, you must have a good teacher."

Tessa was an unusually dark colour.

It was her being almost black that first caught my eye and made me ready to bring the quiz session to a close and turned to the farmer and framed the question intriguing us, "Andrew, I see that Tessa is growing well, and already seems to have her mother's character, yet surely she is too strong to be pure bred Jersey?"

Andrew looked rather sheepishly at me and after a short pause, a generous grin spread over his face then, in a somewhat halting manner, he allowed an interesting story to unfold, "Well, it was one of those accidents, Rachael (Tessa's mum) was bulling; a term indicating a cow's readiness for mating, and we were busy with the sheep shearing and she went looking for a boyfriend, and somehow managed to find her way into the field with the Galloway bull," He surprised me by pointing to the calf with an extravagant flourish of his cap, "And here we have the result, and now we are wondering what will become of your great work?"

Theresa was engrossed and missed the sense of humour that flickered across my face before my follow-up remark was delivered in a tone sprinkled with a bit of tongue in cheek humour. My opinion on the calf's parentage was spot on and the temptation to tease Janet simply could not be resisted so I gave her a huge smile, and remarked, "Now Janet, I don't think that was an accident. I am sure Rachael was in control of that situation and I am sure she knew very well what she was doing with the bull. Isn't it a fact that love will always find a way?"

My teasing question hit home and Janet's face instantly went a deep shade of red to indicate Cupid's arrow was securely lodged in the bull's eye, "Oh Mister Vet, don't you be speaking of such things like that in front of an old married woman?" Janet; a lovely prim and proper Presbyterian lady in her sixties, could always be made to blush, as indeed I do, and I enjoyed pulling her leg when the opportunity arose.

Galloway crossbreds are not milk cows.

We were curious to establish their attitude to Tessa, "What will you do with her then? Will you try her with the beef cows or will you move her on?"

Andrew took off his battered old deer stalker in a manner that suggested he was slowly considering the question. He took his time and perhaps the manner in which he gently scratched his head aided him in finding an answer, "It's a bit difficult really. After Rachael's death this little one was brought up in the kitchen for her first two weeks then she was moved to this special place next door to the kitchen," He paused for a few moments and gave Janet another great smile, "So you see, according to this special lady here she's not really a normal cow, she's more like a big dog." He gave Janet a quick cuddle and continued, "That is also partly due to the fact that Chance hardly left her side during those first two weeks and so you see we think we will give her a chance at producing a bit of milk, and then decide where her future lies".

Tessa was special; she had to be, as her birth, the manner of her naming, and the early days when she required intensive nursing, all contributed to her being extraordinary. Her progress was one we followed with almost paternal curiosity and during our regular visits to the farm we always enquired after her progress. She had an almost dog-like run of the homestead and energetically greeted every visitor. As the centre of attraction she probably considered herself at least partly human anyway.

Tessa was raised as a member of the family.

During her first months she had a dog-like attitude to the other animals and certainly to the people on the farm. Her fondness for people ensured she was always present when we visited, and always had a chat with her special family. Some cows are remarkably vocal, and Tessa developed her own repertoire of soft, amusing sounds which convinced Janet she had special calls for different people. On one occasion she said, "I have raised many calves on the bottle, but this one is special, I think she understands every word I say."

CHAPTER 19

A BOX ON THE NOSE

S HE WAS EXCEPTIONALLY attractive; in fact the lady was spectacularly beautiful.

Tessa was; and sorry I also meant to include Theresa, was exceptionally attractive! The calf was blessed with the typical contoured face of the Jersey with a longish nose that dipped and widened from the forehead before ending in a very generous and humorous mouth. It was Theresa who picked up that feature, "Have you ever seen a calf as pretty as my Tessa? I think it is that lovely, almost kissable mouth that makes her so special."

I agreed with Theresa's opinion on the calf's mouth, although for me it was her eyes that were amazing, "Now you pretty thing, I agree with your aunty, you do have a beautiful mouth, but your eyes are also lovely, you have the longest, thickest, and most wickedly curved eyelashes, I have ever seen." They were framed in deep liquid pools that ensnared me, and everyone else, with an invitation to come closer. Her irresistible enticement for the hapless admirer was those eyelids; when one is subjected to that ultimate in feminine coquettishness; the fluttering eyelid, the trap is complete and one is a Jersey fan forever.

Tessa developed quickly.

She was a beauty in a parish of beauties as her distinctive markings made her striking and stunningly attractive. She enjoyed being spoken to and listened intently by striking a pose that caused her head to rotate to the side with an upward tilt of her muzzle. She particularly enjoyed being told how beautiful she was; nothing unusual there! "Tessa you are looking very attractive today, your skin and hair are shining beautifully." That was one of the comments she especially enjoyed, and would pause for a few seconds, as though basking in the compliment.

I remember one occasion when Theresa had addressed the heifer in that manner, and she made me catch my breath; it must have been my feminine side coming to the surface and that allowed an unguarded moment to impress my lovely wife. I fascinated her by expressing some of my thoughts on female beauty and informed her there were many beautiful women in the county, "I know lots of truly gorgeous girls," I must have been drifting away from the real world as I continued, "But there are only a lucky few who possess the true stamp of individuality, a few who have that something special that makes them particularly attractive," I caught a bit of a strange look in her eye that made me think quickly, and I sensibly followed that statement by also placing Theresa into that category, "Yes my dear! It is just the lucky few, *such as yourself* who are truly attractive." That was a close one; my explanation was more than comfortably accepted,

Tessa and Chance continued with the remarkably close attachment they had formed and although his role as a working dog meant some separation, they always slept snuggled up together.

Orphaned animals are often a nuisance.

They tear at the heart strings of all connected with them by calling up the most basic of maternal instincts. The practice of rearing orphaned lambs and calves is a necessary, well established one that is an integral part of most stock households, but there are dangers, as it does have to be attended with a sense of detachment. It is always interesting to watch fostered animals mature, as most that were fun when small, change with time to become a nuisance.

The pet ram lamb raised on the bottle may often turn out to be a dominant monster, with a tendency to head-butt, and mount people from behind. As this usually happens unexpectedly the effect is often less than amusing and we fondly remember an incident when Theresa's brother, Francis, was mounted by an obviously hand reared, Impala buck that was roaming free in the picnic area of a small game reserve. His wife Pamela was either shocked or confused; it was difficult for her to quite make up her mind! Her excited comments were along the lines of, "I never knew whether to be affronted or jealous, it's funny when you see someone else that finds your man attractive." We laughed about that one for many a night.

Tessa was less than perfect.

She developed one bad habit, which, although it was initially amusing, soon proved a real nuisance. When working on farms it was often my practice to leave the car boot open, in order that I might easily fetch various items from my veterinary kit. This was impossible when Tessa was roaming, as she had a fascination for the human species, of which she was after all, an honorary member. She had to conduct a detailed investigation of all things human wherever possible, and if an open car boot was an attraction, an open veterinary boot was irresistible. In order to conduct a detailed examination of the contents each package had to be sniffed, licked and even chewed over. As many drugs were in soft cardboard packages she could make an impressive mess that was not just annoying, but costly, in view of the damage that made some products unfit for sale.

She produced many fond memories.

On one occasion she trapped her muzzle in a strong walled, plastic box. I noticed her when she returned to where we were working with a puzzled look on her face that clearly suggested her embarrassment. She stuck her long neck out towards me, and gently mooed in a manner that clearly meant, "Please take this thing off my nose".

We laughed at her, an action that compounded her sense of loss of dignity. Although feeling a bit miffed with us she patiently allowed the box to be cut off. I mumbled away to her while working at the box with a pair of heavy scissors, "My dear, dear Tessa, you really are a most interesting lady, but I do wish you would stop fiddling with my drugs."

Those who say that cows cannot smile would have changed their opinion that day as we believed Tessa, when she had taken a few moments to compose herself, grinned from ear to ear. Theresa said, "I think it is amazing how she just stood there so patiently while you took the box off her nose," As she stroked the heifer's neck she continued, "I think Janet is right you understand every word we say."

Tessa pointed her nose to the sky and then bent down towards Chance who gave her soft muzzle a serious licking of reassurance more than anything, and then she gave a long soft moo that we thought meant, "Naturally!"

Her tendency to fiddle with things meant that special precautions had to be taken when attending Balgowan and that being her only flaw meant we loved her to bits.

If the Princess of Balgowan had offered us some simple entertainment in the past, she amazed us in the future.

CHAPTER 20

THE COW AT THE WINDOW

H ER JUVENILE DEVELOPMENT was uneventful then Tessa's story continued and it was fascinating.

When she had blossomed into a strikingly beautiful lady of about two and a half years of age we visited Balgowan to pregnancy test the entire herd.

In those days the test was a manual one and was performed by me inserting my well lubricated arm directly into the cow's rectum in order I might palpate the uterus and its contents. Lest the more sensitive reader feels faint at the thought it is important to state, my entire arm was protected by a long, fine plastic glove. Most cows show hardly any reaction to this and I suppose it is not too dissimilar to some of the procedures ladies experience at the gynae; another good reason for being male.

I caught Theresa quite by surprise the first time she assisted me as a recorder, when I turned to her and announced, "Now dear one, perhaps you should pop into the crush, and I will check that all is well with you." That was too close to the bone, and the lady did not take kindly to that remark, and, as it was thoroughly enjoyed by the attendant farmers, all male, it caused her not just a little embarrassment. I had even offered to use a new glove and that did not help extricate me from a very dangerous situation and the good talking she gave to me afterwards ensured that mistake was never repeated!

It was a balmy day at the end of August.

Our drive up the long track, via its many gates, was a pleasant one and at the first one I squeezed Theresa's thigh and remarked, "So glad you are with me my dear."

"Are you enjoying my company, or merely glad to have me here as a gate opener?"

"What a silly thing to say, you know how much fun we have together." I tried to keep a straight face.

She frowned at me and as she offered me a half smile she gave me a hard backhanded slap on my chest that made me wince in surprise and caused her smile to become a delicious one.

There were lambs everywhere; the fields were full of small bundles of wool enjoying a bit of rumble and tumble on the well grassed slopes. Although it was early in the morning Theresa could not help thinking the setting was perfect for a picnic, "It would be nice if we could take a few hours off and that patch of soft looking grass would be just right for a bit of lunch . . ."

She was jolted back to reality when I called through the window, "Hello! We have a few cows to visit."

We arrived on time and found everyone ready for us.

Theresa initiated our conversation in the usual manner, "Greetings everyone, and how is my darling Tessa this morning?"

Andrew was the first to greet us and he said, "She and Chance were around this morning when we worked the herd to bring them down from the hill and then they disappeared."

"She is very well, although I haven't seen her or Chance for the last hour or so," Janet gave us a cuddle and said, "No doubt she will pop round to see what we are up to."

Theresa showed her surprise, "I think this must be the first visit where she has not been here to see me; I hope she is not hiding somewhere because she is sick?"

"Now then Theresa, stop being a vet's wife for a few minutes. She was perfectly normal this morning and I am sure she will join us shortly." Andrew gave her a huge, reassuring smile.

Janet said, "Although we will have to find her and she must also be tested."

I surveyed the scene.

The air was full of the normal sounds and smells, of penned, anxious cattle. As always, the elderly matriarchic was determined to be the first cow through, although she took some time to be encouraged into the crush; the black, Galloway cross, with a splash of white on her tummy, was not impressed at the change in her routine. Patience won the argument, although her sudden and powerful decision to go forward made the crush shudder violently, an action that caused Henry, a temporary farm worker, to exclaim, "Jings vet, that old bitch nearly brought the crush down on top of you."

My reply, released with just a touch of alarm, thoroughly agreed with Henry's reading of the situation, "Bloody Nora, you're not wrong lad."

Theresa's concern for her breadwinner's health was a factor, as the herdsman assisting at Balgowan that day was an elderly chap. Although he was a likeable fellow, Henry did not actually inspire confidence that he would prevent the cows from flattening her husband. The look on Theresa's face declared she had seen the incident and it was not long before her quiet, earnest advice followed, "Please be careful."

The herd soon followed their leader.

The group of noisy calves practiced a perpetual motion technique and constantly jostled Theresa who watched them carefully; at times her evasive tactics gave her the appearance of a ballet dancer as she constantly shuffled her feet to prevent her little toes from being trodden on and one particularly good pirouette made me say, "That's it my dear, if you keep your eyes open, and protect your little tootsies, this job will soon be over." I admired the manner in which she attempted to hide her distress from the farmers.

"I suppose I will be fine, the more I work with cattle the more I appreciate I have to be constantly on guard." She managed a weak smile in my direction until one of the larger calves barged into her, forcing her to jump to the side and made her exclaim, "This is not going as well as it usually does, are you sure it is safe?"

"Not to worry my dear, we will soon get through this."

The older calves were vaccinated, dewormed and weaned from their mothers as they passed through the crush. As the animals were released through the front of the crush, a strong gate was swung to direct the animals into pens designated for their groups; to direct the calves and the non-pregnant cows to the right, into Theresa's pen, and to the left went the pregnant cows that were to return to the hill.

Cattle work is noisy.

As weaning was taking place at the same time it was extremely noisy with calves calling to their mothers and cows bawling to their calves.

When all had gone through the crush, the main pen gate on the left was swung wide open to allow the herd to return to their pastures on the hillside. From the manner in which the herd steadily drifted onwards and upwards it was clear they would soon relax, and that same Galloway cross cow again indicated she was indeed the herd leader as she almost marched them off into the heather.

Theresa was watching their departure closely and remarked, "That old lady does look like the herd matriarch and is determined to get away from us as quickly as possible."

Janet said, "You are right. Maggie may be getting on a bit, but she is still the boss," At that point I saw Janet gently touch Theresa's arm, before continuing, "See the other black cow beside her?"

Theresa was well into the conversation by then, "The one that keeps looking back at us?"

"That's the one; she is Maggie's first daughter and when the old lady moves on she will become the next herd leader, the daughter of the leader often becomes the next boss cow."

A few of the cows were hesitant, still hopeful their calves would join them and, as the herd instinct took over and drew them onwards and away from us, it caused Theresa to voice an interesting thought, "I wonder if they are actually pleased at the weaning and perhaps they feel the same sense of release parents do when their children move on to college!"

"You are probably right and it's interesting you should be thinking about that when our own family hasn't even started yet."

We looked intently at each other, and dwelt on an idea that was becoming increasingly important to us, "Well," Theresa smiled at me, "Maybe it's time it happened."

I also smiled at that happy thought.

The entire process went well.

As the final cow left the crush I pulled off my glove and congratulated the team, "Well done everyone that has gone very smoothly, a great job."

Theresa as scribe, had recorded my comments alongside the ear tag numbers that Andrew read out, and she passed the notes over to Janet and said, "Here are the figures, how do the results look?"

Janet took the notes from Theresa then searched her pocket for her spectacles. She perched them on her small, sharp nose and studied Theresa's notes with a mannerism that, while funny, was also reminiscent of the glare of a wise old owl. After a detailed examination of the work sheet she exclaimed, "That's grand! Everything seems to be in order, and yes, it looks as though we have had a good season," Janet continued, "All we have to do now is test Tessa, I am sure she is pregnant, but she should be checked." Naturally the Princess of Balgowan had not been mixed up in the mêlée, as a lady she set impeccable standards.

Tessa and Chance could not be found.

During a morning working with the common cattle Tessa would normally have been in our faces and she, who was always lending a willing hand, could not be found. A thorough search of the homestead proved fruitless and I wondered if she had ambled off down the lane, and volunteered to go and search for her, "The last gate into the farm from the drive has been left open and perhaps she has wandered down into the home paddock, I will jump into my car and look for her." My return found the others standing by the house and the manner in which I shook my head indicated my search was fruitless.

Andrew was also puzzled, "Now this is a strange situation, where is the creature?"

We were standing beside a smallish tree.

About five yards from the kitchen door stood, of all things, a miserable, disgruntled looking walnut tree; one of the very few trees on that upland farm and that one, an untidy sort of an individual, was the only one I knew of in the region. At my approach a number of small birds, among them a pair of starlings took to flight and perhaps their rapid departure was due in part to the fact I was becoming agitated, "Where can this silly creature be? How can we lose a cow on a small place such as this? There are no real hiding places can she have gone onto the hill with the rest of the herd?"

We had many questions, but no answers as on that small farm there were no hiding places. We had lost a cow after all, not a rabbit or a dog that might have gone off hunting and Andrew did one of his head scratching sessions, "Where can my little heifer be?"

"Odd, very odd, she is always here making a nuisance of herself so where can she be?" Janet sided with her husband.

The farmyard at Balgowan was typical of the region and we were standing outside the kitchen door that was set in buildings of dark, greyish coloured heavy sandstone blocks that time had granted a well weathered look. The steading was formed in a u-shape with the mouth of the U opening generously as though set to embrace whoever might approach from the road.

Andrew searched in silence while the old lady constantly called, "Come along Tessa, where are you my pretty girl?" My mind was whirring when Janet interrupted my thoughts, "I am puzzled, I cannot understand where she has gone," She paused as another thought came, "I wonder, I wonder if she hasn't gone into the house?"

Andrew scratched his head and said, "It's possible."

Janet turned and faced the house and we followed her lead as she headed for the open door. Our silent attitude was disturbed by a long, soft, moo and we looked at each other as Andrew stated the obvious, "Why that sounds like Tessa, where can she be?"

As he said this, Janet solved the mystery, "Gosh, there she is," She pointed skyward, a movement we all made as though it were a well synchronised action and there indeed was the brown heifer, its distinctive face peering at us from an upstairs window.

In our career we saw animals in many strange places.

There was the odd, odd lady in Drofter, who had a hutch filled with rabbits on the end of her bed. In her flimsy negligee she locked the bedroom door behind me and I had visions the end of my career was imminent; that situation took some getting out of.

Tessa' situation was also an odd one, "Well I never . . ."

My thoughts were interrupted by my excited wife who continued, "What in the name of fortune has made her wander up there in the first place?"

Her curious question was echoed by the others as we all wondered what an adventure that must have been for this little, but still about six hundred pound lady. How had she managed to get safely up the winding staircase? How had she then had the cheek to push at a poorly fastened window until it happened to open?

The anxious vet in me came to the fore as my training and experience caused me to blurt out, "Thankfully her efforts have not found her nose crashing through the thin plate glass of those windows she could easily have slashed her face."

"Dear me, this is an odd sort of a predicament," Janet was worried at the way our morning was threatening disaster.

Theresa's trembling voice added to the scene, "How will we get her safely down from that room?"

"*Mooooo*," Tessa smiled at us.

I calmed the situation.

"Listen everyone Tessa seems relaxed and it is important we consider the problem in a slow and gentle manner. We must not do anything that might cause her to become upset." Experience had clearly demonstrated that when animals were trapped the last thing they, or anyone working with them needed was to get excited. Any suggestion of anxiety particularly when associated with raised voices, encourages the fear and flight reaction that leads to panic.

Our musings were left in the background when the elderly lady of the house took charge of the situation and in that confident and determined manner of hers, she decided how best to conduct Tessa' rescue, "I have an idea. I know how this heifer's silly little mind works, leave her to me," Janet decided the spoiled Tessa would do anything for a piece of food, "I will go and fetch some fruit, perhaps an apple will do the trick," She chuckled to herself, "When dealing with this silly little animal I have found she is best controlled by her stomach," Janet left us and popped into the kitchen.

·Theresa whispered, "Do you think Janet is right? Do you think she will be successful, do you think . . .?"

"Slow down woman, Janet knows what she is doing."

Janet emerged flashing a bright Top Red from the Cape.

She set her plan in motion and the remainder of us were helpless spectators. "Watch what this silly girl will do when she smells this apple?" Slowly, while quietly, and confidently, chattering away to either herself or the cow Janet climbed the stairs.

The rest of us felt insecure as we watched her bottom disappear into the unknown. We followed her, but remained at the foot of the stairs where, although out of sight, Janet's voice held our interest, "Now Tessa, you really are a silly child getting yourself into such a fix. Why ever did you climb these stairs and you probably with a calf inside you? It really is very silly of you."

I felt someone's nails doing their usual thing in a crisis and Theresa whispered in a voice that was softer than the force being exerted on my forearm, "What is going to happen, will Janet be all right, what if Tessa knocks her down the staircase?"

There was a moment of peace when we could not hear Janet talking. We stepped outside and looked up at the window and found Tessa still there, and when I fixed my gaze on her face, I swear I detected a trace of amusement. Suddenly she withdrew her head from the window and for a few moments we neither heard, nor saw anything.

The nails bit deeper.

They relaxed somewhat when we heard Janet say, "Just as I thought, you never could resist an apple."

"That sounds promising," The nails were less aggressive.

"Mind your feet, this staircase is steep, and if you are not careful you will fall on top of me." Janet came slowly backwards, down the steep twisting staircase and joined us in the courtyard.

My wife rambled on and on and whispered, "Do you think Janet is going to get her down safely?"

The lady blathered away to the heifer, "You must understand Tessa I am actually too old for your pranks, I must be stricter with you in the future."

Chance came flying out of the doorway with the apple driven Tessa followed closely behind her.

The old lady pulled it off.

Tessa walked into the yard and gave us a much shorter greeting than we usually received; she hardly took time to acknowledge the good hug we gave her. Theresa looked from the heifer to me and said, "I cannot believe she has come down those stairs so easily, that was lucky," Theresa's smile was a huge one as she continued, "Look at the cheeky thing now, she has dumped me, her aunty, for an apple."

That remarkable incident ended with Tessa acting the normally well behaved lady she usually was and she followed the apple round to the pens, and popped into the crush. Only then was she rewarded with her juicy prize, which so occupied her attention she never even flashed her tail at me during the examination. I pulled off my glove and turned to drop it on the ground when Chance smiled at me and, believe it or not, she winked at me with the white eye.

Tessa was about three months into a normal pregnancy and as a pregnant lady her meanderings were severely curtailed in the future. She was delivered of her calf safely at the appointed time and did fulfil her role as the house cow for many years, but never again was she given the opportunity to repeat her performance as the cow at the window.

We took our leave of that special place.

The many gate openings did not seem a problem. I was driving and Theresa gave me the impression that nothing could upset her. She joined me after closing the last gate, turned, looked at me and gripped my left arm, "I am still so thrilled about them naming Tessa after me. It really puts me in the mood for having my own babies."

CHAPTER 21

PETAL

EVERYONE WAS COUGHING and sneezing as Drofter was in the grip of a bad outbreak of the common cold.

Half of the superstore's staff had failed to make the starting line and I was in my usual tearing rush, but necessity insisted I sneak off for fifteen minutes to get a washer for a badly leaking kitchen tap. The young assistant was most helpful and I thanked him, "You are a star, I think that is exactly what I am looking for," The overworked chap by the maintenance section had done his best and expertly helped me in spite of the irritable cue around us.

I turned and headed for the check out.

A powerful hand grabbed my shoulder hard and shook it, "No man! Will a clever fella like you be able to fit that by yourself?"

I turned and looked up into a huge round face, "George Tomlinson, how are you man?"

"Great Alex, great, but surprised to see you here at this time of the day, should you not be out saving lives or something?"

"To tell you the truth I have a busy afternoon round, but this is an emergency, the kitchen tap is driving Theresa nuts, and, well you know what they are like."

"For sure man, for sure."

He had the friendliest of all faces and the way he rolled his eyes and shrugged his shoulders made me smile as I said, "I am actually passing your driveway now and I must get off." I remembered our last meeting and asked, "How is Petal since her adventure?"

"Interesting we should meet, because my lovely boss was thinking of ringing you about her," He pulled out a huge, bright red hanky with one hand and motioned for me to keep back with the other. The blow he produced would have saved a ship from being wrecked on a rocky shore, "Sorry about that Alex, this damned cold has also touched me." The intensity of how he examined the contents of that hanky suggested he might have lost something up his nose and was looking for it.

"It is a nuisance, but sorry George you must excuse me, I must get off," I shook his hand; probably a dangerous thing with the amount of dodgy looking snot he had in that hanky, and a thought stopped me in my tracks, "Sorry George, you mentioned Petal?"

He folded up the hanky as though it were a family heirloom.

"As I said, the boss; she who must be obeyed; Flo herself, said the pony has changed since that incident with the fire brigade."

"I thought that went well, changed eh, what do you mean?"

"Well!" He sort of stood back and looked at some fasteners on the near bye shelf and thought for a moment, "She is not nearly as well behaved as she was," He tapped a packet of plastic plugs against the knuckles of his right hand and said, "Now you know I am not the horsy person in the family, you know I am swamped by all the women in my life . . ."

"Come on now George you are the most blessed and spoiled man I have ever met. You have a beautiful doting wife and three fabulous girls."

He smiled and slapped me on the back; thankfully with only a little of the power his six and a half feet could muster, but it was enough to make me take a step back, "Yes indeed I do enjoy my girls."

"The pony George, you were going to tell me what is wrong with Petal?"

"It's a funny thing!" He waved the pack of plugs around in the air and then tapped them against my chest, "It is as though the noise of the machines the fire brigade used that day have affected her ears, it's as though she is going deaf."

"Deaf!" I was regaining my balance by then, and his suggestion that Petal might be going deaf made my own ears prick, "Deaf you say, deaf."

"That's what the girls say, deaf."

Bang!

The answer dived into my mind and I slapped George hard on the shoulder, twice. It was as though a light had come on in that filing cabinet which is my brain, "I know what is wrong, I am immediately going to the farm and I will have her up and running as well as normal by this afternoon. God bless friend," I turned and fled the scene, but took a left round the end of the aisle instead of a right, and had to reverse my journey.

George was still standing in the same place staring at the spot where I had rushed away from him; he was still investigating that hanky when I apologetically slapped his shoulder, "Sorry George I will sort her out."

Six weeks ago the pony had a problem

Petal; an eight year old grey, Welsh section B, had tried to wander away from their property and had failed to negotiate the steel bars of the cattle grid designed to prevent such an escape. Nancy; the eldest of the girls, spotted her and called out to her, but, as the pony turned, she took a step backwards and her hind legs slipped between the spars of the cattle grid.

When I arrived my friends from the fire brigade were in attendance.

I ignored everyone and scratched Petal on the wither.

I said, "Sorry to see you like this my friend. We will soon help you."

Only then did I acknowledge those present and shook hands with Inspector Dickson; one of the firemen, who said, "Thanks for coming and so glad you got here so quickly, we need your expert assistance to free this pony from the grid."

"I suppose when you switch on any of your scary machines she gets excited?"

"Oh Alex it is a shame to see how the precious little thing reacts, she is a show pony, and if we are not careful she is going to damage her legs . . ." George's wife Flo was working herself up into a bit of a state and I paused as the same thought again hit me. Every time I saw her, or better still when I was with both of them at the same time, I could not help thinking how life is funny. She was the most gorgeous of Barbie Dolls, five feet on her tip toes, with the loveliest of long, silky blond hair and with the perfect figure she was everything George was not.

"Do not panic we will soon have her out of there," I turned in the direction of the Saab to fetch the Domosedan she needed.

Ted; the fireman who had helped me in the past, held her head like the expert he was and I smiled at him and said, "That's the way, you have helped me with this before." My injection; a tiny dose of tranquiliser, was easy to administer.

I motioned Mum and the three girls forward.

"She will need about ten minutes for the tranquiliser to do its job, so it's over to you."

"You are leaving it to us!" The middle girl, Gloria, a pretty eight year old with a scraggy mop of curly ginger hair was surprised, "What do you want us to do?"

"Do what you must always do when a family member has a problem."

"I do not understand."

"Georgina; the youngest and already the tallest, who was every inch her father's daughter, moved to Petal, put her arms around her neck and said, "Uncle Alex needs us to love her."

"Ready chaps the drug has done its job."

I stood back and motioned to inspector Dickson, "Right sir it is your chance to get the job done."

The cutter roared into life and although Petal was a very sleepy pony she still reacted to the noise and I stopped them and said, "Wait lads give me a moment," Her reaction was slight, but, as she had almost fallen over with the noise of the thing, I decided to add plan B, "Hold it," I nipped back to the open boot of the Saab and grabbed some cotton wool, "I think this will be the final piece of the puzzle," I said that as I filled her ears with the stuff, "This should help."

Gloria said, "How is that going to help?"

Georgina again took over, "Because if she cannot hear the noise!" She did that thing that smart people do when they roll their eyes at everyone, "She will be much happier." It was clear she had not only inherited her father's looks, his intelligence also claimed her as his own.

The cotton wool worked like a charm, it usually does and the massive cutter had her safely out within three minutes. I finished the job off by smothering the many slight abrasions on her legs in calendula cream, and then wrapped her in stable bandages. Gloria walked her gently back to her stable to sleep off the tranquiliser.

Everyone was happy, or so I thought.

Ten minutes after I zoomed out of Hilliard's car park I pulled up beside the stable, "Afternoon ladies, where is Petal?"

"Hello Uncle Alex," Grace smiled at me, although her confused expression framed the unspoken question of why was I visiting them. She pointed a long slender hand at the paddock closest to the stables and said, "There she is."

"Hello Petal, how are you today?" As I climbed through the fence I changed my attitude and shouted, "*Hello Petal.*"

The lovely creature whinnied at me, and, as a real lady she allowed me to do the necessary without a head collar. I pulled the cotton wool out of her ears.

Job done, and everything was back to normal.

CHAPTER 22

THE SWILL MAN

M Y SOLICITOR POINTED his finger at James and said, "Would you take a look at that fellow?"

I recognised the man, smiled and said, "Without doubt that is one of Drofter's most famous sons."

"To you he may be a famous son! To me he is a tramp, a mess and he parks his disgusting van right in front of my practice, twice a week. It is so out of character with the rest of this fine row." Bernard inclined his head to indicate the fine buildings to the left and right of us.

I had visited Bernard over a bit of business.

He helped me tidy up a few bits of this, and that, and after concluding our business he walked onto Carolgate with me, to see me off, in the way solicitors do. Their attitude always made me think of being escorted away from the Locarno nightclub in Glasgow, by some beast of a bouncer whose intention was to ensure my egress was permanent.

I called out, "Afternoon James has the market been kind to you this week?"

The tall, fat man looked at me and peered at me with eyes reminiscent of those normally trapped on either side of the long nosed creatures that turned the swill he collected into bacon. His eyesight was not the best, and it took him a few seconds to spot me even though we were within five yards of him.

His specs were dangling round his neck on a thick piece of string, and after he fitted them to his eyes he smiled and said, "Hello there Mr Veterinary, I didn't recognise you in these unusual surroundings."

The devil was in me.

I thought; this is a good chance for me to put the wind up this larny friend of mine, "Spare us a moment James, I would like you to meet a solicitor friend of mine." I felt the sudden tension, and it was easy to imagine Bernard bunching his senses up protectively, and looking for a stone under which he might shrink, for fear some business men might spot him liaising with the underworld.

James was never the snappiest dresser when collecting swill, and that day he was rather less than sartorially elegant. One of his ancient welly boots was torn at the top and I remembered his story of how an old sow had tried to chew a bit off his leg, and got a sizeable chunk of rubber instead; at least both boots were of the same colour and make, a fact that was not always the case. His old jeans were heavily soiled from the day's work, as was the ancient, possibly green cardigan he sported, that almost covered his rotund abdomen. The loud checked shirt was from the stable of a fashionable manufacturer, although the torn collar, and blanks in the pattern, indicated such a heritage was from the distant past.

James reached his hand out to me and said, "Well now, one never can be sure when such a useful gentleman's services may be required, and indeed it is my pleasure to make your acquaintance sir." He doffed his ancient flat cap and proffered the slightest of bows to Bernard.

"My, pleasure sir, and of course, my services are always available."

James caught the wink I threw his way.

It must be remembered we had been regularly connected for a number of years, and knew each other well and he quickly guessed I was up for a bit of sport, and again offered a humbling bow that any labourer might extend to a professional, an extremely smartly dressed professional. Why I would not be far off the mark to suggest that Bernard's fashionable pin stripe suit was worth a month of many a man's wages.

The smell of James' business drifted nicely towards us on the gentle breeze skipping down Churchgate and the solicitor's nose indicated how the rest of his body was reacting; he gave me the impression that flight might soon be the order of the day.

In this short introduction the reader may already have formed his opinion on James, but, and perhaps to avoid you slipping into the same mould as the solicitor, that opinion requires a bit more sustenance, err it can be accurately formed. James was a highly educated, well-bred character, with more than a few bob to his name, but there were circumstances in his history; of an unrequited feminine nature, that had caused him to take on his present lifestyle.

James returned the wink.

The game was well and truly on, with Bernard very much destined as the meat in the sandwich, "I do have fifteen minutes to spare so perhaps I should pop into your office and we could chat over a cup of tea about a bit of business?"

Power to the man's elbow, our friend Bernard was himself no slouch in matters of conversation, indeed his well-honed court room skills prepared him for most events, but this was too much and he wilted, "I, I, would love to," then his smooth tongue got into gear, "Do just that, but of course such weighty matters need careful consideration," He stepped forward, gave James a strong handshake and looked him straight in the eye, "Please pop this business card into your bureau and do give me a ring sometime. Unfortunately, today is impossible as I have back to back appointments, you know how it is?"

Bernard turned to me, "Thanks to you also Alex for your visit, and now if you will please excuse . . ."

James stood tall and attempted to tuck some of his belly in.

He interrupted Bernard, "That's a grand idea as I do have a problem with all of this inherited wealth." That was a cracker, a comment that made Bernard snap to attention, as though five fingers had been brushed vigorously across the soft white skin of his cheek and James continued, "There are piles and piles of these share certificates coming in from the estate of poor old Aunt Matilda, and, well a swill man, such as me, is getting bogged down by all of it."

Bernard almost reversed the half turn already executed, his mind no doubt already considering the fat commission to be found there, caused him to hesitate until the wind freshened even more. The smell was too powerful, and encouraged our man to continue on his original course, "Interesting! Sorry I must be off, but when you get the chance you must ring me, we must get together, and yes perhaps I should visit with you."

James bowed again, turned to me and said, "In that case Alex, I also must get back into the world. When you get a chance pop in and check out my old boar for me. Ferdinand is looking a bit sore on the old pins. Cheers guys have a good day, and God bless."

Only when I was alone on the pavement did I allow the heartiest of chuckles to escape.

"My, but you are a bad man!"

"Moi, a bad man, and a good morning also to you, Mr Veterinary."

"How could you disturb poor old Bernard as you did yesterday?"

"I think we both enjoyed rattling his cage did we not?" It was early the following morning, a good time to catch my friend before his many duties dragged him hither. James had a small farm about fifty yards on the left down Bolham Lane, it was a small higgledy piggledy place where he fattened a few pigs, and had the space to indulge in his pride and joy; a large collection of English Game Fowls.

"Tell me about this poor old creature?" We were on our way to the pigs, "What have you done to it now, have you worked it to death?"

"Ferdinand the Fearless is now about seven years old and he has done a good job for me, and, sadly I fear you will tell me it is time for him to go," he scrunched his face up and continued, "Yes, perhaps he will have to be replaced."

I smiled at the boar's imperious name as we stopped outside the large pen and James said, "There's the man himself."

As I studied the huge, almost pink Landrace boar that rested peacefully atop a sizeable pile of fresh, clean straw, I could already see the left hind leg was swollen." He pretended to ignore us, but, as a trained observer, I saw enough to spot the twinkle in his eyes, and guessed he was watching us, biding his time in the hope of creating mayhem.

"It will indeed be a shame if I have to retire him".

James shook his head and scratched hard at a similar checked shirt to the one he wore yesterday and said, "Although he is very difficult to deal with I am fond of the old man, and it will be a pity if he has to go." There was a very soft spot to Bernard that few ever saw.

"I wonder what is going on with his foot, it looks swollen on the outside, above the coronary band, have you noticed that?"

Bernard had a short stick in his hand and he gently prodded the boar, who leaped up and banged hard against the pen door, "Come now you old rascal let the kind gentleman look at you," He turned to me, "My eyes are not so good, and now that you have pointed it out I can see where it is swollen."

"Let's get him along the passage and then I can have a better look." We encouraged Ferdinand to walk along the narrow passage, and it was a noisy journey with both parties doing a fair bit of grunting and swearing. James had a small heavy wooden board which he used to block any attempt the boar made at reversing. As he reached the end of the passage the boar put down his head and began eating and I complimented James on his management technique, "Clever man, you already were set up for this."

"Come now Mr Veterinary we have been down this road before, and, although your solicitor friend thinks otherwise, in this game we have to learn to survive."

"That is for sure."

Pigs and Labradors are great eaters.

As long as Ferdinand had something to guzzle on I was able to examine his leg and thankfully it was a back one, and therefore much easier to inspect than the front, where, directly underneath his huge mouth of big teeth, that would have been more difficult. I grabbed the leg by the hock and pulled it backwards and upwards. The strength a heavy boar has in that area is prodigious, and I was blowing hard by the time I had it under control, "Doesn't feel like arthritis or injury and, ah, from the heat here, I would say it is likely to be . . ." As I manipulated the foot and squeezed it, a ripe abscess burst and shed its contents; a thick, bloody green mixture, in front of us, "That was lucky, a dose of penicillin into this huge bum and, you can pick up his foot, wash it well three times daily, and bandage it overnight with Epsom salts."

James laughed heartily and clapped me hard on the shoulder, "Nice one Alex, we won't forget that in a hurry."

The injection was in and done before I finished talking.

Ferdinand, now that his food was finished, no longer played the perfect patient. He reared up on his good hind leg, put both of his front legs over the wall of the adjoining pen, and made some of those horrible noises all pigs are expert in. His fury was taken up by the dozen or so sows in the pens and it was another occasion when ear muffs should have been standard practice.

"Get back Alex!" James' strong advice was unnecessary as I was already heading well away from the scene; I knew Ferdinand of old and took no chances with him. Only a mule could reverse faster than that boar and within ten seconds he was safely back in his pen.

We stepped outside.

The morning held the promise of a welcome drop of rain to break the dry spell that had held Drofter in its grip during July and most of August, "Well done Alex and that is good news indeed, well done. Do you have time for a quick coffee?"

The farmyard was a scene from the aftermath of a *Star Wars* strike, but the house was its antithesis. It was a pristine, beautiful and expensively furnished refuge, a perfect residence for the man-about-town that James intimated he would be one day. He was in expansive mood, "Bathe it three times daily indeed," He laughed that lovely, rounded laugh of his, it was infectious and easy to enjoy, "What was his name?"

'That was Craig he had only been qualified about three weeks when you met him for the first time."

"I will never forget the look on his face when I told him he was an idiot."

"You shook him up that day and he learned more about handling pigs in one thirty minute session with you than he did in the whole of his Liverpool University days."

"Sometimes nature knows best and there is no doubt in my mind that farm animals often do best if we leave them to get on with it."

I had time for a quick look at his fowls.

They were top show birds in a wonderful array of colours, and in magnificent condition and the beaming smile on James' face was followed by a confident statement, "I am hoping to do well on Friday."

"I might take Andrew in that direction." The big poultry show at Nottingham Showground was a fascinating event, and, as we were quiet I had decided to take a bit of a look, "Why don't we go together?"

"That's a good idea and I will take you for a spin in my new Mercedes and the young man will enjoy the trip. This bird," He walked about five yards to the left and placed his hand on a large wire cage, "Unless the judge is half blind will take the championship."

"Excellent, let's make that a date."

When I told Andrew what was happening he jumped at the chance to join us.

We were greeted by a very smart James who had outfitted himself as any country gent would have expected, "Good morning Master Niven how are you today?" His bright green Harris Tweed jacket almost matched the bright orange silk cravat that caught the eye.

"I am well sir, and you?"

"Also well, and excited about the prospect of doing well at the show."

"Can we do anything to help?"

"Not at all, at all, but thanks Alex, the birds are loaded, and you are on time and I think we should hit the road."

The new 500S Mercedes pulled the trailer as though it did not exist and the showground arrived at such a rate of knots we hardly had time to enjoy its luxury. We helped unload the birds and left James busily caging, and dressing his fowl for the judges.

"So Andrew, what do you think thus far?"

"It is a fabulous car, but gosh dad, does he always drive so fast?"

"Yes, but he does get a few tickets. Never mind, I think we should start with the big birds and work our way down to the bantams, OK?"

The exhibition was in one huge hall that could have held aircraft never mind the smaller flying versions we studied. From pigeons; both fancy and racing, to ducks, geese and a myriad of domestic fowls, there was plenty of interest.

We caught up with a beaming James about two hours later. His six game fowl were so heavily covered in tickets it was difficult to see the stars themselves. He had taken best female on show with a Black, while his Black Breasted Red, the cock that was the love of his life, had indeed taken the championship.

"Gosh Uncle James you have had a great day."

"Yes indeed! I have had such fun, and, I am in such a good mood that you young man are in for a treat."

"Now James, I know you would like me to have a few of your birds on the place, and while we thank you for such a generous idea, we simply cannot cope with such flighty creatures, they will be up and off."

He patted Andrew on the head, gave him a great smile and said, "I agree with you, so I was thinking about something of a more manageable size. Come Andrew I am going to find you a nice pair of bantams."

Andrew's eyes were like saucers in a face that was beaming from ear to ear and he decided on a pair of Silver Sebrights; small, white feathered bantams with lots of black lacing. Bernard approved of his choice and said, "Well Andrew I think your mum will agree these tiny birds are just too beautiful."

"Wow Uncle James, these are the prettiest birds anywhere." Our son was very excited.

"Great! I knew these would be perfect. OK, here's the plan, my mate Fred will drop the birds off at my place sometime this week. That will give you time to organise a bit of a run for them and I will drop them by you later, possibly at the weekend."

"Thanks James that is an excellent idea." I also love bantams and was excited at having a pair in the garden.

Following a bit of lunch we packed up and headed for home.

"I must say this car is a real flying machine. Andrew was amazed at how fast you drive and curious to know if you ever get into trouble?"

"Well, if truth be told I do get a few tickets, but, as my road sense is good, I am usually able to spot . . ." As though it had been choreographed one of the boys in blue jumped out in front of us, and waved us down. The usual pleasantries followed, and afterwards a very disgruntled James climbed back into the car, scrunched up the ticket, and threw it into the back beside Andrew.

As we drew off he let rip about the inadequacies of the police force, their policy on speeding, and his own thoughts on how such a situation makes all of us Government lackeys, and so on. Two minutes later the car slowed down by a country lane, "Yes! I know exactly where we are, I will get them this time," He mumbled to us or himself.

"Now James, what hair brained scheme do you have in mind? And remember, we have little ears with us."

"Beg your pardon young Master Andrew, but, I am going to get my own back this time."

James made a sharp right into an overgrown country lane.

Forty yards later he took another right into an even more overgrown lane, "Yes! This is the one, nearly there," We were running parallel with the main road and he obviously knew exactly where we were, and, after a few minutes he brought the vehicle to a halt and said, "Excuse me for a moment gents, a man must do what a man must do!" He grabbed a pair of pliers from the glove compartment and disappeared into the long grass.

Andrew asked, "What is Uncle James doing?"

"In all honesty I do not know, although, by my reckoning we are very close to where the tapes that trapped us speeding lie across the road."

"Gosh! I would never drive a beautiful machine like he does."

"I could never drive this Mercedes into a country lane like this and would even think twice about bombing up here with the Saab, but, well, that is James."

He returned after about four minutes, with a grin as wide as the Forth Road Bridge and said, "A wee souvenir for the farm," He brandished two pieces of wire some two yards long, "That should take them some time to repair and it certainly makes me feel my speeding ticket was worthwhile."

"No! You haven't cut the trip wires, have you?"

"Sure it was nothing. They were round the corner from me and could never spot such a fast worker as me, a snip here, a snip there, and we best be off."

"I think James, that maybe just maybe it might be a good idea for you to have a proper chat with Bernard. You must remember him the solicitor? If you get caught doing this you will need his professional services."

We prepared to receive the bantams.

That Saturday we made up a serviceable house and pen for them, and expectantly awaited their arrival. On Sunday afternoon we were out for lunch at a fortieth birthday party bar-b-cue. We had a lovely time, although the long awaited rains came down constantly, and in buckets; there was never any need for a rain dance in Drofter as the mere whisper of eating outside always did the trick.

We arrived home at about six and found a large, brown, cardboard box sitting on the doorstep. Bearing in mind its construction and the nature of the weather it was soaking wet. Melissa was the first to take a peek, "Chickens? Gosh Andrew it must be your bantams, but, no! Look, I think they are dead."

I opened the box properly and found six tiny bantams lying on the bottom of the box, they were seriously chilled, almost dead and when Andrew saw them he burst into tears.

Mum responded the fastest, "Quick, let me get the oven on."

Melissa cried, "No mum, surely we cannot eat these little birds?"

Andrew had regained his composure by then, and said, "Don't be daft Melissa we are going to put them into the oven to dry them and to warm them up."

We watched them through the glass of the oven.

"Look, one of them is beginning to move," Andrew was sitting on the three legged stool directly in front of the cooker, "And another!"

Melissa was jumping up and down with excitement, "They are all beginning to wake up.

Theresa said, "Who needs vets when there are mothers around?"

CHAPTER 23

PRAY FOR THEM

"**H**IS NAME ESCAPES me for the moment."

Our receptionist was anxious to get things right.

"We have three young vets at present can you describe him for me?"

"Well he was tallish, slim and with short hair and; no hang on a moment, it was the vet who prays for them."

Ever been misinterpreted?

Do people always listen carefully to what you say? Do they always fully understand what is going on, or, are you like me often surprised at, and confused by, the fellow members of our species? The fact of the, *I thought you meant complex* has been an almost daily occurrence in my practice.

Mrs Audrey Ealing's request was nothing unusual; she requested a vet to examine a pony that had a leg problem. She was not a regular client of mine as her string of valuable ponies and horses were normally under the care of John Dunlop, the specialist equine vet from Doncaster. The lady's needs were specific; it had to be the same vet she had met six weeks previously, she had enjoyed working with him and she reiterated; the vet was male, Scots, and he prayed for the pony.

Penny, who took the call, was fascinated and when she traced back through the work diary it was there in black and white; I had attended them, and she entered the call in the day book beside my name for the next day. She was busy working on the month end accounts and completely forgot to ask me about the prayer session that had cured the pony's bronchitis.

The property was on the fringe of Drofter close to the hunt kennels.

I never met Mr Ealing, nor did I ever learn his first name. He was not that bothered about the creatures himself, but he was in that fortunate situation where he could keep Audrey and his daughter happy by indulging them in the best available horse flesh. His job was simply to pay the bills; and may God bless him and the many others like him for their support.

Mr Ealing had spent a fortune on his portion of Drofter where he had built; to the most exacting of specifications, a huge six bed roomed house. The stables were constructed to a similar standard, making it apparent that if he had to live on a farm, at least it would not look like a farm.

A horse was being exercised.

As the Saab drifted up to the stables I paused to watch Elizabeth; the daughter, who was completing a lesson under the tutorage of the famous Marjorie Dewlap. Dressage teachers, with the obvious exception of my many friends, are an interesting breed of animal, and that lady was no exception. Marjorie was sporting an enormous, dark brown, leather, and very weather beaten hat that almost managed its task of disguising a face that had been exposed to the sun, for far too many lessons over far too many years. Expert with horses she may have been, but she was typical of many of that genre of old, dried up, dressage ladies. On the odd occasion I had been in her presence she intimidated me with her air of disdain, and imperiousness. Yes! Intimidated is a good word for how we felt, those rather inferior mortals, who were graced by her presence.

She made my heart race again and I bit my lower lip and thought; this consultation might be a tad difficult, it might spoil my otherwise lovely day / week / month, and then I told myself; stop being a wimp get a grip and be natural and, as my car pulled to a halt beside the stables my insecurity lifted. Events over the last year or so had taught me to recognise dressage teachers for being the experts they are, but I was now able to appreciate there was also a lot about horses where my knowledge was better than theirs.

Sporting a comfortable tweed deerstalker, the light rain was of no real consequence, I wandered over to the fancy gazebo that flanked the dressage arena to watch the end of the lesson. That was a good move as afternoon tea, with scones and chicken sandwiches had been brought out by their manservant; wasn't that a touch of one-upmanship?

Audrey's greeting was a warm one.

"So glad you could come, we were running a bit late and your timing is perfect." She held my arm firmly and led me into the gazebo.

"That's good news, I hate being late," I hinted at the buffet, "My, but this looks a lovely spread, are you having a party?"

She was not really an attractive girl; her face was sallow, thin, and more wrinkled than it should have been, but her smile was comfortable and genuine, "I am sure a hard working young chap like you is ready for a wee bite to eat?" She said that in a manner designed to accent the *wee bite* part, as a drunken Scot might.

"That is a splendid idea, many thanks." The jam was raspberry, easily my favourite.

Elizabeth was riding!

The pretty fifteen year old girl was riding a horse, yet even a quick glance revealed it was not just a horse! It seemed a virtual machine as it appeared to glide round the arena. As I bit into my first scone, the pair performed an extended trot across the diagonal, it was perfect, and caused me to exclaim, "I have never seen anything as beautiful as that in my life." I had never seen the creature before; he was a 16.3hh, magnificent, copper coloured chestnut stallion with one white sock on the near fore, and the most regal of bearings with a fluid movement that literally took my breath away.

My obviously genuine comment delighted Audrey who eagerly volunteered the information her husband had bought the creature only two weeks previously, following his winning a major competition in London. The figure that changed hands was not mentioned, although her raised eyebrows suggested the vast sum involved. That action was complimented by the remark, "Mr (always Mr) Ealing very rarely goes to horse shows, but, when he does attend he likes to see his daughter well horsed, and winning," She gave my arm another squeeze and continued, "Arctic Wonder was his idea, I am glad you appreciate a good bit of horse flesh."

To this day he is still one of the best I have ever seen and it was difficult to take my eyes off him. A real wonder horse with a good temperament to boot; he was one of those excellent buys who won just about everything and was blessed with many years of soundness before going on to a successful breeding career.

I did not talk to Marjorie at that point.

Following the briefest of greetings; a nod of the head at a distance, from the now drenched old frog, Audrey and I left the pair of them to what was still a very ample offering of bread and confectionary and we walked through the slight drizzle towards the stables.

If examining horses in the rain is not much fun, it is still a hundred times more comfortable than working with dirty, smelly pigs during sunny weather. Yes! Indeed horse practice does have its advantages and I was getting used to the fact that almost half of my time was spent in such employment.

The yard was decorated with huge hanging baskets; magnificent copper planters that were immaculately tended, and I had to pause and remark on their beauty when my interest was met with a totally unexpected comment, "To me they are only flowers, I would never spend this kind of money on fancy stables, and gardens, and flowers, but Mr Ealing has to be kept happy." She gave me a coquettish wink that made me blush; obviously Audrey had other accomplishments that appealed to her husband. She had a good body and a good way with men and I could only imagine what other qualities she possessed that helped her captivate such a successful man, and, as this work is directed at the family environment let us assume that it was her expertise in . . . oriental art!

Mavis the groom was a gangly lass of about eighteen.

She had an unusually dark complexion, that contrasted oddly with a mop of wispy, straw coloured hair trapped under a wide brimmed, cowboy style hat.

I recognised the pony as being the same strawberry roan I had previously attended to and; as with everything else in the yard, Dorset Dandelion was stunning and it was clear that she, Clarisse by her pet name, was a member of the family. The fourteen year old mare had seen Elizabeth through most of her childhood career, enabling her to gain national colours in various disciplines.

My examination began and was immediately interrupted when Audrey chimed in, "Do you remember Clarisse? She was the sick little soul you helped us with late one evening? When we got back from London? She had a case of bronchitis if you remember?" The entire story was retold and I exercised some patience as the woman, who was in full flow by then, ranted on about her breeding, her successes and her future; as they do!

At last we got onto the present problem, "So, when she came in from the paddock last week almost hobbling on three legs, we panicked," Audrey finished in a flourish, "I called John Dunlop to check her out. He breezed in here in a desperate hurry, hardly looked at her, diagnosed a shoulder problem and told me quite bluntly to retire her," She again snuggled up to my arm and I was beginning to get a feel for what captivated Mr Ealing.

Jings, that woman could talk.

She hardly took time to breathe, "He said she deserved a long holiday before going off to stud in the spring," She did that horsey thing they all do when asking for a second opinion, you know the one? Where the head goes up, and the shoulders go back, and the eyes roll? She eventually ran completely out of air and almost allowed me a little respite and then she dived in again, and continued talking at her normal fast pace. During her delivery she constantly, sagely, nodded her head, "Elizabeth was quite disappointed in his attitude. She felt that he had not treated her as the member of the family she is and it was she who suggested we should ask you to examine her. You were so kind to Clarisse when she had the bronchitis."

That flattered me and made me smile. The pony stood at a perfect square and I circled her slowly from a distance of about three yards, to gain an overall impression of her condition and conformation. She looked a perfect example of the type and I spoke to the groom, "OK Mavis she certainly looks good, but let's see how well she walks."

It was at that point that Elizabeth and the old battle-axe joined us and the young lady impressed me with her manners, as she immediately walked up to me, kissed me on the cheek, and said, "Thank you so much for coming to see my little friend, I am so worried . . ."

Marjorie; however, took over, as is the want of the dried up old dressage ladies, "No Mavis! Not like that, leave her head loose and trot her away from us."

The temptation to tell her to pee off was resisted and I thought; anyway she will probably tell me what and where the problem is, they often do, and they are often right! Sure enough there came the diagnosis, "Just as I thought! She is lame on the near fore and Dunlop is right, he usually is and it is her shoulder. Yes indeed that's the ticket, give her a holiday then send her off to stud, that should do the trick."

I said nothing; sometimes I can have the forbearance of a martyr although it helped when I bit my lip and prayed silently; dear Lord, keep me safe from this woman, please!

Mavis, to her credit, ignored Marjorie.

The groom followed my instructions and when she walked the pony on a tight circle I noticed she was cramped up at the start, but soon loosened up. My partner Seamus had taught me the art of *festina lente*; that quietness and masterly inactivity are valuable veterinary tools, they make the owners think a real gem is coming, that something profoundly important is about to be divulged.

It is fair to say my immediate impression had already formed some agreement with Marjorie and we did at least agree on the correct leg, but as I watched Clarisse my opinion wavered as something niggled at me, telling me that perhaps the problem was lower on the limb.

Marjorie couldn't stand the silence and again shattered it, "Yes I thought it was a waste of time calling in a second opinion, the problem is obvious."

My self-control was again impressive as I walked up to the mare's shoulder and scratched her withers. She enjoyed that; it is the best way to say hello to horses. The temptation to walk straight up to the front end and pat the muzzle does not have the same meaning to a horse as a firm scratch on the withers does, as it tells them, "Hi there, I know you and we are friends." I spoke quietly, "How are you my little ray of sunshine?"

My respect for Mr Dunlop was great.

When I needed a second opinion he was always kind, never condescending, and treated me as a fellow professional. He wasn't always right, and, in this case he had obviously been under pressure and could have missed something. I studiously ignored Marjorie and said, "OK Mavis, please trot her away from me for about twenty yards then turn sharply to the left, and trot back."

The patient was moving reasonably well, but the sharp turn caused an obvious shortening in her stride and I exclaimed to no one in particular, "Looks well, but did not enjoy that sharp turn," I motioned for the groom to come closer, "Thanks Mavis I will examine her now."

My left hand palpated the head and neck of her right side and then it cruised down over the various muscle groups of the lower neck and shoulder. I worked over her from the lower part of the neck, via the withers, and on down the rest of the spine to the pelvis, and then I carefully checked out the acupuncture trigger points and found sensitivity over the right Sacro-Iliac joint, as evidenced by obvious muscle twitching. That was also noticed by Elizabeth who put her arms round the pony's neck and said, "Shame, but Clarisse looks to have a sore back"

I enjoyed the child, whose upbringing suggested more than a touch of quality that was not quite as evident in her horsy mother. I had to restrain her as it was important not to allow her to either distract me, nor to conceal any reactions the pony might make and I touched her on the shoulder and suggested gently, "You obviously are very fond of this little one and yes, she is a bit sore, but please don't touch her until my examination is complete, it might cause me to miss something."

"Oh! I am so sorry," She eased herself away from the pony and went back to her mother's side.

I moved to the near fore and continued my examination. The shoulder was slightly tense, particularly over the tendon of insertion of the biceps muscle. My exploration travelled downwards and found some discomfort behind, and below the carpus, oddly enough called the knee joint in the horse - although it is the front leg!

I picked up that left leg.

My left side was against the mare's left side and I allowed her foot to slip between my own, slightly flexed knees. That meant the lower part of her limb was held in a horizontal position and extended backwards and away from me, and that allowed me to use both hands to explore the interesting structures of the limb. The upper suspensory apparatus was slightly swollen and painful, and she flinched when I palpated it with the tips of my thumbs. With my right thumb I moved the superficial tendons in a lateral direction then pushed directly over, and into the suspensory and I maintained the pressure for about twenty seconds while giving Mavis her next instruction, "Get ready Mavis. When I put the foot down I need you to take her straight into the trot."

As I released the foot the girl took her away from me and the little mare almost stumbled for the first couple of paces and was obviously lamer than before which made Audrey say, "That's touched something."

"Just as I thought, she has tweaked the high suspensory ligament and I will now do a nerve block to confirm it."

I enjoyed my short walk back to the car.

That pause from people gave me time to reflect on the success of that examination and it gave me a most pleasant feeling in terms of its accuracy, and also in the manner in which it had been conducted. I collected drugs, needles and syringes and returned to the pony when I again picked up the sore leg and held it between my legs. Elizabeth was holding the pony by the bridle and I said, "Now you can help me," I gave the girl a big smile, "Now I need you to talk nicely to Clarisse, to distract her from the treatment."

The area over the sensitive ligament was soaked liberally in a mixture of alcohol and surgical spirits and its slightly pink tinge gave it a professional look. 5ml of lignocaine was then infiltrated over the inflamed area, using a very fine needle to which Clarisse hardly reacted. I nodded to the girl, "Thanks Elizabeth that was well done."

She laughed and gave a short bow, "Thank you kind sir."

"Lovely, and now as Mavis is busy with the other horses you can take her again," I instructed Elizabeth to walk the mare round the school for fifteen minutes, a timed pause that would allow the numbing effects of the local anaesthetic to take effect.

Audrey took me for a tour round the other horses.

They had been brought into their stables early due to the increasing rain. At that stage Marjorie was quiet, very, very quiet and even thoughtful.

Exactly fifteen minutes later I instructed Elizabeth to trot Clarisse up and down, and also on the circle. The nerve block had worked and, as the mare was completely pain free, she moved out like a dream. My diagnosis was correct and suddenly, and to my great surprise, Marjorie said, "Well Mr Niven I am impressed. I have heard good reports about you from a number of sources and now, having witnessed you at work, I am truly impressed. Well done indeed."

The old head was beginning to swell and I countered her comment with, "I am sure Mr Dunlop was having one of those bad days, we all get them." It is important not to fall into the trap of criticising anyone in the horse world; we are a small, closely knit band, with a tendency for gossip that is only rivalled by the Women's Institutes.

Mr Dunlop was slipping into his sixties, still working far too hard, and covering an enormous mileage to service his many clients. My courtesy call to him afterwards caused him to say, "Things are too much for me now. You should think about coming to work with me, we could have some fun together."

That was a cheery conversation as horses were becoming an increasingly important part of my life.

I was feeling ten foot tall.

The fall came, and later I remembered the admonishment in sacred scripture; *He hath taken the mighty from their seat and hath exalted the humble.* It was then it happened; from out of nowhere came the following astonishing comment from Elizabeth, "That is tremendous news, does that mean that you do not have to pray for her?"

They told me afterwards that my mouth opened as wide as the Kimberly Hole, and they said I stared stupidly at them and I was unable to think of anything to say.

They were soon as confused as I was and then the story unfolded. On my previous visit to Clarisse she had been affected by a chest infection. My examination had departed from the normal plan, as I had misplaced my stethoscope and, in order to listen to her lung sounds I resorted to the oldest stethoscope invented when I listened to her breathing by squeezing my ears tightly against the walls of her ample chest.

I offer the reader a nice little challenge.

Pose the following question to your friends, "Why was the stethoscope invented?" The answer is an interesting and very practical one. Physicians of a bygone era appreciated that a diseased chest or lungs is inclined to produce abnormal sounds, which are a reflection of the altered airways that develop following many types of disease. Originally such an examination was conducted by the physician placing his ear directly onto the patient's body. The hygiene of those days was not as it is now and in particular people were much more commonly the host for lots of little beasties. Legend holds that the stethoscope was originally designed as a means of protecting the physician from personally collecting the lice that frequently adorned their patient's bodies!

Clarisse was a pony of diminutive stature.

That meant it had been necessary and practical for me to kneel down beside her. As is my want, I must have mumbled away to myself and I can easily imagine how I must have droned on, "My dear little pony, please be a good girl while I put one of my big ears against your chest, I need to listen to your lungs."

The penny dropped and I appreciated how the family had construed my rudimentary method of auscultation as me inviting the Good Lord to give his input on the case. I happily admit that, in all honesty, it is not uncommon for me to invite the Holy Spirit to help me in many problems, of either a human or animal nature. It is not something that causes me any embarrassment whatsoever.

That case was certainly one that really floored me.

I still pray over the more difficult cases.

My successes will never rival those of the great Saint Francis who of course blessed me with my Confirmation name.

CHAPTER 24

A CHANGING DROFTER

W E WERE REAL vets and farming was our game!

Drofter was a contented rural community.

Our patients were mainly cattle and sheep with a few pigs and the odd dog and cat thrown in, but farm work was the game. That was real veterinary work and we shrugged our shoulders at some of our colleagues and wondered how they could consider themselves vets, if they were not racing about the countryside attending to calvings and milk fever cases.

The green wellies, the flowing parturition gown, and the off-dirty car were the tools of the trade. We were up to our knees in mud and excrement for half of the year and our clothes were tainted by the flavours of the job. It was often the sweet fragrance of the newly calved cow and it could also be the oppressive, clinging smell that remained after removing retained foetal membranes.

No poncing about in neat clinics with cats and dogs for us.

The big boss was a local character / hero / talent.

The lady boss told stories of how they had developed the practice nothing, "He was the hardest worker I have ever known," and, "he is the best vet I ever met."

The more I knew him the more I agreed. He was an expert at treating horses with colic by expertly manipulating his pharmacopoeia of ancient drugs from arsenic to strychnine and a master at the art of delivering cows, an exacting process that requires sensitivity to minimise uterine damage. That skill takes time to master and the boss taught us a lot and by the end of my time in Drofter Seamus was almost as good as the boss. Birthing the cow is an art and in those days; prior to the emerging science of modern animal medicine, calvings were the criteria on how a vet was measured. It was these gifts that resulted in the boss building up our wonderful practice; and what a great practice it was, and still is.

Veterinary practice is a business.

Excellence in practicing veterinary medicine is not enough, in the real world the vet has to be a business man. Practice in Drofter began to change and Seamus had the makings of an astute business man, and saw how the nature of the beast was changing. He brought up the subject, "Alex, I have been thinking."

"Oh no Seamus, I get nervous when you start a conversation like that, it usually ends up with me getting into something . . ."

"Hold on there," His smile interrupted me, "Stop thinking about the odd little occasion that might have gone wrong . . ."

"Might have gone wrong, listen to me for ten minutes and I will make a list of all of the weird clients you shifted in my direction? I could write . . ."

My friend patted me on the shoulder and disarmed me with that great smile of his, "Now relax man and listen to me for a minute." He took a deep breath and motioned me to a chair, "Come let's have a proper chat about business."

He sat down in that odd manner of his, the one where he almost crossed his legs and I thought; well that's a good sign, he only does that when he is serious.

"I need your opinion on something," He introduced the subject of how small animal practice nationally and locally, was developing. Seamus was a bit of a veterinary politician, not one of those haughty ones as he was genuinely interested in the profession, "I found our last BVA meeting at Grantham interesting, it's clear the future is in dog and cat practice and there's money to be made."

I agreed with Seamus and we decided to research the matter carefully, and to formulate a business plan. The public needed modern small animal medicine and we had to decide how best to incorporate that into our existing organisation.

University had prepared us for such change.

The longer I was qualified the more I appreciated the excellence of my vet schools philosophy. Glasgow vet school had a strong agricultural base yet Sir William Weipers, the Dean of the faculty, was a forward thinker whose teaching methods were streets ahead of the other vet schools, and caused Glasgow graduates to be highly sought after. The course had a very practical basis to it and within a few weeks of graduation, we could be relied on to roll up our sleeves, and get on with the job.

A number of logical reasons supported a progressive view including the fact that Britain was becoming more civilised in its attitude to pet animals whose value to family life was obvious.

Was Drofter ready for such a change; that was one of the many questions we asked; was our environment ready for that expected growth? For me personally my own involvement with our farming and horse clients had made me popular and therefor busy and I wondered if I could fit small animal medicine into my life, and did I really want a career shift?

Importantly, Drofter was growing as a town; the single traffic light on Bridgegate would soon be joined by others, and the numbers of household pets was increasing dramatically. The town held an air of prosperity and people, at long last, had the finances to look after their animals correctly, and indeed the desire to so do.

There were other appealing differences between farm and small animal work; the animals visited us and small animal business was conducted in a modern, indoor environment that cocooned us from the ugliness of everything the vagaries of the British climate threw at us. That was a huge cost saving factor as we did not have to travel for miles in expensive cars.

Owners; including ourselves, were emotionally attached to their animals, and agreed they deserved the best treatments available. Farming slumped in summer while dog work, also of a seasonal nature, was busiest in summer. The final deciding factor was that small animal business was cash based, and very unlike farming practice where accounts were usually settled two to four months in arrears.

The change was formidable.

In spite of detailed investigations our hopes and aspirations for the future were wrong as small animal practice boomed; it actually exploded and rapidly became a major contributor to business profitability. The addition of another vet helped, and our new hospital, converted from an old restaurant, was a great success as business exploded.

It was not perfect and the great man, the big boss, found change difficult. He saw the advantages of the changing nature of things and made his feelings clear, "Well done guys, we must push on with this," then he added a cautionary note, "My only concern is we must be careful that expansion into dogs will never be at the expense of our established farming clientele," He nodded a few times, "A cat is a cat, and while I would never like to see one neglected, it will always be a cat," I waited patiently for him to finish, "We must never keep a farmer with a sick cow waiting in order that someone examine a cat".

However! Mrs Boss did keep a few kittens and she was a clever lady and she offered her thoughts, "I agree with you to a certain extent. For many years we have worked hard with our farmers and can never desert them, but what about some of the wonderful dogs we have had in the past whose lives could have been saved with better medicine?" She had him there, and, as the boss nodded quietly, she continued, "We will have to go fully into this new venture and our plans must factor how best to protect our existing clients."

He nodded at us and said, "Seamus, are you listening to this woman? If you have half the business brain she has, you two will be able to grow our business when I retire. Yes! Clever women that, you must do both sides of the business, and do them well." He looked intently at the clock, "Yes and now you will understand our thinking. Yes, and come along mother, it's time I gave you another thrashing over nine holes."

They were gone in a flash and I said, "Well Seamus, that seems to have gone well, I think."

"I wonder what he will say, if the golf goes badly"

I sympathised with them.

The following morning he was in expansive mood, "I think my ideas about taking this practice into the next century are sound. You young chaps must pay more attention to this dog and cat business, and take careful note of what I say." He turned on his heel and walked out.

Seamus and I looked at each other, and there was a pregnant pause until we both opened our mouths at the same time, "That's the boss!"

At that point he stuck his head round the door and offered a final comment, "Yes! That's it, get on with things, but, never forget farm animals are more important than dogs and cats."

In spite of the phenomenal growth we achieved in business he never changed.

He always had a problem with us; as he described it, wasting time treating cats and dogs, and that opinion came out very clearly when the case of the constipated cat upset him a wee bit.

Well!

Rather more than that!

CHAPTER 25

A CONSTIPATED CAT

E VERYONE PLAYED A part in this story.

Animal, owner, vet and the big boss were involved.

It was the input of the big boss that continued my education in the University of Life.

The consultation began, "Please, please Mr Vet, you have to help me, my old cat cannot make a poo!" Mrs Thompson's plea was a common one, and I wondered how many times I had heard an owner's worries expressed like that? It is fair to say the workings of the animal gut were important contributors to the education of our children.

Mandy and Betty.

Betty the cat had a problem with constipation and then diarrhoea; the digestive twins. She was a non-descript, domestic cross bred, a medium haired individual of about thirteen years of age; she was a dirty, unkempt looking, dark tabby with a miserable personality who did not like people much.

Betty's mother; Mandy Thompson was different; a lovely Yorkshire lass with a bubbly personality who had an interesting story or two to tell about Seamus' first job in her native town of Thirsk; stories that improved with the telling. She was not in the mood for reminiscing as she was worried about her little one, "She sits in her favourite part of the garden for hours, and tries and tries, but doesn't seem to get anywhere. Just a few little bits of poo that look like dried up nuts, they are hard, dark, and crumble up and she sits there for ages."

Stools are good indicators of health and, as I knew Mrs Thompson well, and was surprised at finding her so upset, I felt a bit of firmness – a different kind that is, was in order and tried to bring her back to reality, "Now Mandy, stop being a drama queen you are a Yorkshire lass and can cope with anything."

She paused for a moment, then with a hint of the old girl in that rugged face explained her feelings for the scruffy thing, "You are right. I can hardly believe my own feelings for Betty as in the past she would only have been a, well, a cat!" She paused, and sensibly I remained quiet, "It was an accident really, she walked in and took over my life. It was two days after Albert's funeral and I was very low and in she waltzed like she had lived with me forever. She came straight up to me, wrapped herself around my legs, and, well, took me under her wing."

Cats are interesting creatures.

The more one works with them, and studies them, the more interesting they become. One Christmas season early in our married life I brought home a gorgeous ginger kitten; a feisty little creature and, for the first couple of days, it nearly made itself a permanent little Niven. Our residence on Tiln Lane; the vet's house, was our first home and will always have special memories for us. We had a large pantry with many shelves and a red tile floor and two days after the kitten arrived, the industrious Theresa painted the floor.

The kitten picked her way over the fresh paint and added a charming stippled pattern to the beige coloured, hall carpet. Have you ever tried removing red floor paint from a beige coloured carpet? I was in luck when the phone summoned me to attend a lambing and I had to consider that request for help very carefully in relation to the massive, cleaning process that was underway. I had to decide to either continue cleaning the paint off carpets, or to deliver a healthy pair of Suffolk lambs; a tough one!

The next day kitty climbed up the Christmas tree where she wrecked half of our diligent efforts at Yuletide decoration. We never lost touch with her as Ginger had a long, happy life with June next door.

Cats are different.

They are more aware than most animals and in my articles on homoeopathy I discuss how cats have the uncanny knack of turning up, and disappearing, at the right time. That was the case with Mandy's friend Betty and she delved into her feelings in more detail, "I have never been one for cats, but Betty is a friend, she sits and listens to me and I talk to her. I tell her all about my life and she means a lot to me."

My left arm slipped comfortably round Mandy's shoulders and gave her a reassuring squeeze, "I will examine her right away."

A large, cardboard box was placed on the table. Betty was inside the box and although it was not designer transport, she was at least confined in a container, from which escape was difficult. It is important that animals be suitably restrained when visiting the vet as we have on a number of occasions experienced the escape artist, whose flight causes grief and disruption. Hunting down animals that have run away from the clinic are problems I can live without.

We had one incident that involved chasing through the streets of Drofter with the gracious assistance of the local constabulary as we searched for a large Dalmatian who had escaped from his owner in our car park. His left front leg was encased in a heavy plaster cast and our peg-legged friend took some finding. When our exhausted, anxious band, finally caught up with him we found the plaster cast still perfectly in place. Now that was a bit of skill or was I using up a lot of my luck account?

Andrea lifted Betty out of the box.

She placed her on the table and my assessment began, "She is looking well and certainly her usual cheerful self." Never one to enjoy her clinic visits, she growled away like a small dog, and glared at me with deep, yellow, penetrating eyes. Difficult cats can be scary, although not as dangerous as the bigger ones I dealt with much later in Africa.

My examination continued in a logical order when I checked through her circulatory and respiratory systems; heart, lungs, pulse and the colour of her mucous membranes were normal. The abdominal part of the examination commenced when I palpated the kidneys, "Good, I can feel both kidneys and am happy with them."

The anxiety in Mandy's voice heightened and her voice displayed a hint of impatience, "You did say they were fine the last time I was here, but what about the constipation, what can you feel there?"

The lady was distressed and I made another attempt to calm her, "Mandy, I must be thorough so relax a bit woman, I am getting there."

"Sorry, don't mind me I will try to be patient."

The liver seemed normal and although there was no pain over the stomach it did not feel right. My nurse Andrea, who was restraining Betty, held her up by the front legs at the shoulders and my practiced fingers walked through the bowels. There was a large mass in the stomach, but she hardly flinched when I squeezed it, "Good, I know what the problem is," My assessment was over and a diagnosis had been reached I knew would satisfy the cat's mother and I said, "Thanks Andrea, I have finished and now Mandy I can tell you the story."

Betty interrupted me with a smart swipe of her paw and I laughed at her, "Nice one girly, good job I was watching." I popped her back into her box and said, "Most importantly there is no evidence of cancer, nephritis or liver disease. She does have a medium sized hairball in the stomach and that is what is causing the constipation."

All clients love a diagnosis, even if the news is bad they feel more content with an answer. The tension from the lady's voice went and was replaced with her usual enquiring nature, "A hairball you say, what is that, can it be fixed?"

Many cats develop hairballs.

The process by which cats collect hairballs is interesting and I explained the problem in detail. Grooming results in the ingestion and swallowing of loose hair, which is either subsequently passed in the stools, or vomited up. When there are excessive amounts of hair present in the stomach or intestine, the cat may be unable to successfully clear out the foreign material and the hair gradually accumulates and sticks together, forming a mass which is usually ovoid in appearance. It becomes a space occupying problem and clinical signs develop related to its size and the space it occupies. There may be regular throwing-up; the bold and investigative owner who inspects the unpleasant vomitus may be rewarded by finding that the sticky little mass contains hair. If the unfortunate creature is able to pass the hair further down the tract then constipation may be significant.

One case eventually found me removing a solid ball of compressed hair that resembled a tennis ball in size and consistency and the cat made a complete recovery after surgery; they usually do.

In Betty's case the treatment was simple.

The vast majority of cases respond to dietary manipulation and internal lubrication with liquid paraffin and I was confident Betty would respond to three mls, given orally until the obstruction cleared. I explained my thinking and said, "Are you with me so far?"

Mandy was relieved! (Sorry about that one). She listened carefully as I outlined my plan for Betty's treatment, "Andrea will bring us a small bottle of liquid paraffin and a plastic syringe and she will demonstrate exactly how this must be administered. I will also give her an injection under the skin of B vitamins that will help protect her normal gut bacteria, and give her a system a bit of a boost."

Mandy liked that idea and said, "I am feeling much better, my sister's cat had the same problem, the vet treated it, and it went very well, so yes I feel better."

Andrea wrapped Betty in a towel.

Cats are rarely easy to dose with any medication and the best plan is to consider treatment as a military operation. They have to be held firmly, and confidently, and time is of the essence. I grasped the skin of her neck with my left hand, and pulled her head back until her nose was in the air. With my right hand I poked the syringe tip between her side teeth, behind the long sharp canines and the front teeth and the liquid slipped gently into her mouth. That took about three seconds to accomplish.

Mandy felt that she could cope with such a plan, "I should be able to manage that, and I am in luck. My sister arrived yesterday to stay with me for a few weeks. She is good with cats, and will help me to handle Betty."

The injection of vitamins was swiftly administered under the skin of the neck and Betty was replaced in her cardboard box.

I began repeating my treatment instructions.

"OK Mandy. Let's be absolutely sure you understand what must happen. Betty must be given 3ml of liquid paraffin four times daily and . . ."

CHAPTER 26

THE SITUATION CHANGED

THERE WAS DRAMA in the waiting room, and the voice of the big boss boomed out.

"Why has nobody been to see this sick cow in Beaton? What the hell is happening, are there no vets here?"

The three clients in the waiting room had the privilege of watching the Boss do his nut. He was in full flow and those clients; dog and cat owners after all, meant nothing to him and they had to take a back seat to the cow. A back seat! In his mood I don't think the back seat of a bus would have been far enough away. Luckily the girl on reception was his favourite, and, more importantly her many years of experience working with him allowed her to take the edge of his attitude. Penny's voice held a note of calmness she did not feel, "Alex is in consulting room one and I am expecting Stuart back at any moment. The call has only just come in and one of them will visit the cow now."

I opened the consulting room door, and, at the same time, Stuart arrived via the back door and I blurted out, "It's not a problem boss, Stuart can finish the consultations and I will visit the cow."

He was most upset.

The boss was not in the mood to let the matter rest and he carried on with a display of his temper that embarrassed everyone in the building, "It's not a problem he says, this is happening too often and these bloody cats and dogs will ruin my business," He stormed off.

It was an embarrassing situation and, as the boss disappeared Penny put down the phone, "That was Beaton again their cow is deteriorating badly," Her serious face that was normally serene, angelic even, was set hard, "Go and see her now!"

The call was a matter of urgency, and appreciating the particular farmer was not a softy I took control, "Stuart takeover, I will shoot off to Beaton."

I returned to the consulting room where Mandy and Andrea's shocked faces stared at me and I apologised for rushing off, "Sorry ladies, you heard that, this is an emergency so please excuse me?" I finished off the consultation by rushing through what were, I thought, clear instructions, "Ok I am away now, Andrea please book Betty in to see me again in three days."

The journey to Beaton took ten minutes.

Fred's cow was in trouble with grass staggers, and was rapidly deteriorating. Dangerously lowered levels of blood magnesium were affecting her nervous system and she staggered around aimlessly as though drunk. She needed an intravenous infusion of saline containing magnesium and calcium and her large size and agitated state meant we had to fight to control her. The degree of restraint required to manage one thousand pounds of very active cow is considerable, and it was an unpleasant task and her necessary, and unwilling treatment, ended up with us agitated and sweaty; no doubt the attitude of the boss contributed to my state. The cow soon improved, no permanent damage had been done and I moved on with my life.

Mandy's next appointment arrived.

She was obviously upset and stressed as she presented me with the same cardboard box and as I placed the box on the table the outburst came, "I am so worried about Betty. I have done everything you suggested, but this cannot be right and we now have a serious problem."

Even before I opened the box a terrible stench rolled up and attacked my nose. The contents of the box revealed a most distressed Betty who was covered in diarrhoea; she was a frightful mess and, as it says in the old joke; she was going through the motions.

I was sympathetic for Mandy's distress and was puzzled that the case had taken a significant turn for the worst, "Tell me what has happened? This looks very bad, I cannot understand this?"

The problem unfolded, "We have had a battle with her. We have dosed her with the liquid four times daily and, as you suggested, we have kept her in the box all of this time. Every time we open the box to treat her or to feed her it really is a terrible job. Can we please let her out of the box?"

What had gone wrong?

I thought; how have my instructions failed, what has gone, when Mandy interrupted me, "Is it my fault, have I done something wrong? I listened to your instructions carefully."

Andrea slipped in a comment, "I think I know what has happened," She looked at me and actually smiled, "When we were giving you instructions the boss arrived and blew his top. It must have been then that things went wrong."

I remembered that incident vividly, how I had been dealing with Betty at the time the boss had thrown his tantrum. Whatever instructions I delivered had either been inadequate on my part, or had been completely misconstrued. Mandy thought I had advised her to continue dosing, and, not to release Betty from the box until we met again.

Wrong!

Wrong, very wrong! I was embarrassed and sorry for both of them, and babbled on with an inadequate apology then turned to the ever faithful Andrea for help, "This is a mess, what are we going to do about it?"

I repeat myself! Nurses are wonderful people and with her remarkable ability to do the right thing, at the right time, and to do it well, Andrea took charge and said, "Come with me Mrs Thompson, let's get Betty tidied up in the new treatment room. We have only just finished it and Betty will be famous as being the very first patient to be treated there."

The matter was taken out of my hands and all three ladies ignored me and disappeared in the direction of the innards of the clinic. I thought; what would I do without that girl in my life? I was happy to be free of the problem confident super nurse would handle the situation.

My appointments were soon satisfied.

The last appointment, another Cocker Spaniel with infected, smelly ears, was discharged and left me thinking; I cannot put this off any longer. It was with marked feelings of curiosity and nervousness I went in search of Betty and company. My first destination was the treatment room where I found a single large cage, inside of which was the newly bathed Betty licking her feet dry. She looked calm until she recognised me when she responded in her usual manner to my polite enquiry, with a hissing that was if anything more powerful than ever.

It was not difficult to work out where the ladies would be and my anxious progress towards the office was soon eased when I heard the happy sound of laughter filtering down the staircase. In the office Mandy, Andrea and Penny were doing that wonderfully feminine thing, the one that pours balm on every crisis. They were enjoying a cup of tea, with a biscuit, and lots of chatter and everything was under control.

Mandy appreciated the Boss was difficult and that it was his attitude that had thrown everyone out of kilter.

It transpired that Mandy was leading a rather lonely life, and she enjoyed the company and being fussed over by the girls. The consideration shown to her by our ladies was much appreciated and often in the future she dropped in for tea and cake with them. That worked both ways as she enjoyed mothering them and they enjoyed being mothered.

Betty was none the worse for her experience as her hairball problem had most definitely been cured.

If communication is not everything in business, it is a great part of it.

CHAPTER 27

DO HORSES KICK

T HE HAUNTING CRY of the angry gardener rang out.

Theresa caught me early, before breakfast.

It was a crisp April morning and her voice must have awakened a neighbour or two, "What are you doing to my trees?" The sudden interruption made me startle as most unexpected noises do, and also it was the realisation I had been caught out; nipped in the bud by Theresa's unexpected appearance. I immediately put on my humble act, "Hello there my darling I didn't expect to see . . ."

"Don't you my darling me, what are you doing?"

Sometimes I make unilateral decisions.

I knew that had my intentions been set out for her approval, she would have objected to my correct application of the pruning shears. My mind was made up and the pros and cons of my intended actions had sent my actions along the path of righteousness. I was doing the right thing and, as I had been sneaky about it guilt came knocking and I acted as any wrongdoer skulking in the night would have done.

I was carrying out a pre-determined plan; one that had formed in my mind over the previous few days. It centred on me surreptitiously sneaking most of the tangled branches off before her ladyship rose for breakfast. That plan had been formulated in the hope that such a busy woman as my lovely wife is would only notice the intervention of the surgeon later in the day; when my daily adventures as a vet would have me safely out of arms reach.

My artistic rearrangement of the privet bushes had been the first target, followed by a gentle bit of TLC for the adventurous fruit trees and on and on I went, enjoying the freedom and stillness an early morning immersed in nature brings.

I was content; the job had gone nicely and the coming spring would bring regeneration and healing and that gave me the confidence and vision to know the odd rather exposed architecture of the basic plant superstructure of the garden would soon be handsomely adorned with fresh, healthy and vigorous growth. "Yes that is about right, so right!" I continued with the clearing up and continued chatting to the thrush who was my new best friend as she enthusiastically filled her crop with the many wee beasties my efforts had exposed.

I had dallied too long and was caught in the act and I knew exactly what was coming; the woman's wrath was about to be fully expressed. As our marriage developed I was learning to accept my faults, and a number of well-honed facets of self-preservation made me try a soft touch, "Good morning my precious one, how are you this lovely spring morning? Did you sleep . . ."

My gentle, caring approach was forcibly rejected, "I thought we had agreed those hedges were fine and they did not have to be interfered with, and here you are, a demented hatchet man pulling them to pieces."

Animal husbandry and Behaviour had been fascinating subjects at university.

The excellent lessons learned had proved during my early years in practice to be effective, and their frequent implementation had extricated me from many a tricky situation. When faced with the possibility of direct confrontation with a difficult animal a full appreciation of that species normal behaviour patterns offers a system for downplaying problems. Most species do everything possible to avoid direct physical contact as fighting equals damage and often results in a less than optimal ability to survive.

Not only was I well versed in animal behaviour, but a few years of marriage had better equipped me to appreciate the rules as laid down by the Lord in the management of the angry nest builder. My experience had clearly established the best plan when the matriarch is on the rampage is simply to adopt a posture of abject humiliation. A clear example of this can be found in the attitude of the submissive dog; where the head down, bent neck and exposed jugular vein offered to the alpha bitch are a sure mechanism for defusing an argument. Please note, the use of the word *bitch* is meant purely as the vernacular term for the female dog, and under no circumstances is it intended to convey any dishonourable thought for the head of our (sorry dear one) your household.

My well-practiced defence mechanism swung swiftly into gear when I lowered my head and brought both feet together without fidgeting, and said nothing.

Theresa enjoys her garden.

The previous summer of '83 had allowed her to appreciate it to the full, and she eagerly awaited the fruit crop from our tiny trees. Gooseberry tart had been mentioned and she was daily and earnestly inspecting the budding bushes for the tell-tale signs of early berries.

We had been in our home in Elm Walk for about five years. A brand new four bed roomed, detached house and we were at last at the stage where the garden had begun to establish; the naked walls and conspicuously obvious, ugly fences were fast becoming covered with the more natural and attractive plant life that contributed to our immediate ecology. A song thrush had even set up home in one of the privet bushes where her four pretty blue eggs and subsequent chicks allowed the children free access to practical biology. The now discarded nest was rather clearly, even starkly exposed as a result of my efforts at; in view of the depth of my chastisement, it is with some temerity I tentatively call it topiary.

It had been time for a good tidy up.

The surprising aspect to Theresa's opinion on my pruning is that she does like to have her house neat and tidy; a place for everything and nothing lying on the floor. The garden must also be spick, but she does take a long time before deciding how that should be done and that is where the expert horticulturist of the family comes in; that is me by the way. My botanical knowledge gained at Glasgow University always came to the fore in matters of a plant nature.

That reminds me of a strange little lecturer we had at one time, a botany teacher who was a truly dapper little chap. Although he was an extraordinary person in many ways there were two main features of Cyril's that amused and irritated us. Adorned with his ever present sports jacket, checked shirt and smart cravat, the one was his funny little habit of mincing all around the stage. The second was his attitude to correctness, which did not allow him the opportunity or freedom to ever smile. No one had ever heard of him either cracking a joke or responding to another's attempt, many of which were indeed quite good, as we did have more than a few wags in the class. On the odd occasion when he had inadvertently created some humour we all quickly saw the amusing side while he either never picked up his *faux pas* or demonstrated his ability to control himself. In all honesty he did not like students and actually lectured in a manner that suggested the room might indeed be an empty one.

A couple of the guys came up with a clever the idea.

They thought of surprising him by presenting a Valentine's Day gift. The subject for presentation may seem rather macabre to some of you but heck, remember we were vet students and we did have hearts. In the spirit of that ancient and probably inaccurate festival whose worldwide theme of romance is placed clearly on the value of the heart as being much greater than that of being merely a pump, it was not difficult for us to focus on that day as a special one.

A carefully washed and dried fresh lamb's heart was pinned to his lectern and we waited in expectant hope, chattering eagerly as we attempted to estimate his likely response. There was an immediate and very expectant hush as the side door to the lecture hall opened and Cyril strode onto the stage towards his throne. He immediately spotted the offering and without any change in his normal facial expression he addressed the ceiling and announced, "There will be no class this morning and today's work will not be repeated." Without any show of emotion he flounced from the lecture room, leaving us to initially laugh, but quickly to realise our stupid prank had seriously misfired and we were the ones who had lost out.

That morning's pruning effort had to be completed.

My fingers and hands had received a few minor pricks and scratches from the rambling roses that had put up a bit of stern defence, and there was a little bit of blood about, which again meant that further admonishment, and this time it was fully justified, was delivered. "Alex we have agreed time and again that you must wear gloves when working in the garden. Your hands are your biggest asset and you cannot risk them being damaged when you expect to spend four hours in surgery every day."

Now that was an expertly converted penalty kick and my lovely lady was spot on, as every time pruning or heavy gardening came around, the little and not always so little, cuts and bruises that injudiciously appeared irritated me for the next few days. Scrubbing up prior to an operation was uncomfortable, and if this was associated with any swelling of the digits, this easily caused a reduction in the manual dexterity required for some of the finer procedures. Thus any of the more exacting operations, such as those involving changes to the structure and shape of the eyelids or cats willys, could indeed be rendered more difficult. There had even been a number of times when some infection had made surgery impossible.

That was followed with an interesting suggestion, "You are also on call this morning and really you would be better out working than messing me about and getting your hands into a mess." Theresa could not have expressed the moment any better and I was in luck; my rescue was at hand when the phone summoned me out to an interesting problem.

The problem related to a four week old, part bred foal.

It had suddenly gone very lame and as it transpired the case also had a gardening theme and it was for Ute von Hummel who was always a pleasure to visit. Almost as tall as I was and with a strong well rounded figure the long haired lady in her early forties was at that lovely stage in a woman's life when her maturity saw her at her very best. The normal problems of life, of having children, the development of a business and the nonsense of a hectic social life were behind her and her lovely children were already well along the road to achieving the state of happy independence which frees up parents to take up their own lives challenges again.

Ute had easily slipped into that period of womanly grace which encouraged me to think of her as being attractive, indeed handsome, although that is not normally a term used for ladies it described her good looks and her serene bearing rather well. She and her husband Hermann were second generation Germans, which gave them that touch of correctness and efficiency that goes well with the exactness of horse keeping, particularly breeding. Her husband had done well in business during the last ten years and their company; manufacturing good quality reproduction furniture, had provided them with the significant disposable income required to keep a few thoroughbred mares for covering by Warmblood; mainly Trakehner stallions.

As I had been their small animal vet for several years they naturally turned to me for support in their equine venture, an area that had become of increasing interest and value to me. My budding interest in that species was nurtured by the expert himself, the big boss who often treated me like a son.

Ute was normally a well informed and independent lady.

She was not one to get especially excited and that morning our telephone conversation easily indicated her concern and the anxiety in her deep, rich voice was easy to notice, "Oh Alex I am so glad you are on duty today and so sorry to interrupt you on a Sunday, but there is a problem that might not wait until tomorrow. Cheryl's four week old foal is very lame this morning and she can hardly put her right front leg down and is quite distressed by it. There is nothing obvious to be seen, do you think it could be joint ill?"

A little jaunt into the country to see the von Hummel's seemed an excellent idea; a chance to slip away from a verbal beating from Theresa. My attitude must have seemed slightly out of character as my reply boomed along the line, "Splendid! See you in about fifteen minutes."

Joint-ill is a nasty problem.

It is one that can rear its ugly head in all neonatal animals and even people. When the little one first enters the world the attachment of the umbilical cord must sever. This has been its lifeline throughout pregnancy; a two way channel that transmits food and oxygen to the foetus and removes waste products back into the maternal circulation for recycling and excretion. With the birth of the small creature that cord separates and then contracts down, thereby controlling any possible haemorrhage and, importantly, by sealing in such a manner, it reduces the opportunity for any bacterial contamination. There are always plenty of dormant bacteria in most environments simply biding their time, waiting for an opportunity to invade exposed tissue where they can develop, multiply and generally continue with the things that make bugs, bugs.

The cord in the new born foal is over a half inch thick and has a rubbery feel to it, like a piece of soft garden hosepipe, and it is for fear of infection that the cord is disinfected with an iodine solution.

In the simplest form there may be obvious swelling and pain centred on the naval itself which if readily observed, and if treatment is quickly initiated may be soon controlled. If the infection gradually slips inside the abdomen and grows towards the liver via the remnant of the large blood vessels, the problem becomes a more insidious one. Bacteria proliferate and, by spreading throughout the blood stream, gain access to many parts of the body. The soft cartilaginous lining of the immature joints is an exceptionally attractive site for bugs to set up home. This process may take ten days and more to become obvious and must be considered as an emergency.

A foal thus affected will often, but not always, be depressed, may be lame and have at least one swollen joint. If they do not respond quickly to drug therapy then surgical intervention is required. The anaesthetised foal has its joints inspected via arthroscopy whose large bore needles allow for thorough lavage with saline containing more drugs. The opportunity to breakdown and remove any of the products of infection, including any thick fibrin deposits that may form, markedly improves the chances of long term success.

The problem is common enough and dangerous enough to warrant Utc's concerned call that morning.

My journey took me towards and past Eaton College.

That quiet route found me turning left and climbing gently uphill past a pleasant little spot on the corner that is fondly remembered for its bed of soft grass that is heavily interlaced with blooming cowslips. They are important indicators of the health of the local environment and the final flush of their pretty bells were basking in the filtered spring sunshine, yet sweetly protected by a backdrop of shrubs and trees that followed the sharp bend in the road.

The boom of the railway crossing invitingly opened on cue for me, allowing me to bend towards the farm that always, and still does, made me smile. The incumbents were a couple of happy, generous characters who always had a joke and a smile even when things were not going well. That farm is fondly remembered as the place where JT took our first pictures of a very successful caesarean operation on a cow.

The journey easily slipped past that morning, swinging left again and on past the lovely garden centre at Grove. The farm was set on the fringes of a pretty little farming area; a further few miles before the journey would have taken me further on and into the flat arable land towards the Lincolnshire aspect to the practice. Was it right to call my destination a farm? Its twenty acres or so were much smaller than most farms in that area and its modern house and buildings were always smart and clean and the short, tree lined driveway was always welcoming.

It was a busy place.

The open plan stable block held a surprising collection of people as, in keeping with the nature of the part time owner and breeder who were becoming more and more common, the support system of friends and trainers was already well in evidence. Of an entirely feminine nature most of the gathering were well known to me and Linda, Joyce and Brenda were the ones easily recognised. There is something about horse society which readily encourages the grapevine network to make a hearty welcome to all of a similar genre who are interested and concerned; a powerful empathy at work. Indeed Linda had come from her own farm about thirty miles away to give an opinion.

The broad grin on my face illustrated my amusement at the situation and I said, "Good morning girls, is the morning coffee session for the local Church open?"

The mare and her foal were presented to me.

Cheryl; being a regular patient of mine was well known to me as a suspicious, often difficult character who could be very naughty when nursing. A sixteen hand, bright chestnut mare with flashy white legs, her face was dominated by a deep blaze and the penetrating look she directed at me indicated she was not in good humour. As I entered her box she presented me with her ears flat on her head, further confirmation her attitude was going to be a problem rather than merely indifferent. Ute quickly fitted her with the necessary bridle and head collar to give her more control while we were working with the foal.

I stood back and observed the mare and foal quietly. That is for me a necessary process, one that makes my eventual diagnosis easier and the mare relaxed during this period, while the little one who was obviously lame on the off fore leg, hopped round the stable. Her breathing was good, she was alert and there was no obvious evidence of joint or naval swellings.

We can all agree that foals are cute; it is due to their large eyes being set in a well formed head with long and generous forward pointed ears that help make them so. Her strong, apple shaped rear end gave an impression of the strength that was to come and the limbs supporting the body were correctly proportioned. The pasterns were short and the knees that were nicely forward at this stage would come back a bit with growth. I liked her even more than my first impression when she had received her first health check at about four hours following her birth.

Two of the girls expertly trapped the foal.

They held her by a short lead rain attached to the small green, fluorescent head collar that enclosed her head. A thick piece of towelling was slipped horizontally round her body from brisket to hindquarters and formed a bandage-like restraint which gave good control and also by its very nature encouraged relaxation. Breeders had at last learned that when foals were handled correctly from birth, they quickly learned a life-long respect for their human partners and all forms of handling were rendered simpler in the future.

My examination began at the head where the colour of the mucous membranes lining the eyes and mouth were checked for any changes that might indicate fever, toxaemia or anaemia. That being in order I felt her pulse where it runs along the course of the large artery that lies underneath and parallel with the jaw line. The tips of my sensitive fingers suggested it was a little bit fast, but the firm even rhythm was reassuring. During this process my own little bit of horse talking continued in order to help keep both animal's relaxed, by making soft and confident conversation with them. The palm of my hand flowed under her belly and gently palpated the umbilical region where again only negative results were obtained and I announced cheerfully, "Everything is looking good thus far, let's take her temperature."

Joyce said, "I took it about forty minutes ago and it was normal at that time."

"That was a good idea and if it has changed it will offer us interesting information, so we will check it again." The foal's tail was held upright and firmly while the thermometer was slipped into the rectum, where after the full minute allowed for an accurate temperature to be recorded it was read, "Good news here, it is still normal, so infection is unlikely."

I then examined the legs and feet.

I flexed the joints to check for any painful reactions and only after the normal three legs were examined did the last part of my examination focus on the obviously painful right fore. My fingers slipped over the shoulder then continued down the limb to palpate the tendons and she allowed me to pick up the foot and flex her joints. All parameters were normal and my final act was to conduct a thorough study of the foot. The foal resented my cleaning its foot and that confirmed my suspicion the source of the pain was indeed in that region. The light was not good in the corner of the stable where we were working and I dropped the foot and asked the girls to manoeuvre the foal round towards the stable door where the morning sun provided good illumination.

I again picked up the foot up and my examination continued when the happy cause of her lameness was soon recorded when I noticed a large rose thorn embedded in the frog of the foot close to the heel. It had not actually dug its way deeply into any tissue, although its irregular three pointed shape was causing pressure and therefore pain. The good news that a probable source for the foal's problem had been found was received by happy smiles from the attending nursing staff, "That's lucky, there is a thorn caught in the frog which is causing the problem so let me fetch a pair of forceps from the car."

The happy, relieved chatter of the ladies followed me.

Brandishing the seven inch long pair of stainless steel artery forceps I had procured, my instructions were delivered with a confident tone, "Right ladies these should do the trick and please take up your positions once more." The thorn was quickly found and yielded easily to a quick pull of the forceps. I found only a mild degree of bruising and decided we should be patient, "Let's leave them alone for a few moments and then watch how she moves."

In the normal fashion of young foals whose routine has been disrupted the filly went straight over to the milk bar where she had a quick suck, more for reassurance than hunger, after which she moved round the box and gave a little hop and a skip. The foal's other mother was delighted to see her little one already walking almost normally and the relief in her voice was evident, "Thanks so much Alex that is a big relief. I was convinced she had joint-ill and we would lose her. Does she need some medication?"

"I think we should take a break and then decide, so let's have a cup of coffee then I will check the foot again. That was declined by two of the girls who, obviously content the foal was out of danger, felt they could leave for their own business. The remainder of us enjoyed a rich, stolen cake with our delicious, freshly ground coffee amidst the conversation that included the normal buzz of the equine aficionados.

Our short break was soon over.

We returned to the stable and the mare and foal were once again caught for me to conduct my final examination. The foal's head was towards the back of the stable, my right hip was against her right shoulder and I was still holding up the foot and turned my head to talk to the girls directly behind the foal, "That's grand, there has been no bleeding and her dam has been well vaccinated against tetanus, there is no . . ."

Wham!

It was not really a wham it was more of a gentle tap. Being now bored of the situation the filly exhibited those inherited behavioural tendencies that were more appropriate for her mother and, making good of the old adage which states a man must not marry a woman until he is confident the girl's mother is what he would like his wife to be at that age, she demonstrated that Cheryl was indeed her mother.

She kicked me! A four week old foal kicked me. So! What's the big deal about that? She was only a tiny little creature anyway. As I was facing her hindquarters I actually saw her foot coming for me as the tiny foot of the right hind, lifted into the air and proceeded straight forward in my direction where it made a perfect contact with my special parts. Dead right! Had the foot caught me on the knee that gentle tap would have made me rub it a bit. But wham! With the precision of the county darts champion going for the triple twenty she hit me on the spot. It was a precise little tap that caught me in full flow, directly onto the source of my masculinity.

The pain was immediate, exquisitely intense and caused me to drop to the floor. The girls witnessed the incident and reacted with hysterical laughter into which even the mare herself seemed to join. Did one of them offer support? No! Did they offer to rub it better, or even kiss away the pain? Not on your life, they thought it was the funniest incident that had happened in the parish for many a long month.

I gradually stood up.

I hobbled painfully out of the stable door and towards the car, a move that took me out of view of the still very happy throng and offered me the opportunity to examine myself, to take stock. My own equipment was thankfully still intact and as the nerves to the insulted area were ceasing their insistent clamour I was soon able to re-join the girls and to take part in the fun of the incident.

Foal and doctor made a complete recovery and the incident soon made its rounds of the local horse community. Oddly enough the incident caused a marked change in Cheryl's behaviour towards me and she tolerated me with more understanding in the future. Was it out of sympathy or was it because she had reacted to the unrestrained laughter of the girls by softening her attitude to people, or did she believe that one balls-up was sufficient for her vet?

Mrs Niven also enjoyed that story.

Her sympathy ensured my morning's adventures with the pruning shears were fully forgiven. That tap was an acutely painful one, a straightforward risk when working with horses, whose very size, weight and power means they are an endless possibility for injury. It has to be admitted that the majority of bad accidents actually occur from riding the creatures, rather than as a direct result of bad behaviour on their part.

Another incident was even more bizarre.

A kick from a dead horse caused me weeks of discomfort.

CHAPTER 28

ONE SOW, ONE PIGLET

H ER ATTRACTION FOR me was boundless, and the brazen lady was unable to control herself.

She displayed her wicked intentions by coming after me and I panicked; I was spoken for, engaged to Theresa and there was no room in my life for another female. Yet! This girl meant to have me! Her intentions, if not exactly honourable, were abundantly clear and I was the chosen one. What does a well brought up boy do in that kind of situation? There was only one way out for me. I ran away, I unashamedly ran away.

Candice called me after supper.

"I have a terrible problem with Winnie."

"Please relax and tell me what is happening." The back to nature people were everywhere including odd birds such as Candice who was a single mother, and her weird boyfriend, the tenant at number 38 Longmeadow. Apples, pears, plums and a generous portion of small fruit bushes covered most of the land, and their vegetable and flower gardens took up an acre or so. The remaining land was one big untidy field that housed their stock of lambs, hens, geese and ducks.

The plot was yielding well, and generating enough vegetable waste matter to feed a pig or two. It was a common situation, and most people handled that profitably by purchasing a couple of weaner pigs aged around the six to eight week mark, and fattened them. Candice and, what's his name, her odd man, had decided to go the whole hog as it were! They bought themselves a pregnant gilt and set her up as, well yes, dare I say their piggy bank?

"Only one baby you say?"

"That's right and there is no sign of anything else happening."

"That is very unusual."

The farrowing seemed wrong to me and during our telephone conversation Candice explained how Winnie had gone into labour during the early afternoon, "It has been over six hours since that baby was born and nothing else is happening."

"That is too long a pause between babies, is she still in labour?"

"She seems so comfortable and when nothing was happening I called the farmer from whom we bought Winnie, and asked his advice." He informed her his gilts averaged ten or eleven piglets for their first litters, and, in his experience, for Winnie to pop one piglet was unusual. He declined the invitation for either himself, or a member of his staff, to pop round and take a look and made the excuse he ran a closed herd and on principle, never visited other pigs for fear of bringing infection home to his pristine unit. I guessed that was his excuse not to get involved.

"Please vet, please come and examine her."

I sensed the desperation in her pleading, "Please come, I am worried her babies will die if they are not born soon," Her final plea hooked me, "Pleeeeeeese come, we really need help and all of my friends say you are the best, and the kindest, and always help sick animals."

The urgency, the concern, and the flattery, had me reaching for my shoes.

She kissed me on the cheek.

I thought; that's a good way to start a consultation and my arrival was heralded by squeaks of joy from the pretty thing; the girl I mean, "We are so grateful you are here, come and meet Winnie."

As a lonely single man, the warmth of the greeting from the good looking woman warmed me. I could feel her excitement through the closeness of her body, and the soft pink blouse with a cute frilly collar she wore made me look. As the top two buttons were open over what was clearly an excellent bosom that encouraged me to keep looking.

She linked her arm through mine and led me into the barn and when we reached the sow she dropped me, slipped through the gate of the pen and knelt on the straw by the sow. I was disappointed at how easily her charm slipped from me and was now solely focused on the huge animal. She spoke softly to the sow, "Now at last Winnie, here he is, come and meet the nice man who is going to help you."

I missed the comfort of her embrace, and thought, that's a pity! I was enjoying being fussed over. I smiled at the cute little thing; the pink piglet I mean, as my focus was firmly on piggy matters by then and said, "Excuse me, give me a moment to get organised." I popped back to the car, and changed into the usual clothing required for obstetrics.

They were still in the same place.

I reflected on the scene; would you look at the two of them, what a mutual admiration society. The huge creature was comfortable on her warm straw bed, and, as I checked her out, she hardly acknowledged my presence. The single little porker was a healthy little chap whose fat pink body was snuggled up against her huge swollen udder and I said, "She looks completely normal, I will now examine her internally and that will give us the full story."

"What will that involve?" Candice; still stroking the sow, hardly looked at me as she asked that question.

"I will slip my well lubricated arm into her breeding passage."

"That doesn't sound so nice will it cause her any discomfort, is it really necessary?"

"Most sows hardly react to such an examination, and yes it is necessary. If the second baby is stuck I should be able to release it and that could allow others to come rushing out to greet us."

"OK. That would be lovely you are the boss, so let's do this!" Candice made herself comfortable by sitting down beside the sow and then gave me a nod, "OK Vet we are ready and you can do your thing," Her smile lit up the barn.

"I cannot examine her here, like this!" I explained how the sow would have to be securely confined, "We will have to pop her into a farrowing crate?" The farrowing crate is the standard method of confining sows at the time of birth. It is a secure, purpose built, metal container that is not much longer or wider than the sow, and is designed to restrict her movement, to help prevent her tiny babies from being crushed. The sow may weigh over four hundred pounds and the tiny, perhaps only two pound babies, run the real risk of being flattened or crushed if she inadvertently lies down on top of them.

"We do not have a crush."

"Hmm!" I scratched my nose and thought aloud, "That is a problem."

My eyes were already roving and I said, "Let's have a look around there must be a narrow passage in which we can trap her." After a thorough search my problem worsened as no suitable device for restraining the sow was available. There was no doubt in my mind I had to conduct an internal examination although I was unsure how to proceed and I explained my thinking, "As a rule it is dangerous to attempt an internal examination on a sow unless she is well secured."

"My Winnie is a family pet and she thinks she is human," Candice pouted her lips at me, as any spoiled child might.

"That might make things easier. You must appreciate that although she has been well socialised she is still a large and potentially dangerous lady." As I said that I looked at her great, peaceful body; flat on her side, resting peacefully and with the little one snuggled up to her warm, pink belly, she was the essence of contentment.

I examined the sow again.

As I prodded away at her abdomen she made happy little noises, and, particularly when I scratched her tummy she appeared the most gentle of creatures. There was no doubt in my mind this lady was indeed a well behaved girl. Pigs are amenable to training, and, under the correct circumstances may be as easy to handle as dogs. I wavered and that allowed my inexperience and common sense to be diluted by the scene of domestic bliss.

My varsity experience had given me an extensive introduction into pig behaviour and management. Animal Husbandry at the University farm of Cochno clearly taught that safety for the vet and all others working with farm animals is a major factor. An injured vet is no good to himself, his family, and his clients and I could hear the venerable Prof's advice, as though he were standing watching over me, clearly telling me, "Listen to me student and listen carefully. Get her into a confined space, a passage where she cannot turn round. Find somewhere to examine her without being in danger of an accident happening to either the pig, yourself or to the owner."

It was easy to agree with such sage advice and I said, "This could be difficult, dangerous."

The big drip of a boyfriend was very quiet although his manner of constantly smiling at me, and hovering in the background, irritated me. He almost spoke, but Candice beat him to it, "She will be good, I know her so well."

There was absolutely no possibility of suitably restraining the sow.

She was the quietest gentlest pig that anyone could find, wasn't she? Brought up like a dog and often walked out on a leash, she was even house trained to do her smelly pig business in one spot. The lady of the manor turned her attention back to me and exuded an attitude clearly designed to ensure Winnie would get the attention she deserved, "She is a real pleasure to work with, we love her to bits and she loves company. At no time has she ever demonstrated aggressive or difficult behaviour and I am sure she will allow you to examine her, no problem."

The pretty blonde turned on the charm and Candice, a lady at the very height of her femininity was in full flow. She gazed at me with big, gorgeous blue eyes that sneaked out from their hideaway in a mess of long blond hair and captivated me and charmed me with that feminine softness that ensures women have power over men. I later realised it was a combination of the smile and the fluttering eye lashes that pushed me over the top?

I gave in, and against my better judgment I decided to make an attempt to examine the sow, "She does seem a pleasant lady."

Candice picked up on my indecisiveness and drove home her argument, "That's it I knew you would not let me down?"

I thought; what kind of a wimp will she take me for if I walk away now and then Candice delivered the final blow that turned the discussion totally in her favour. She left the sow, walked over to me and snuggled up close to me, then linked both of her arms into mine, and gave me the sweetest of smiles, and another faint flutter of her eyelids, "I will sit beside her head and stroke her chin, she loves that and will relax nicely for you."

Caught! I swallowed not just the bait, but the hook, and the line and the sinker.

Candice wandered over to Winnie.

The girl sat down beside her, and stroked her and spoke gently, "There you are my sweet thing. Is that nice?" Winnie grunted her appreciation and it was clear the underside of her chin and throat appeared to be the blissful spots and Candice continued, "I am sure you will not even notice anything when the nice vet inspects you and then he is going to bring your beautiful babies into the world." Winnie wriggled herself snugly into the deep straw.

I was a bit jealous, and thought how a bit of that tender treatment would do me good. My mind was made up, "OK! She does seem a gentle creature and we are wasting time, I must do something."

In approached the sow with the stealth of a Scottish Wild Cat on the trail of an unsuspecting rabbit. My approach was a slinking, quiet one, as noiseless as any vet could be; allowing for my wearing a long green parturition gown, and wading through six inch deep straw in cumbersome wellies. I reached her, and paused for a few moments to allow my rapidly beating pulse time to relax.

I acted very carefully, determined this would be the most gentle internal examination possible. I slipped one well lubricated finger inside her breeding passage, no problem; then the second finger; no reaction and then I allowed my entire hand to slip comfortably inside her, right up to the wrist.

That's when everything went wrong!

It was the noise that sticks in my memory.

Squealing like a stuck pig! So that's what the expression means! It was the extraordinary combination of loud, high pitched squealing, strained breathing, and a sloppy splurging noise as she raced over the yard that will remain for ever in that part of my memory dedicated to scary things. It was the heavy breathing that was most obvious; hang on a minute, the heavy breathing was mine!

The sow was suddenly a wild animal and was on her feet in a flash, and accidentally knocked Candice onto the floor. Her long body hurtled into motion as she went looking for the fiend that had disturbed her happiness. The speed of her reaction was incredible, as from lying blissfully on her bed of straw that huge bulk was immediately on its feet and she twisted and turned into the streamlined instrument that hurtled towards me with the speed of a ground to air missile.

The swiftness of my own reactions surprised me.

Long distance running proved to be the sport that was my forte, I could never sprint to save my life, or so I thought! Yet life threatening situations bring out the best in survival mechanisms and the automatic factors which controlled my Fear and Flight system were operating efficiently before I knew what was happening. Those few yards to the boundary wall were reached in a superman style of speed, as the fear of being mauled had me exiting that place quickly, very quickly. Had she reached me, her huge bulk would have hit my lower legs with a force that would have dropped me, and the damage could have been great; a pig has a dog-like mouth, only bigger.

The jaws opened wide as though demonstrating her huge teeth, and caught my right boot a glancing blow as my body disappeared over the wall. Had my departure been a fraction of a second later; not a nice thought!

The big drip spoke for the first time.

He added to my painful and miserable condition when he said, "Jings! That was amazing, I never imagined she could have moved so fast, her mouth was huge and she nearly got you, amazing," He was really animated, his eyes were wide with excitement and his flushed cheeks confirmed his fascination with my escape, as he blabbered on and on in the manner of a six-year-old who, having opened her Birthday presents, doesn't know which one to play with first, "You should have seen her react? Her response to you was lightning fast, it really was amazing, simply amazing."

Although I can be a short tempered man it is uncommon for me to be aggressive and he got me close to the brink and I thought; if he calls this unpleasant scene *amazing* once more I will punch him; all I wanted to do was hit him once, a good one on the jaw. If that would have been a very unprofessional manner action, it was certainly one that would have cheered me up.

I was in a mess, stiff and bruised all over and apart from the physical damage, it was the knock to my ego that upset me. He picked up my belligerent attitude, recognised the look I gave him and wordlessly slunk under whatever rock he normally called home.

The message echoes loud and clear.

Do not take chances when working with dangerous and highly unpredictable animals! Animals often beat up young vets and that incident with Winnie was the first of many veterinary encounters in my career where the animal came off best. It served as an introduction to the many situations where my attempts at ministering to them failed completely, leaving me with souvenirs in the form of kicks, bites, fractures and lots of bruises.

Time is a great healer.

As my mind and body began recovering I gazed over the wall where the scene was rapidly regaining its former air of domesticity. Winnie was back on her bed with her anxious baby stuck noisily onto a front nipple and Candice was scratching her belly and soothing her, "There, there, my lovely girl. Please relax, that nasty, nasty man has gone away and mummy will never let him come near you again."

The nasty man never did go near her again. That call turned out to be a complete waste of time as for the only time in my career a sow delivered a single piglet. Had it in fact been a waste of time? No!

It was a hard earned lesson in the University of Life.

CHAPTER 29

HIPS

WE LIVED IN Elm Walk Our home was in Drofter close by the hotel with the same name as the street.

I was as fit as a Greek, butcher's dog due to a bit of squash and a heavy long distance running program as my main exercise. Most of the locals recognised me, and often greeted me cheerfully as I whisked past them on my training runs, even when we never really knew each other. My runs were usually conducted early in the mornings, and one lady and her dog were regular *hello* partners of mine. The dog, a middle aged, yellow retriever was one of the most unusual examples of the breed I had ever seen as she had a small white blaze running down her face.

I walked over to reception, picked up the case notes for the next client and called out, "King, please."

A lady walked towards me and said, "I know you." It was the first time I had properly met Alison King and her lovely dog Rebecca and they followed me into the consulting room where we caught up on who we were, and where, and why, and got through the usual questions vagrant dogs ask when they finally sniff each other. Business was quiet, and that gave us the chance to chat for longer than normal.

"I must be honest this is our first visit to your clinic as we usually go to Clayworth. They have examined Rebecca, and, as I am unsure about their findings, I would like you to give me another opinion."

"That is fair enough although best if I contact the vet who has examined her previously, in order that . . ."

She interrupted me, "I have already spoken to them and they have kindly given me a report authorising you to examine her."

"You have been most professional."

"They also gave me the radiographs."

"I am impressed at how organised you are."

"It was easy for me to keep it professional. My husband is a radiologist at Worksop Infirmary and he is used to doing things properly."

"I agree with that approach, and you have certainly caught my interest so best if we start at the beginning."

Rebecca was eight years of age.

She had been gradually becoming stiff over her hindquarters; nothing unusual there as many of us follow that same path as we mature. Alison sighed and said, "Mr Coates has been very good for our dogs and has been helping us with the problem and Rebecca has been going along as well as one could expect, until last week."

"Let me back track a wee bit," I made a few notes on the clinical record, and asked, "I have regularly seen you walking with her and have never noticed anything markedly unusual."

"Well!" She did that womanly thing, where they hitch themselves up and take a deep breath before speaking, "This is where it gets to be a puzzle. I think Rebecca has actually been doing well and as you say we walk every day. We often see you doing your Chariots of Fire thing as you flash past us."

"Thanks, what a lovely way to put it and I will bear that in mind every time we meet." I had to smile at that happy thought, "I sometimes see you as far out as Eaton College, which means she is capable of a good four or five mile walk, so what is the problem?"

"This is what happened."

The lady took over as they often do, "It was last week, Tuesday, after breakfast at about nine when it happened," Alison had been tidying up in the living room when she noticed Rebecca sitting awkwardly, "I called to her, and she took a few minutes to stand and was so stiff and tired I was concerned about her."

"Did she seem in pain?"

"Well, I have had dogs all of my life, and she did not seem too uncomfortable."

"How long did it take for her to get back to normal?"

"Not long, I would say within five minutes she was up and about and back to her old self."

"That is interesting, were you with her for some time afterwards?"

"I was at home for the whole of the morning and she seemed fine, normal. It was then I took her through to the vets."

"And what did Mr Coates find?"

"Unfortunately he is on extended leave and we saw his locum, a Mrs Williams. She examined Rebecca carefully, most correctly, and admitted her for radiography."

"What were her findings?"

"You will see from the radiographs her hips are in shocking condition, they even made my husband whistle when he looked at them," She handed them to me, "Here they are, please tell me what you think."

"Thanks, I will look at them, but only at the end of the consultation. I am afraid that X-rays often confuse me so I leave them for later."

"That is an interesting statement, why should X-rays confuse you?"

"I have been in practice for long enough to know the patient has to be considered as an individual and holistically and thus I like to do a complete examination first."

"Fascinating, I must mention that to my husband."

I ran through my detailed examination.

Rebecca; in common with many middle aged Retrievers, did not have the best of hips and when I put a hand on each of them and encouraged her to walk I sensed a degree of abnormality there and said, "Yes! There is some instability, but not markedly so and there is very little muscle tension." Apart from that she was very well and I congratulated her mother, "My compliments to you Alison, I think your regular exercise pattern is spot on, you both look fit and trim."

"Thanks! We have been enjoying our walks so this came as a bit of a shock."

We were both seated and I steered the conversation to the nitty gritty of the day, "OK! What is the other vets opinion?"

"Well," she paused, and I saw a tear form in her eye as she continued, "Mrs Williams feels Rebecca needs immediate surgery to remove the femoral head on the right side, and then, when that has healed in another five months she would like to do the other side."

"Oh!" I rubbed my chin and bit my lower lip. My friends know that to be a sure sign that my mind is in overdrive and my first thought escaped, "That is major surgery."

"I know. When my husband looked at the radiographs he agreed with the vet, and the first operation is scheduled for next week Wednesday."

"That is major surgery! Its time I examined the radiographs."

The X-ray viewer was in the pharmacy, behind the consulting room.

I took the envelope from Alison and said, "Thanks. Let's pop them up." I opened the back door of the consulting room and placed the pics on the viewer in full view of the owner, "Yes! I see what you mean they are not nice," I pointed out the areas for concern.

"That is exactly what Mrs Williams said. She did take her time to point out what arthritic changes were taking place."

I felt like a tennis player as my head flashed from radiograph to dog, and back again. Something nagged at me, telling me all was not as it seemed and I said, "I am unsure. The radiographs are bad, Rebecca does have advanced arthritis and yet it is almost as though these pictures do not relate to this dog."

"No! Have they given me the wrong . . ."

"Sorry, sorry to interrupt you like that. No! I am sure a quality clinic such as theirs would never make such an error. It is just . . ." Another bout of chin scratching, and lip biting followed, before I continued, "The clinical picture and the radiographs don't match," I nodded my head, "Please pop her lead on and follow me outside, I would like to watch her moving."

Rebecca wagged her tail, as only Retrievers can.

"Walk up to the wall and back again," I studied them closely as I did when examining a lame horse and encouraged them, "That's it, again, and a bit faster," She moved fairly well and did not appear to show any discomfort, "She could move better, although I am not picking up any pain. That of course could be the gentle, uncomplaining nature of the breed."

"Yes they are very special creatures."

"And now, finally, I would like you to run with her and when you get near the wall please try and turn her sharp." We did that little test a number of times and the old girl seemed to enjoy the game, "OK let's pop back into the room and we can put our heads together."

"This is an interesting case."

Alison nodded her head at me then looked at Rebecca.

I continued, "I have come to a conclusion and it is time for me to explain how I think we should proceed with Rebecca," I sat beside Alison and we both constantly watched Rebecca as we talked to each other, "I agree she is affected by chronic, bilateral osteo-arthritis of the hips."

"I was afraid of that."

"Yes, but let me finish, please?" The lady almost stood to attention and fiddled with the pearls that hung loosely around her long, slim neck, "However! I do not feel it is in her best interests for surgery to be conducted, at this stage."

"So you do not think the radiographs are so bad?"

"As I said previously the pictures are bad, my problem is I cannot tie them in with the degree of pain that she . . ." I stopped, rose from my chair and said, "Did you see that?"

"What! I saw nothing, what did you see?"

"The muscles of her left ear, and the side of her face, and the eyelids all twitched."

"Twitched, why would she do that?"

I ignored that question and my eyes never left the dog and I probed the owner for more answers, "Have you ever seen her twitch like that? Has any of the family ever noticed her twitch?"

"No! I have never seen her twitch, nor do I remember anyone else mentioning that."

"I wonder, I wonder."

"Gosh Alex, but you look like a Jack Russell who thinks a rat is under a shed, what are you thinking?"

"A Jack Russell indeed, well that might be so. I wonder if what happened that morning might have been something very different, I wonder if we are looking in the right direction, if . . ."

She interrupted me, "A fit, is there any chance she could have had a fit?"

"Interesting thought that as it is exactly what is going through my mind. Tell me though, why should it suddenly jump into your own mind?"

"I have maintained regular contact with Fred Hafez who bred Rebecca; we did some training with him for a few years, and when I spoke to him the other day he said one of his lines was having a problem with a very mild form of epilepsy. He wondered if Rebecca, as she is of that same line might also be affected."

"Bingo!"

I clapped my hands together which caused Rebecca to jump up and head for the door, "This might be a red herring, but I think we should be patient." I was excited by then and after scratching the dog on her head I turned to Alison and said, "If I remember correctly you have two sons?"

"Aloysius is sixteen, and Francis is fourteen."

"Are they also into dogs, I mean do they play with Rebecca?"

"They both love her, but Francis adores her and would have her sleeping in his bed if he got the chance."

I thought for a moment and said, "OK then, here is my suggestion. Postpone surgery for the present, and then I need you to talk to the family, and to do so when everyone in the household is relaxed. Please bring up this topic without being dramatic or excited and be gentle." I knelt beside Rebecca and gave the lovely creature a cuddle, "I would like to know if any member of the family has ever seen you have any twitchy episodes, or any funny balance things."

Alison was thrilled at my suggestion and both of them wagged their tails as they headed for home.

The problem slipped from my mind.

Five days later when they returned I pulled at Rebecca's ear, smiled at them both and said, "Hi chaps, and how are we all doing today?"

"Well Alex, we are simply wonderful, wonderful." The smile on Alison's face was so big and cheery it instantly reminded me of the happy faces that often decorate Halloween cakes.

I grinned in harmony and said, "Tell me then, what is making you so happy?"

"I asked my husband and Aloysius if they had seen anything unusual," She paused and looked serious for a moment, "I did it carefully and gently as you said I should. Neither of them has ever seen anything unusual." She was still grinning by then and I was sure something special was about to unfold, "Francis was away on a school trip and only came home yesterday afternoon. He and Rebecca greeted each other as long lost lovers might and within thirty minutes they were lying on the lounge carpet wrapped up in each other's arms."

Alison's smile got bigger and bigger, "It was such a happy sight and I left them to it until the young man awakened and came looking for food." She paused and then her face took on another smile, a different one, one of those smiles that mums reserve for their children, "Gosh he can eat that boy. He is growing and it's all that sport."

I was a helpless bystander.

"Anyway! He was munching through his second sandwich when I gently brought up the question, *the question*." It was an effort, but somehow I managed to remain quiet and allowed her to continue, "His answer! 'Mum she often does funny little shaky things when she is sleepy. I suppose I notice them because when we are cuddled up together they tend to wake me.'"

My diagnosis was mild epilepsy that did not require any treatment.

Alison and Rebecca continued to enjoy their walks for a number of years before advancing arthritis; and I can never remember whose came first, slowed them down.

Phew! Careful observation saved that one from the knife.

Hip, *hip*, hooray!

CHAPTER 30

A WEE-WEE FACE

A NGELA HAD A cat called Thing
His name was pronounced
Thleeng.

He was affected by cystitis, inflammation of the lining of the bladder. Do you know anyone who has been afflicted by that disease? Worse still, has that condition actually ever preyed on you? A colleague so affected once remarked, "You have no idea how uncomfortable it was, I felt as though I were passing chopped up razor blades."

Och! That is enough to put you in the picture.

Cystitis is common.

The cat may have an infection in the bladder wall and this may be associated with gravel or crystals in the urine that can block the urethra. Standard veterinary treatment applies antibiotics and anti-inflammatory drugs. The homoeopathic route is of value where remedies such as Berberis and Cantharis are of immense value.

The problem occurs regularly in the male cat as Tom has a long, narrow urethra that lends itself to block easily. When this happens it prevents him from weeing normally and he may be found sitting for long periods in the garden or on his litter box. He may have a very strained expression on his face; cats are normally shy about their toilet habits and I often wonder if they feel a certain loss of dignity.

The diagnosis of a blocked urethra is simple and treatment is very successful if it is carried out early. Light anaesthesia allows a more detailed examination to be conducted, then the tip of the penis is gently, ever so gently, cleaned and an attempt is made to pass a catheter through the urethra, and on into the bladder to drain off the pent up urine. The technique requires experience, patience and above all a gentle approach.

Thing was a handsome character.

He had visited me on a regular basis over the preceding two years. He was very much a full Tom and, although not destined to be a stud cat; Angela had decided against this and her foot went down very firmly on the subject, she would not have him neutered. He was very much a male, a real man about town, with more than his fair share of testosterone. Were he a male of another species he would no doubt have been driving about town in a convertible, in winter, with the top down, and the wind gently caressing his balding head.

Thing had an attitude, a characteristic flaw that often goes hand in hand with high hormone levels. He was a fighter of note, a gangster with a Bruce Willis lifestyle; a swashbuckling character with the physique to match his mind, and often arrived home in the mornings after a night on the tiles with wounds to his face and neck.

At a time when purebred Siamese were uncommon in Drofter, Thing left his mark productively and colourfully on the local breeding scene. We had noticed a number of distinctly oriental looking kittens coming from the suburbs close to where he lived and I was confident he was making his presence felt, and must confess to having more than a sneaky admiration for him; go Thing, go!

His kittens were stunning and always found good homes; a far cry from the modern situation where many unwanted and beautiful kittens have to be euthanased. *Please, please have your cats neutered!*

Angela contacted me by pager at seven a.m.

She had found Thing sitting in the garden on a patch of soil and he was straining, mewing pathetically and obviously in distress, "His hindquarters are all wet and they look blood stained."

"Gosh Angela, I do not like the sound of that."

"Sorry Alex for disturbing you so early, but I am anxious."

"Please! Don't worry about me and anyway I am a morning person and have been out already." I had just returned from an early visit to John Hogg's large dairy herd at Tarlton where I had brought yet another calf into the world.

The lady was sympathetic and very understanding, "Now that is a shame have you had your breakfast yet? I am sure we can wait for an hour or so."

"Very kind of you my dear, but no, I will meet you in about thirty minutes."

My breakfast was a quick gulp on the run.

I made my way to the clinic in reasonable time and found Angela and a very vocal Thing waiting for me and, as we freed him from the wire cat basket I said, "Come now my friend, what have you been up to now?"

"He seems blocked up behind and is feeling very sorry for himself." Angela was on the point of tears.

"You are spot on Angela, I am sure small crystals are blocking his urinary passage and preventing him from passing urine."

"Is that why his tummy is swollen and hard?"

"His bladder is enormous and, as you pointed out he is in a lot of pain."

Andrea, our senior nurse, had arrived early for duty. She was the best of the best and certainly of much more value to our practice than Simon, a new graduate who had recently joined us.

An Englishman! The cheek of it! In a practice that was traditionally full of Scots he was one of them, an English vet at a time when everyone knew the best medicine was from North of the border, but, I do keep forgetting we were working in England, so I suppose that bit of prejudice is unwarranted. Anyway! Our invitation for Simon to join us had not been a success and he was an unpopular lad for a number of reasons. Top of the list was his attitude; he thought he knew everything and he had graduated with flying colours from Cambridge University where they all thought they were the cat's pyjamas anyway.

Among his many irritating mannerisms he had a bad habit of peering over my shoulder. Peering over my shoulder; he would literally, and actually, get up my nose when I was dealing with something a bit complicated, a bit different, but try to get him to assist when I was doing something routine such as chopping the horns of calves! Then he would be nowhere to be seen.

Oh well, another cat with a blocked willy!

Andrea had already prepared for the procedure to unblock him. We were working in the annex to the big boss' house, prior to our move to the swish new veterinary hospital we were converting along the road. The Land of Nod beckoned Thing following an intravenous injection of a wonderful anaesthetic called Saffan and, as he slipped off to sleep Andrea volunteered her thoughts, "I bet that's the most comfortable he has felt for ages."

"I love this anaesthetic, I often wonder what they think about, or dream about, when we put them under."

"I hope never to have one, although I think we must make an effort to try and remember what we think about when they put us under." Andrea nodded her head in that determined manner of hers.

She had positioned Thing on his left side and I directed a bright light onto the sensitive areas and was able to examine his bladder and penis properly, "It is a big one, but we have seen worse and it is not tense enough to suggest imminent rupture."

"That's good news, I like this cat."

A song sprang to my lips, "Now then pussy cat, wow, wow, wow, now then pussy . . ."

I was interrupted, "Alex please do not make that horrible noise! You know you cannot sing we know you cannot sing, please!"

"Sorry friend, it helps me to concentrate and I thought that Tom Jones number would be perfect for this . . . hang on, hang on, this urethra is blocked fast." I was unable to work the plastic catheter into his urethra and I worked patiently and quietly; by then Andrea was humming out something from her hero Rod Stewart, probably *Maggie May* and she made a much more soothing sound than I did.

The necessity to be fastidious, when attempting to unblock that urethra caused me to become tense and I soon felt physically and mentally drained, "Damn it Andrea, but this is a difficult one and it is getting to me, best if I take a short breather."

"That's a good idea. I don't want you getting rough with this special creature. Yes, best if you take a break."

"Hmm!"

I straightened my back and stepped away from the table.

Confident that our patient was being well monitored I wandered to the window and glanced outside in time to see him arrive. Yes, that one, the know-it-all, and he made me mumble, "Oh no that is all I need this morning."

"Why, what's wrong?" Andrea rushed to see what was happening.

"It's him, you know who has arrived."

"Oh no, that's all I need this morning!" Andrea popped back to Thing and as she checked the colour of the mucous membranes inside his mouth she muttered, "I must agree with you, I thought you were being hard on Simon at first, but we would be better off . . ."

The man prevented Andrea from stating the obvious as he burst into the clinic and said, "Now then chaps, what is causing such excitement at this early hour of the day? Something interesting I hope to prevent us slipping into the tedium of a routine day. Eh! What!" He was soon in his normal position, perched over my shoulder and his unsolicited advice soon followed, "Why don't you try rotating the catheter a bit more, give it more lubrication with the gel".

I kept my cool, "How many of these have you successfully deal with?"

His confident reply was delivered with his usual loud voice, "Never actually seen a case before, although I have read up on all the latest published works on the subject. Yes! I do feel I have a good working knowledge of the problem."

Academically Simon was brilliant.

He could come up with the most fascinating theories and ideas and one way to gain breathing space from him was to ask him to check his varsity notes for some information. He would have enjoyed being a permanent student and in all honesty, from the practical point of view that was the obvious route for him to follow as his brains stopped at his wrists! He was not designed to be a surgeon, when he did get scrubbed up and allowed a bit of blood and gore to get onto his pristine body, there was a change, a marked deterioration, in his attitude.

"Hmm!" I looked at Andrea.

"What are you thinking?" She mouthed the question at me; we had been working together for so long we understood each other.

I signed back to her, "Let's test him," I gave in to temptation, "I have had a hard morning with an early calving out at Tarlton and maybe you are right, maybe you should scrub up and take over. I will have a cup of coffee and support you from the side lines. There's a good chap, let's see the Englishman in action."

"That is an excellent idea, you take a break and I will show you how a Cambridge graduate does things."

Flash Harry was soon scrubbed up.

He dived into the fray and worked gently with Thing for about ten minutes. Gentle! He was so careful and nervous he hardly touched the creature while I remained quietly on the side lines until one of his comments indicated his lesson should come to an end, "The catheter doesn't seem to be able to penetrate through the calculi in the tip of the penis where the mucous and gravel have formed a solid blockage." I saw his obvious distress and embarrassment and knew I had found him out with this case. I did not have time to gloat as we had, after all, a living, breathing creature in our care that needed help and I made some encouraging remarks to help him learn.

Andrea was monitoring the patient's vital signs and she gave me one of her sighs, looked hard at the clock then spoke to him, "Time is getting on, do you feel you are getting anywhere?"

Our nurse made it quite clear she was unhappy about his handling of the case and that increased his distress, "I am making some progress, but he might be a candidate for surgical intervention."

I also checked the cat's vital signs and said, "Everything normal thus far." Finding them to be within normal limits I continued to monitor Simon's progress.

Simon's stress levels went through the roof and at last he admitted he was making no progress, "I cannot understand why the catheter will not go through the blockage because I am doing everything by the book. I give up, it is solid and you better take over."

"OK let's have a look." I donned a fresh pair of gloves, picked up the catheter and explored the problem. I noticed, mainly by feel, that he had in fact made some progress, that the obstruction was beginning to yield to his efforts and in the interest of teaching I suggested he make another attempt, "Come and have another feel at it, I think you will be able to see you have made progress."

Simon followed my instructions and soon agreed the situation was improving, "That does feel better, if I continue to rotate the catheter will it slip into the bladder?"

My reply encouraged him, "You are almost there," I raised the tone of my voice, "Remember! That urine is under a lot of pressure so be careful."

Simon made a mistake!

Simon made a big mistake because as usual he thought he knew better than me and he did not listen to my advice and made a simple error, one I guarantee he never repeated. The blockage was breaking down and he should have advanced the catheter along the urethra with his left hand and gently squeezed the bladder with his right hand which would have allowed the escaping urine to pass steadily into the stainless steel bowl awaiting it.

"That's it Simon, that's the way. You are learning fast, but please remember the pressure in that bladder is great."

"Not to worry Alex, you can leave this to me now."

"Well! Are you sure you are under control, will you be able to release it gently?"

"I have it and now you can watch the Cambridge boy in action and here she comes."

What he did was actually completely different when he did the reverse of the accepted approach, "That is much better, I can feel it, I am nearly there and we are about to make the breakthrough."

"Excellent, but please *go gently*." My voice lifted in volume by a couple of levels, but to no avail. Simon removed the catheter completely with his left hand and squeezed the bladder at the same time with his right hand which had the desired effect of clearing the obstruction in spectacular fashion. He was mantling Thing's little body in the manner of a golden eagle with a hare, and the release of urine was a beautiful sight to behold, a great joy for all who witnessed it. Well! Most of us!

Simon's face was only eight inches from the tip of Thing's willy. He was directly in the line of fire as a magnificent stream of urine left Thing's bladder at fifty miles per hour. It was torrential release and we stared open mouthed at our assistant's face being drenched in urine.

Simon leapt into the air.

He ran off screaming some weird English ejaculations that were probably ancient war cries about the lack of suitable parentages of some of my Celtic forebears and Andrea and I almost fell down laughing.

The big boss was been heading for his car when the flying vet almost ran into him and he came rushing in to see what the excitement was about, "What's going on, what have you done to that ejit now?"

We were in such a state it took us some time to offer the explanation. The big boss thought it was hysterical, and disappeared into the house to tell the lady boss.

It really is odd.

Simon didn't last much longer with us.

I think something about general practice must have . . . p****d him off!

CHAPTER 31

THE LION DOG

SIMBA WALKED IN took over and, He acted as though he owned the place.

His owner; John McGregor was also a veterinary surgeon, accompanied him. McGregor's employment as the Divisional Veterinary Officer for the Ministry of Agriculture in one of the neighbouring counties resulted in him traveling a lot and, being a bit of a miserly Scot, he always found an opportunity to overnight with anyone he could sponge off. In the song Delaney's Donkey, sung to perfection by our late uncle Dani, there is a line that fits him perfectly; *with a grip just like a Scotsman on a five pound note.*

Our modern hospital impressed and he watched me pin a fractured humerus on a Retriever, a black, flat coated one, and then over a cup of tea he waggled his enormous black eyebrows at me and commented, "I travel a fair bit around the country and I must say you are as good a surgeon as I have seen anywhere."

His odd facial expression; it was only then I noticed how the left side of his mouth was markedly lower than the right, made me hesitate, and then I said, "Well, I have had some good experience over the last ten years or so, although I know there are plenty of vets who are better than me and our own Greg is a good example."

He cut me off, "Nonsense Alex, you do not realise how good you are."

Every enjoys a bit of flattery and that made my head swell.

His visit was followed by a telephone call a few days later.

When his complimentary attitude continued I guessed he was softening me up for a favour; his well-practiced telephone manner exuded the command expected of a top administrator and it made me rise from the desk and respond as a private in the Army might when addressed by an officer, "Thanks Sir that is very kind of you and our hospital is going well; sir."

"Good," He paused for a moment then continued, "I need your opinion."

"Yes Sir, how can I help?" I shook myself, annoyed at how he was manipulating me.

"Have you had any experience with Ridgebacks and the dermoid sinus problem?"

I was under control by then and said, "Why Mac that is an interesting condition, and yes it is one I have some experience of."

"That's grand. Your boss said you were the right man to talk to, I am coming over next week and need you to look at my wife's dog."

Mac was looking for a freebie. One evening over dinner, the boss disclosed our success in managing the problem and Mac confided his own fourteen month old male was affected, and the vets he consulted recommended euthanasia. They felt surgery was impossible owing to the advanced nature of the disorder, and, in view of his wife's great attachment to the fellow he requested a second opinion.

Dermoid sinus is a congenital defect.

It occurs in a number of animals, and is of most importance in the Ridgeback breed. It develops along the dorsal spine of the neck or tail as a sinus; a tube or funnel of skin that grows from the vertebrae to the surface. The open sinuses produce a purulent discharge and it is such an undesirable problem it is common practice for breeders to examine their tiny puppies at an early stage and euthanase them, but a few sneak through.

I was interested in the phenomenon, and, with several successful operations under my belt, was keen on looking at more cases.

Ridgebacks are interesting creatures.

Their history; formed in the heat and dust of the Dark Continent is the envy of most breed societies. It was the need for a strong hunting dog that would fend of jackals and other stock predators; of the two and four legged varieties, that led to his development as a strong, muscular creature, and the many stories of their great bravery; most of which are more than legends from the veld, helped give the big fellows their sparkling reputation. One such story describes how, when old Oom (uncle) Jacobs of Nelspruit was badly mauled by an angry lioness, his brave lion dogs saved his life; two of his five dogs were killed, sacrificing themselves to save him. The others protected him during a vigil that lasted twelve hours until his family found him underneath the vast spreading canopy of an umbrella acacia tree.

With such a history it is hardly surprising the breed achieved a popularity that is still high in the savanna, the correct environment for them as they are not lap dogs!

Oom Jacobs big male Frikkie was a cracker and he rightfully became a favourite with local farmers and it is estimated he fathered in excess of thirty litters, amassing well over two hundred puppies. Such fame was deserved, yet the other side of the coin was disappointing as Frikkie was badly affected by the sinus problem, and this became a significant problem in his progeny with courage and sinus passed on in equal measures.

Simba was a good example of the breed.

Ridgebacks are an impressive mixture of ruggedness, aloofness and masculine good looks and even the females are tough; they are also very feminine.

Simba stood about thirty inches at the shoulder, and bore a long, muscular frame that indicated his athletic potential. He was a real man's dog; although I say he was a man's dog there is no doubt my friend Gill would have liked him; she knows about these things! His walk, as he strolled through the clinic, held a swagger that further expressed his personality and he calmly took in everything in a manner that suggested he was inspecting the premises and Andrea was the first to comment, "Would you look at him, is he vetting us?"

Patricia stood looking at him and her mouth was partially open, "He is magnificent, he almost takes my breath away," She paused then continued, "I wish I could find a man with that charisma."

I laughed, but Shelley bit her lower lip and nodded in agreement.

I met Craig at reception a short time after the big dog left the prep room.

He said, "We have passed the test, Simba has given his approval and we may operate." Although he was a farm dog who only rarely found himself indoors, he had no problem in coming to terms with the unfamiliar look, feel and odours of our hospital. An immediate favourite with the girls he deigned to be patted and stroked once or twice, before suggesting such fawning was unnecessary. In my home town of Dumbarton people would have termed him a *stoater*! He had a rich colour; a dark reddish-brown shade reminiscent of the ancient, well-polished imbua wood of his ancestral home.

As Simba eagerly devoured a couple of large tranquiliser tablets McGregor, to our disappointment, informed me he was definitely going to peer over my shoulder. That information was most definitely not welcomed by any of the staff whose hope was that he and the boss would have spent the day chasing the wee white ball. At least I did have an hour or so to compose myself.

Patricia popped her head round the office door and smiled, "I have a message from our Happy Highlander we are ready."

I smiled at her use of Greg's pet name and said, "Excellent! Tell him to tap Simba on the head with his chanter and I will be there in five."

CHAPTER 32

DERMOID CYST

T HE BIG DOG was spread all over the table.

He lay on his chest.

His front limbs were stretched out comfortably in front of him on either side of his neck, which was itself supported by a number of sand bags. The skin over most of the neck had been shaved which gave me the opportunity of examining the problem in more detail and two, large, open sites glared at me and I said, "They look even more unpleasant now."

"I have never seen anything like that before." Patricia stared at the lesions her pretty face with its pale, flawless skin was crunched up in distaste.

"If you clean them up as you would any infected tissue you will feel better for being involved."

She squeezed them to evacuate as much rubbish as possible, then irrigated them with a hibitane solution, "Thanks Alex you are so right and I feel better now."

"Excellent! Let me have a good feel." I introduced a steel probe into each of the sinuses to estimate their depth, and smiled on finding that one of the problematic ones clearly extended close to the spinal cord, but ended bluntly before it made contact with bone and I said, "This one is deep, but I am sure it should not be too difficult," I moved to the next one and grimaced, "The second is more of a concern as it could be connected directly into the vertebral column."

"That is what you were worried about," The owner nodded at me, "How does that change your thinking?"

"I expected this would be a difficult case and it doesn't change my plans." The fact that some of the sinuses might originate close to the spinal cord had been explained to McGregor. Spinal surgery involving the opening of the actual vertebral column was uncommon in those days, and beyond even our adventurous attitude.

The owner made a suggestion.

"Why don't you remove the simple ones first then decide what to do when you approach the big one."

In some ways that seemed a reasonable approach, but my attitude was different, "No Mac. I am going to explore the bad one first, for two reasons. Firstly, if that proves to be inoperable there is no point in continuing with treatment. Secondly, I do not wish to risk the contamination that might come from the other sinuses discharging pus into the environment of what might be major surgery."

"Good thinking, I like that approach."

The usual gowning, gloving and draping process were soon concluded. A final check on the gleaming instruments and the drapes and swabs set out on the instrument trolley suggested we were ready to proceed, "That looks good team, and everything seems in order."

Surgery has little time for pleasantries, nor should the operating theatre be a place of discord or rudeness. Regular training ensured our A-team would perform as a well-oiled machine where the surgeon is in charge and heavily dependent on the anaesthetist. Dependable Patricia would take no nonsense, she missed nothing. Our pre-op discussion had focused on the possibility of the wide ranging swings in the depth of anaesthesia that can occur whenever tissues are manipulated in the region of the spinal cord due to the brain being intimately connected to it.

Mac was informed of his place, "Nearly ready team. Now Mac, please stand back and do not talk unless I ask for your contribution, I am lucky to have this excellent team assisting me."

"Righty ho Alex, I will make myself small by the window."

"Ok team does anyone need to add anything?" I made a point of looking around at everyone, they all shook their heads.

Please Lord, help us today.

I began with my usual practice; although I have to admit that in those days my Christianity was not as easy to express as it is now. I bowed my head slightly, closed my eyes for a few seconds and invoked the expert assistance of the Holy Spirit then said, "Well Greg, if Patricia is comfortable with her sleeping beauty we can go; probe and forceps." A stainless steel probe was slapped firmly into the palm of my left hand; when dealing with potentially dangerous instruments a confident approach is important. We always worked with top quality instruments as surgery always flows better with good equipment.

The round ended probe slipped down the entire length of the sinus and its progress came to a halt when it grated against bone and it made me grimace, "I have reached bone and it feels solid, although I am not yet sure if it is anchored in, or around the canal. There might be some tissue between me and the vertebrae, scalpel."

The first incision was in a circular fashion, 5mm from the edge of the sinus. By holding it up with rat toothed forceps I was able to detach the external opening then Greg placed a heavy pair of artery forceps over the exposed sinus to seal it, and give him a better grip.

My deliberate exposure of the sinus continued with Greg pulling steadily on his forceps while I used scissors to bluntly dissect around the tube-like structure. It was becoming obviously exposed and I saw how the route of the tract was somewhat tortuous and angled towards the spine. It was delicate, steady work as I attempted to remove the maximum amount of diseased tissue, and at the same time I had to prevent the tube from rupturing into the clean surgical cut.

"Fifteen minutes, Pulse, respiration and colour are good."

"Thanks Patricia." The vertebrae of the neck were closer and it was difficult not to become tense, knowing how close the sensitive nerve tissue was. The journey become slower and more patient as our destination approached; it was at this point that Mac tried to interrupt me, "Are you always this patient?" I ignored him!

The sinus narrowed.

By then it was only three mm in diameter and still firmly walled. The detached tube had been pulled away and was lying on a bed of swabs and was almost two inches long. The ever decreasing sinus was in the space between two of the vertebrae. My worst scenario loomed as the tract seemed to be directly in contact with nerve tissue and I pointed this out, "Mac! Come closer and see for yourself that we do have a problem." He moved over for a decent look and I continued, "I will work away gently at this thing in the hope that constant traction will bring its tail away cleanly although meningitis and spinal cord damage are real possibilities. What do you think?"

"I do not like the look of this, I am afraid we are going to lose him."

The manner of his reply made us pause quietly and the owner continued, "In my opinion it is time to end the operation, why don't you increase the depth of the anaesthesia, and allow Simba to drift off into his final sleep, that will certainly bring his suffering to an end."

Patricia jumped in, "No! Not yet, we have nothing to lose, sorry."

I smiled at the young nurse's compassionate feelings and said. "Not to worry, you know I listen to everyone's opinion."

Greg chirped in with an offering that swung the balance, "Mr McGregor, it has actually gone well so far, may I suggest you allow Alex to continue, in the hope he gets somewhere with it?"

I agreed, "Let's keep going." My back was stiff as my weak spine was not enjoying the tension and its chronic sacral damage was complaining about me assuming a strained position for too long. My forehead was dripping in sweat and, as Andrea swabbed it for me, I said, "Tell me Patricia, how is he doing?"

"I am happy, he is still stable."

The dog was breathing well and it was time for a short break, "OK everyone let's take five." I needed a few moments to stretch, to dry my face off, and to change gloves, and that short pause refreshed me much more than one would imagine was possible.

"Right chaps let's go again."

Greg; with his normal Scots-terrier-like tenacity resumed his grip on the exposed tissue. I considered very closely the intervertebral opening from which the spinal nerve and the sinus were emerging. Gently, oh so gently, I explored the area with a very fine probe and tiny scissors and was able to remove a little tissue, mainly fat and I said, "Pass me the forceps and let me feel it from this side." I took over the exposed sinus tract from Greg and put some pressure on it in an effort to establish how firmly it was attached. I pulled harder without any impression that it was either coming clear or that it was likely to tear.

As the pressure increased Patricia instructed me, "Hold on Alex he doesn't like that and his breathing and heart rate are accelerating." I backed off.

Simba was in trouble for exactly four minutes.

Only then did his pulse and breathing normalise. That short enforced stop in no way could be compared with the shorter, elected break we had taken and the tension was such the only talking was professional, and the presence of the owner complicated the issue by increasing the pressure on us. Patricia made a soft sound and when I looked at her she gave me a firm nod and said,

"Much better, we are under control again and his pulse, respiration and colour are reasonable."

"Now we can go on," I took a deep breath and continued, "I hate to do this, but we have no choice. Simba is going to react badly to my next move and we will have to let him go dangerously deep." At that point I ordered the depth of the anaesthesia to be increased by twenty per cent; dangerously close to the accepted maximum.

Patricia, who initially had been concerned about the new depth of his anaesthesia was suddenly happier, "That is much better, his heart rate and breathing have slowed down markedly."

"Lucky for Simba as I think all of our pulses are higher than ever," Greg revealed what we were all thinking.

"Ok Greg let's go."

When I asked him to take up the tract, and to slowly increase the pressure my anaesthetist objected, "His pulse is creeping up again."

I felt we were at the final stage where Simba's future, his very life, was hanging in the balance and I expressed my thoughts, "We have no choice, this final effort might prove too much for him, at least he is sleeping and there is no going back now."

"Give me the tract," I decided to take the responsibility on myself by taking the tract from Greg. That decision was made for two reasons with the first a logical one, "Thanks Greg, that will give me a better feel of things," And secondly I made that decision for a more humane reason. Simba's future was then in my hands and by taking on that responsibility there was no chance that Greg could later blame himself if that course of events turned against us.

I took the tract in my left hand and began pulling and suddenly I got a distinct feeling that tissue might tear and I talked aloud to myself, "Too much pressure Alex ease back a little."

"I still do not like it, he is steadily deteriorating," Patricia was vigilant.

The force was gradually and slowly increased until Patricia called, "No!" I again paused and she warned me, "I don't like this, pulse and respiration are shooting up and his colour has gone pale."

I replied in a manner that belied the internal turmoil knotting my guts, "Sorry Patricia, guys, I have no choice, I must continue." I maintained the pressure, and held my stance and grip for a further, very long four minutes and nothing happened, and apart from the almost monotonous warnings from my anaesthetist the theatre was dead quiet. My mind filled with possibilities; should I trim it off at this point and hope for the best, should I give it one good yank and hope for the best, should I euthanase its or . . .!

The sinus tore away.

There was an audible plop and the sinus came away in my hand, and, before I could comment a cry from the ever watchful Patricia warned me, "Alex, no, we are losing him," Simba's pulse and respiration were all over the place.

"Cut out all fluothane."

Her sharp reply had a note of relief in it, "Fluothane is off and he is breathing pure oxygen."

We waited and less than thirty seconds later, a much happier Patricia gave us the good news that Simba was improving, "That has done the trick, his pulse and respiration are better," She waved her gloved hand at me, "You can never win! He is now showing an eye reflex and is beginning to come round.

"Well done everyone."

"Can I introduce fluothane again?"

"Yes! Put him back onto half strength and watch closely, I don't want him going deep, nor do I need him jumping off the table."

I turned to my assistant, "Thanks for your help Greg, I can manage here. Please take this sinus into the lab, open the tip carefully and examine it under the low powered microscope and let's see what we have got."

We, including Simba, relaxed.

It took Greg five minutes to study the object, he was always fastidious, often painfully so, but he missed nothing. His eagerly awaited verdict was delivered with that generous smile of his that dominated a handsome, dark face with an always needing a shave look, "The news is good, the tip is solid and there is no evidence of any purulent material, I think you've got it."

That was fantastic news and Patricia was the first to give a cheer followed by much excited chatter from all of us.

My next task was to contain any secondary problems. I had to consolidate, and ensure that any damage we had caused would be contained. I was concerned about any possible bruising to the spinal cord, and instructed Greg to administer heavy doses of anti-inflammatory drugs to Simba via the infusion line which was connected to a vein.

The main job had gone well, and five additional sinuses still awaited treatment; three were small, closed items that were easily removed from the already huge incision that was almost six inches long and then the final sinus soon joined the others in the waste bin. The operation was almost over and all that remained was to suture the massive wound that extended from his occipital crest; the bony bump at the back of the skull, along the majority of the back of his neck.

The tension of the operation hit me.

Fatigue, tiredness and muscle soreness overwhelmed me and I sat down beside Patricia at the dog's head and nodded to Greg, a simple signal that gave him the privilege of closing. His hands were excellent and he was easily the neatest at stitching, apart from Theresa herself!

"Great! Let me have a go? I can do this." He took the wound from an ugly gaping incision to a straight row of tiny and very neat sutures. My partner Seamus was always of the opinion that surgery could be messy on the inside, but the wound had to look good. That is the only part of the procedure the owner actually sees; it has to be neat.

The owner had had enough.

With about an inch of wound remaining to be closed he tired of the procedure. A much older man than myself, I saw how heavily the excitement was telling on him as his balding head was streaked with sweat, making his few wisps of jet black hair stand out like the furrows on a ploughed field. He was as drained as the rest of us and tired; yet happy and very pleased with us, as indicated by his parting remarks, "What a wonderful piece of work and my wife will be thrilled. We will never be able to repay you for your efforts, thank you. Come lass, let's go and have some tea, and I can ring my wife."

The owner left the theatre with Frances.

The last stitch was being placed.

The swing doors were still vibrating as Patricia's frightened voice rang out clearly, "Oh no, quick! Do something," Her alarm echoed off the walls and in the starkness of the theatre every noise was magnified.

"He's stopped breathing!"

CHAPTER 33

EMERGENCY

P ATRICIA'S URGENT CRY alerted everyone and the procedure entered a new and not entirely unexpected phase; an unwelcome one.

Anaesthetic emergencies can and do arise and we were aware of that possibility and our vets and nursing staff were trained, and equipped to deal with them. Training brings out that which is best in human nature and we had to prevent at best, or reduce at worst, any time that might be lost in dealing with an out of the ordinary event.

There was no time for procrastination; that thief of life and our emergency drill went into action. Phase 1 was implemented within the space of a couple of my quickening heart beats, "Fluothane off! We know what to do so let's get it right," The anaesthetic gas being fed down the endotracheal tube was immediately switched off. The black, rubber re-breathing bag which was about two thirds full of the gas and oxygen mixture that had kept him peacefully sleeping was disconnected from the supply pipes. Patricia gave it a firm squeeze between her hands and it emptied quickly. The empty bag was then reconnected to the black, heavily ribbed rubber tubing that fed the machine.

The oxygen flow was turned up to maximum and I instructed, "OK Patricia, commence breathing for him." As he was unable to breathe naturally his lungs had to be artificially expanded and a life sustaining stream of oxygen flooded into his lungs. It was a difficult and potentially fatal situation, but not yet a catastrophe as the re-breathing bag intimately connected to the dog became his life support system.

"Pace yourself correctly."

I instructed Patricia to begin inflating the Ridgeback's chest with pure oxygen and she compressed the bag every five seconds, and we easily saw how his long slim chest rose and fell underneath the protective green operating sheets.

Part of our emergency setup included a number of drugs sitting on the worktop adjacent to the operating table. The fact they often sat there apparently helpless; until their expiry date caused them to be discarded, was testament to the few serious problems we actually faced. They appeared at times to be a nuisance, a waste of space and an unnecessary clutter in the pristine environment of our theatre, and yet they were an important part of our insurance system; a just in case necessity that if required would facilitate a smoother correction to any problem.

A clear, thick glass bottle containing five hundred mls of bicarbonate was called into action; the alkaline nature of the solution was needed to help prevent the build-up of dangerously high acid levels that develop when oxygen flow to tissues is compromised. Various other drugs were administered including adrenaline for shock and to stimulate his circulation, and that was followed with aminophylline; a dilator of the respiratory tract tubes and the blood vessels. They were injected quickly through the catheter and all of this had probably taken less than twenty seconds to consider and implement.

A stethoscope somehow found its way into my hands and I used it to assess the dog's heart and lung sounds. Andrea; who had been summoned by a call from Patricia, took over the work of assisting him to breathe, "OK Andrea, record the time and heart rate every minute."

"I am already onto that."

The heart was beating regularly, but at about one hundred and twenty beats per minute, it was much too fast and I was desperately concerned. Simba's heart was taking severe strain; its beating had taken on an irregular pattern and I passed the information on, "Keep going everyone as he is now arrhythmic."

Andrea was also worried, "I hate it when this happens it's never a good sign." She read out his parameters, "Pulse is over 140, and all over the place, isn't there anything else we can do?"

Simba's heart stopped!

"We will extend CPR by compressing his heart. Patricia, lift up the drapes, and let us get to his chest," Greg almost bounded to the dog as I stepped aside and removed my gloves.

Greg picked up his timing from Andrea, "3 – 4 – 5 – Go Greg!"

"That's 1 . . . that's 2 . . . that's 3 . . ."

The pattern of filling his lungs with oxygen, and pressing his chest over his heart continued. Time flies during emergencies, "Three minutes. No heart beat."

"I will allow another two minutes before opening his chest to get to his heart," That was a horrid thought as I had never done it successfully. On the previous two occasions where emergencies had led me down that road we lost both of them. I pulled on a pair of new gloves, "Standby Greg. I will give him exactly one more minute before I open his chest and massage the heart directly."

Mac was returning.

The booming, and very cheerful voice of Mac, could be heard as he returned to the theatre. Although my focus was on the dog I could hear him coming, and my own heart almost stopped as I contemplated his reaction. My own disappointment was immense and I could only guess how he would take the news, that after such a marathon and successful operation we had lost . . .

"We have a pulse." Simba, right on cue shocked me and I also detected a pulse, and he immediately started to breathe again. Not just weak little gasps either, the full respiration of a recovering animal came into play and he took a series of great deep breaths that allowed me to say, "Ok everyone, stand back and relax and let's give him some space."

The swing doors opened.

I promise you! It happened exactly like that and Greg looked at me and I looked at Patricia and Andrea. The owner walked up to his dog, and, in the manner of any veterinary surgeon he lifted his upper lip to check his mucous membranes, "Looks a bit pale and perfusion is good. Well done everyone, what's taking you so long to get finished?"

We said nothing and when Simba began to tremble I said, "Excellent, he is recovering well and it is time to get him out of here." Patricia and Greg stripped off the drapes, and, as they prepared to lift him from the table I instructed them to be careful, "Greg! Please do everything you can to support that neck, I do not want it to be flexed either to the side or up and down."

"Got that and yes, we will be careful."

He was quickly transferred to a large, warm, and padded observation cage, with another fresh drip of saline solution attached to the catheter in his vein; a precaution that is important in shock control.

My thanks to the team were hardly necessary.

They understood exactly how good we, as a team had been and we were immersed in an air of pride as we had taken our work to a degree of excellence that would never be surpassed. There was a togetherness surrounding our team as a result of that near death experience in a team that already enjoyed working with each other.

The vets stripped of their theatre gear and there was not much time free for us to bask in the glory of success. There was just time for a quick lunch before afternoon rounds and clinics were due. Luckily my work had been scheduled with the expectation that the operation would have been a very long one.

Mac disappeared for nine holes.

Mac and the big boss went off to flog the wee white ball with him none the wiser about the excitement his charge had generated.

My afternoon was spent on the farms and at around the four pm mark I could not resist the temptation to phone the hospital. Greg gave me the news the big dog had recovered well from the anaesthesia although he had not yet regained his feet, and was experiencing marked back pain. That worried me and made me suspicious he had the spinal shock we anticipated, and we discussed his medical treatment protocol until I was satisfied, "You are doing everything by the book. Continue to monitor him carefully and we can discuss any changes on my return."

"OK! Although the girls find our wait and see approach rather hard."

"I am not surprised. They are more than special people, and, well! Let's wait and see!" I could imagine his smile was tight-lipped one.

I returned to the clinic.

Frances assisted me as I gave Simba a thorough examination of his nervous system, "There is no doubt in my mind his spine is seriously inflamed."

"That sounds bad, how do you assess that?"

"His reflexes down the right side are compromised and his pain levels are high." A stoic creature, he could easily have become aggressive, but he merely peered at me through his large red eyes.

"Is there nothing else we can do?" Frances expressed my own thought.

"At this stage we must be patient," She was disappointed and as she looked ready to shed a tear I explained my thinking, "Let me explain. The more I take away his pain, the more likely he is to move around and that could cause more damage. The situation would be easier were he a human, as strict bed rest and a firm neck brace would be possible."

"That makes sense, he enjoys our company and we spend as much time sitting quietly with him, talking, and, we are also praying."

"Amen! Amen to that." I took a last look at him and wondered what he was thinking. It must have been something along the lines of; what has happened to me? I felt a bit groggy after they gave me some large yellow sweets, and I remember something sticking into my arm, but now! My head hurts, my neck is very painful and I can hardly move my legs, what happened to me?

Girls are much better at TLC than men.

It was two hours later and guess who came to the rescue? Again! Andrea joined me in the recovery room and I said, "Hi Andrea, I thought you finished early today?"

Her look said more than words; she shared our worry over the big dog, our team of dedicated individuals often went beyond the call of duty and she knelt beside him and her soothing voice had a similar effect on both of us.

We adjusted his medication including reducing the level of anti-inflammatory drugs and Andrea had the last word, "I am much happier, his pain is less and his muscles are twitching more."

"That is an interesting observation; is there a chance his pain is less because nerve damage is preventing him feeling the pain?"

"Now then Alex, are you testing me?"

"Definitely."

"Correct, if that were the case the muscles would not be twitching, they would be softer, more relaxed."

"That is spot on, you had good teachers."

We left him in peace, knowing his best vet from this point on would be the ancient miracle of nature. When I last checked with Craig at ten pm his pain levels were slightly better although his nerve signs failed to indicate any positive progress. Craig; the duty vet for the evening, had a dependability that made me confident Simba would be carefully monitored.

The next morning brought no early news.

We deposited the children at school then dropped off Theresa's Volvo at the agents for its first service. The early morning was disappearing although we had time for a quick coffee and then time marched on and I entered the hospital via the side door at around nine fifteen. As I headed towards the kennels Craig's strained face met me and his miserable face worried me, and made me ask, "You do not look a happy chap this morning, give me the bad news."

He took a deep breath, "Simba can stand, but he is very weak and in pain."

He was sad! I however, was delighted as my experience with spinal conditions had clearly indicated the very slow rate of progress they usually show and the fact any improvement had occurred was encouraging, "If he is standing that is a positive sign, come, we will examine him together."

My examination gave me hope. Simba could stand, admittedly with difficulty and managed a few stiff-legged steps. He dragged his left hind leg which made the nails of that foot rattle on the tiled floor. He had passed a good stream of urine and his respiration, although fast, was regular and his pulse and colour were good. As Greg joined us I ended our conversation on a positive note, "So chaps lets cheer up a bit, I am delighted we have seen this slight improvement, we are going in the right direction and I believe the prognosis is excellent."

They soon shared my confidence and we set off on our normal duties.

Simba's improvement was steady.

Over the next three days he gradually improved, and we were able to discharge him to a happy owner and within four weeks he was completely normal.

The boss had suggested that McGregor should not be charged for the operation and treatment; his prerogative although he did suggest the staff would appreciate a nice present.

The disappointment! At no time did Mac phone, write or thank any of us, he never acknowledged the tremendous amount of effort, or the considerable professional and nursing skills Simba had received.

He never even bought the girls a box of chocolates.

Animals are more reliable than people and we had the best possible reward.

The lion dog roared again!

CHAPTER 34

CONFUSED FARMER

THE MODERN FARMER is well educated, but that was not always the case.

We were in practice in Drofter in the seventies and early eighties when many small family farms were still run along traditional lines. They farmed as their fore fathers had done for generations before them and had little inclination to learn modern farming techniques, nor did they possess the necessary education to embrace the exciting developments technology thrust at them.

They were in all fairness real people for whom the term, *salt of the earth*, was coined. They had a problem as the modern world was threatening to run over them and their children were being educated to a standard far greater than they had been exposed to.

Why? I hear you ask, why was that a problem? Their children asked the question; why should we stick around on this small farm, when we can have easier, more interesting and better paid jobs in the towns? They were not inclined to small time farming with its long working hours, nor were they prepared to suffer the hardships of an outdoor lifestyle in all weathers as their forefathers had done.

By our time in Drofter significant changes had already taken place and the local scenery had taken on a different character with fewer small units as more and more were incorporated into big units. I enjoyed working on the small farms and their many characters helped mould my personality and I had lots of fun with them. On many an occasion I took the opportunity to pull a farmer's leg and I particularly remember one that occurred during a pregnancy test, as it caused my sense of humour to backfire on me!

James Anderson was very much a traditional farmer.

He asked for a vet to pregnancy test a cow at his small, mainly arable farm in the Leverton area of the Drofter practice. My journey through Rampton and Treswell was along some of the more pleasant country lanes in the area. The window was down, Peter Gabriel was belting away at *Solsbury Hill* on the radio, and I was enjoying the warm afternoon sunshine as another grand day was coming to an end.

As it was my first visit to the farm I paid careful attention to the directions Seamus gave me, "You are going there from the south, through Leverton. Take a right at the T-junction, then follow the road left and onward," He paused for a moment and did that thinking thing, "Bear with me for a minute and let me get this right. As you hit North Leverton turn right and it is the first, second, yes third farm on the right," He paused again, "The small entrance is dominated by a huge Sycamore tree and you cannot miss it."

I did miss it.

I was so relaxed I missed the turnoff and laughed at myself, "There you go again, daydreaming will get the better of you one day," The red Saab always enjoyed it when I spoke to her and she purred in agreement, "At least I have only missed the farm by thirty yards."

As I rolled into the small farmyard the farmer crossed the yard in front of me. The bale of hay he carried was a huge one, yet the small, wiry old character seemed sprightly under it. My car came to a halt a few yards from the cowshed and I jumped out and said, "Good morning Mister Anderson, my name is Alex. I do not think we have met before, I am from the vets in Drofter, how are you today?"

"I am well Veterinary and thank you, many thanks for coming to help me with this cow."

I remember the manner he stood back and checked me out; it was the look a man might take from the top of the Hambleton Hills in the Yorkshire Dales when he was out of breath from the climb through the bracken and heather to the top. He took his time and had a real good look at me. I read his thoughts; now here we have another new vet, I hope he knows his business.

I had learned how to deal with new farming clients.

Many of them had so few visitors a call from the vet was something they looked forward to. We chatted a bit, about the harvest, the weather, milk yields and so on; it was the usual talk of the time and I finished it off by offering a cheerful comment, "That's grand, your good grass crop will make it easier to get through the winter, farmers do not like having to buy in fodder and you will be happy in that respect."

"I do not know, if I can agree, true, I did cut a lot of grass, but now find I am having a problem trying to store it, most likely the rain will get to it, when March comes, it will be so mouldy, I will have to buy in some fresh stuff."

His speech was painfully halting and of course I agreed, "Farming is never easy," he was the client after all, "There is always something happening to even out the good and the bad seasons."

He nodded his head in a manner that made me feel as though I were an inspector from the Inland Revenue rather than a vet. "You are so right, for a young man, you do have a grasp, of the problems farmers face."

"Thanks for that, I enjoy working on the land and farmers teach me so many interesting facts about life."

He again did that odd head nodding thing of his. I was telling the truth, as working on the land was a fascinating experience that made me happy to go to work every day, "The thing, as you well know, is to do business carefully and gently and in that way we survive another year."

He liked that, and for a few moments we were partners, fellow stock men attached at the hip.

He changed the subject.

"I have this one old lady that is bothering me, if you could please take a look at her for me?"

By then I was growing accustomed to his slow delivery that was gentle rather than unpleasant and I thought; if you talk like that to the cows during milking I bet they relax nicely, another fifteen minutes of this and I will fall asleep, "That's grand, I am more than happy to help you with her, has she had many calves before?"

"She has been a good breeder and this will be her sixth calf, four of them heifers."

There was only one cow to be tested and I do not remember the details as the test had been a routine one. In view of my subsequent problem I later patched the details together and decided my adventure must have played out along the following lines.

I pulled off the soiled plastic glove.

It had protected my arm from all a cow's digestive system evacuates, and then I decided to risk pulling his leg by cheerfully announcing my findings, "Yes! I have good news for you. She is pregnant, the calf is a heifer, it is almost completely black, and it will be born on Dec 16th."

The farmer was most impressed, "Well thank you very much Veterinary, that is excellent news, she is a good cow, I am so glad we can, keep her in the herd."

I of course was having a bit of fun. It was not uncommon for me to take a stab at guessing the exact date for the calving to take place and many of the local cattle were of a black nature, and therefore, to suggest it would be a black calf was logical. As she usually had female calves it was also likely I had a better than average chance of getting the sex right.

The incident slipped from memory and it was brought to the fore some four months later when my favourite nurse, Andrea, called out as I was leaving on my morning round, "Can you fit in another call today?"

"My morning round is busy, what do you need?"

"James Anderson from Leverton has a cow to be pregnancy tested and he specifically asked if you would do it."

"I wonder why? I hardly remember being on his farm before, and a visit this morning is impossible. As you can see from the book I am going to the North, but it would suit me to pop in there this afternoon as I am going to be in the general area of Treswell."

I pulled into the farm.

It was around three thirty and I was in time to miss out on a thorough drenching from the thunderstorm that had been threatening to engulf us for the last hour. I ran the final ten yards from the car to reach the cow shed and said aloud, "Phew! There is a real cracker coming," I called out to no one in particular.

As it happened the farmer was standing unseen and very close to me. I was still looking at the sky, enjoying, yet respectful of the colour changes that were part of the deteriorating weather when the clouds erupted into torrential rain with a heavenly light show that was magnificent. The farmer said, "Yes Veterinary, it looks, like a big storm."

His sudden comment caught me by surprise; I am generally noise sensitive and as the storm had already primed me I jumped, "Sorry man, you quite startled me there. I was too busy thinking about the storm, and never saw you," I recovered, took his outstretched hand and greeted him correctly, "Afternoon Mister Anderson, it is good to see you again, how are you doing and the family are well I trust?"

"Welcome Veterinary, they are fine thanks, nice of you to ask."

"That is excellent news."

At that point I was safe from the rain that was belting down.

I slipped of my shoes, and replaced them with my green wellies; they had been sitting on the floor in front of the passenger seat, and I had quickly grabbed them before running to the cowshed. Luckily there was always a plastic glove or two in my jacket pocket and that meant there was no need for me to fetch anything from the well drenched, and by then almost clean car. I craned my neck to peek inside the byre and said, "I believe you have a cow that needs testing?"

"That is right vet there is one lady that needs your help, I am sorry to drag you out, all this way just to attend to one cow."

"Not to worry, and I am more than happy to oblige you. I trust the cow is snugly inside, and not standing out in the rain for us to work with her?" I again noted his halting speech.

"Now then Veterinary, don't be pulling my leg, you know I would not do that, she is inside, I must confess she is frightened, she might be a bit difficult to manage, because of the storm."

I followed him into the cowshed and paused for a moment to get my bearings and enjoy the atmosphere, "This will be much better than working outside, I love barns and the smell and the noise of cattle."

"Good, well here she is." The farmer seemed even less of a talker than I remembered and his words came out even more slowly and deliberately.

The barn housed twelve cows.

It was a fair sized place and could easily have held double that number. They were chained to the wall in the usual manner, their heads at the front, their business ends closest to us. James walked up beside the second cow from the doorway and began to squeeze himself between her and the first cow and he talked non-stop to her, "OK Lady give me a bit of room . . ."

As he put his hand on the cow she let out with a wicked kick, and her flying foot only just missed collecting him a sharp one on the knee and he blurted out, "Goodness me silly cow you have never done that before."

"That was a bit close!" The suddenness of the kick surprised me, "That could have been a sore one, it is probably the storm upsetting her," I considered our next move, "Will you be able to hold her or should we let the rain die down a bit, and then take her to the crush?"

He scratched himself solidly on his left breast for a moment, and paused, as though deep in thought then looked directly at me and said, "Lady is not normally difficult, let me try again."

He was almost smiling by then and did not appear too concerned the cow might damage us and that made it easy for me to agree with him, "Perhaps if you hold her tail up a bit that will help?"

"That would be best, please be careful." The farmer tapped lady firmly on her massive, black rump, from a distance this time and, as there was no reaction from the cow his confidence returned, "That's a good girl and now I will slip between you and Mavis." She was the pretty red heifer in the stall next to Lady. The farmer positioned himself between the two animals then snuggled up very close to Lady's hindquarter with his left hip pushed directly into her side, in front of her left hind leg.

It takes time to persuade students that the best, therefore safest place to be when dealing with a fractious cow is to be very close to her. The cow was moving, anxiously shifting from one leg to another and I watched them; fascinated at how she and the farmer moved together with the synchronicity of a couple embracing the tango.

He talked to the cow.

"Now then Lady, there is no need for any silliness. I know you do not like the storm so please give us a few moments to work with you." His attitude and speech fascinated me, as he was so comfortable with his cows and his speech, when talking to them, was much quicker and more fluent, than when he addressed me. I liked that as he and I seemed kindred spirits; people who talk regularly and lovingly to cows have to be nice people.

Lady relaxed and the farmer grasped the base of her tail firmly in both hands and was able to lift it towards him and straight up, over her back. Such an action causes a marked pressure on the tail and often assists in calming a fractious cow and I said, "Ok Mister Anderson are you comfortable with her? Can I get on with the testing?"

"She will be no problem, for you now, Veterinary, I have her."

I lubricated my gloved arm with water and soap and said, "Let's do this." I planted my right hand securely and firmly on her right hip to let her know where I was before starting the test. I carefully watched her feet, ready to jump if she tried to kick me, "There's a good girl I am sure you are going to be the real Lady we know you to be. I am just going to have a feel inside for this calf of yours." My gloved hand slipped easily into her rectum and the test began and as usual the moment my hand was inside her rectum she completely relaxed. I cannot ever remember being kicked by a cow during a rectal examination yet I have lost count of the number of times I have been kicked. I continued to stroke her right quarter and talked to her, "That's a good girl and now I will be able to feel everything quickly and we will soon leave you in peace."

I picked up the major blood vessels.

The large arteries that feed the uterus were easy to palpate inside the cow's pelvis and were beating in a manner that suggested her to be heavily pregnant. Rather than pulsating in the standard pattern they thrilled to the touch with a distinctive fremitus that guaranteed pregnancy to be in place, and I smiled and said, "There is lots of fremitus, and, yes! I can palpate the calf itself. She is definitely pregnant, and has only about ten weeks or so before calving."

I withdrew my arm from the cow, turned towards the bucket of soapy water and commenced washing and he surprised me when he said, "That's good, what colour is it, when will it be born, and, you haven't told me if it is a bull or a heifer?"

I straightened up, looked hard into his face and can only imagine the look of incredulity I must have given as I said, "Yes! That would be nice to know, although I cannot give you such information from this examination."

He almost floored me with his next comment, "But you did the last time you tested a cow for me, you said she was carrying a black heifer, and you said she would calve on the 16th of December. You were spot on with everything last time, so why can't you do it this time?"

I was lost for words.

I do not remember leaving the farm or how I excused myself. My practical joke had reversed on me in an amazing manner. I could not believe my estimations had been so correct, nor could I believe the farmer had actually believed my opinion.

I could not believe anyone thought I could be so accurate.

I never tried that one again.

CHAPTER 35

A FASCIST JOINT

I F JUNE DANGERFIELD said it was urgent,

It was urgent.

If it was very urgent she didn't even use the telephone! That woman had a voice, and, as her dairy farm was only two miles from the practice, her foghorn roar could be heard in the office all the way from her kitchen.

I picked up the telephone to return a client's call at the very moment it rang and said, "Good morning and welcome to the Drofter . . ."

June interrupted me and said, "Oh! It's you!" She continued, "I have no choice, its Becky' little dog and I am coming now, get the X-ray machine warmed up I am on my way."

"Right!" I put the phone down and thought; Seamus where are you?

June's farm was one of those places I could not do anything right, and Seamus could do no wrong. It is a fact that you have good clients, lucky clients and you also have unlucky ones, and well, she was my worst.

"Is she coming?"

Roisin, who was standing beside me, was visibly shaking at the thought of June bringing an animal to see us. I shrugged my shoulders at the young nurse and warned her, "We cannot get out of this so let's be as professional as we can, and make sure the decks are cleared for action," Roisin almost ran along the corridor and I called after her, "Hang on lass, hang on, did you manage to clean out the X-ray tanks, and . . ."

"They are perfect and I will be extra careful with the processing."

"Great."

Penny, who was witness to the exchange, patted me on the shoulder and said, "I enjoy the woman, and she is a very good client who always pays on the nail and never complains about anything except . . ."

"Me!"

"What is it about you two that you cannot get on? Seamus and I think it is hysterical; best if we leave it there for the moment and you get your act into gear."

"Too right, I am on my way."

"Good idea and if anything goes badly wrong I will make sure the First Aid Kit is handy," She laughed again and went back to her books.

"Thanks Roisin everything looks . . ."

Bang! The poor front door almost fell off its hinges and the lady's voice boomed along the corridor, "Right Penny we will go straight through."

With her two teenage daughters in attendance this major tour de force swept into the prep-room. I was prepared for anything, almost anything, and yet the woman's attitude and appearance threw me. She was arguably the hardest, toughest woman I had ever met, and yet was always immaculately dressed and turned out. The person in front of me was very different to her usual self, as her shoulder length, normally well controlled brown hair, was dishevelled and stuck down on her tear stained face in many places.

All three of the women were in tears, and the manner in which the normally sensible Becky cradled the box in her arms immediately put me on the alert and as she carefully placed the apple box on the table I said, "Tell me what happened?"

Her reply was so full of pain she moved me right to my toes and when I took a quick glance at Roisin I saw how her sympathetic tears were already rolling down her cheeks; and we did not yet know what the problem was. "Mum ran over him with the car."

"OK! Let's get on with things."

I lifted the dog carefully out of the box and inadvertently winced on finding him in a terrible state. As I laid the bedraggled, mud and blood splattered body, on the table it made me gasp.

"He got up and ran away from us for about five yards and then collapsed and when he tried to get up again we saw his back legs were no good," Bryony spoke for the first time and continued, "He is definitely paralysed and we know you will have to put him to sleep, but it is awful, simply awful."

June who had remained uncharacteristically quiet said, "This is awful, and it is my fault, I feel terrible."

"OK then, let me examine him."

"No! You must put him down and you must do it in front of us, *and you must do it now*," June had rallied and was coming back to herself.

I watched Snooky carefully, hoping to see something that would encourage me and offer him at least a stay of execution. I forced myself to ignore the women and wasted time with my stethoscope and wondered; am I wrong or is this four year old Dachshund's breathing not as bad as it looks? I put the stethoscope down and said, "Are you certain there was no movement of his hind limbs?"

Becky said, "Now that I think about it I am unsure, perhaps there . . ."

"No, and this is nonsense."

June tried to intimidate me as she normally did, "*You must put this dog down now!* He is finished."

I confess I wavered, I almost gave in and then I convinced myself that I saw the slightest movement of the wee dog's uppermost hind foot and took a deep breath and pulled myself together, "There is no doubt he is in a sorry state, but we must not rush in . . ."

"*No!*" June's voice thundered, "He is going to die and you must put him out of his misery *and now!*"

I surprised myself when I almost lost it and slapped the palm of my hand against the consulting room wall hard enough to make everyone, including myself jump, "I will do nothing of the sort until I, that is, until I am satisfied this is hopeless," I strode to the door and, while mustering up a very strong, authoritative voice said, "Out! Get out of here and do not come back until I have finished my examination. *Everyone out!*"

They left us to it.

Roisin was actually standing to attention when I looked at her and her pale face and open mouth made me appreciate how badly this difficult situation was affecting her. I gave her a quick cuddle and kissed the top of her head and said, "Right then, we best find out what is going on here."

Over the next ten minutes I examined the sad little creature and, when my thorough neurological inspection of him had reached a reasonable conclusion I joined the ladies who were drinking tea in the office with Penny.

It was a sad scene and when I joined them I raised my hand at them, to silence them, and then deliberately projected my voice to enhance my air of authority, "There is no doubt in my mind that Snooky has had a severe spinal shock, although the good news is I cannot feel any obvious fractures. I am not going to put him to sleep and I need your permission to tranquilise him and take some X-Rays."

"So you think there is some hope?" Becky had regained her composure. The tall, slim and very attractive sixteen year old who was always a pleasure to deal with had the curious habit of catching the left side of her lip between her teeth and trying to talk at the same time, and it always made me smile.

"The chances are not good, but you guys have to be sure we have explored everything before we take such a drastic and final step."

June nodded at me, and almost whispered, "Yes please, will you do that for us?"

"That's perfect."

Roisin cradled the small dog with the greatest of care, and the tranquiliser slipped unnoticed into his vein. When Snooky spread himself out on the table in the floppy manner of all drugged animals I said, "Now if we give him about thirty seconds I will be able to probe a bit deeper."

I was then able to conduct a more detailed physical examination of his spine and joints, "I still cannot feel any fractures or dislocations and that is good news so this is not a hopeless case." I picked him up carefully and said, "If you open the door for me I will pop him onto the X-Ray table."

The firing button on the big machine clicked out its signal and I said, "Good, if you watch him I will develop the films." The process only took a few minutes, although it seems like hours when anxiety makes one almost afraid to examine the films. They would take some time to be dry and fully fixed, but I shook off the excess rinsing water and held them up to the light.

We had only taken two pictures to start with, one with Snooky flat on his back with the rays shooting straight through him, and another when he was on his side. I studied them carefully and said, "Good thus far as I can see no obvious damage, nothing at all."

Roisin almost danced as she cuddled the small dog's head and said, "You are a lucky little boy and you are going to be . . ." She stopped, looked at me and continued, "He is going to be alright, isn't he?"

"We should have a much better idea by tomorrow so let's finish his medication while he is in here and then you can make him comfortable."

"My Aunty Molly had a horrible back problem."

Roisin who was more cheerful by then exhibited her usual outgoing personality, "It was a terribly painful condition."

"When you think of how complex the anatomy is in the area and how we abuse the spine it is not difficult to understand why so many people have back problems," I used the radiographs to half-heartedly point out the arrangement of the vertebrae to Roisin.

"The chiro said she had a blocked Fascist joint."

I laughed and corrected her, "I think you mean a facet joint."

"Yes! That is what I said."

I explained that the small facet joints that connect the spinal vertebrae together can immobilise a patient and may even cause them to appear paralysed and the nurse said, "The chiro manipulated her back, and she said there was a dramatic click and it popped into place and she was fine." Her fingers flashed to illustrate how the chiropractor had manipulated her aunt's bones and she nodded with some authority.

"Must have felt like magic."

The girl smiled a happy thought, and then asked, "Could something like that be the problem here? Can you try and sort of twist his spine a bit here and there, to let the fascist joint slip back."

I shook my head from side to side.

I said, "No, and no and no!"

"OK, are you against it?"

I explained that chiropractic work on animals was still in its infancy, and that it would be foolish, unprofessional even, for me to take a stab at something like that, "It takes proper training before such corrective procedures may be attempted, what if there is spinal shock or a disc in the process of prolapsing, and I make a mistake and encourage it to move into the spinal canal?"

"Gosh! I never thought about that; are saying if you do not know exactly what you are doing you could actually do some harm," She paused and then almost shouted at me, "I thought I saw a tiny movement of the toes on this leg," She touched the small brown paw and continued, "This one here."

"I hope you are right and it is possible as he is only mildly tranquilised," I again tested his toes by tweaking them with between my fingers and was disappointed he did not react, "I am unable to satisfy myself that much is happening and must now leave him in peace, that's it for today."

The Dangerfield ladies were sent packing.

The next morning, after they had finished milking, June phoned me, "Good morning Alex, how are you today?"

I smiled to myself and thought; now that is a much better way for us to start a conversation. I matched her pleasant greeting and continued, "I do think Snooky has a chance as there is indeed some slight feeling in the paws of both back legs."

"That might be good news, although you will need to keep him for a few days to monitor him before we know for sure."

"Look June, the sad thing of course is that if he does not improve, and we do have to euthanase, it will mean we have gotten everyone's hopes up, and then will have only tears to show for it."

"Yes! And you and I have been there before." I imagined how her attractive face must have taken on a hard, severe look and it was easy to guess she was referring to her Ayrshire cow. The lovely creature had contracted an acute case of mastitis and June had asked me to put it down, but I had a feeling I could save her, and persuaded them to let me continue with some intensive treatment. I was wrong and she died forty hours later; and she died expensively! The memory of that sad case made me think; at least she did not drag up the whole story again.

June said, "We will pop in and see her in about an hour or so."

That was a visit I was not looking forward to as although Snooky had shown a very slight improvement it was not nearly enough.

"OK Helen, please bring Snooky through for me."

The trainee nurse was showing real promise and she was being well tutored by Andrea and Eleanor and we had high hopes for her. She was reliable, caring and most importantly she listened and took advice and she made me smile as I watched her chunky five foot three inch frame head for the kennels.

Scarcely two minutes later I heard the most awful scream and rushed to join her and found Helen sitting on the floor with Snooky in her arms. She cradled him in the fashion of a desperate mother comforting a badly injured child. I knelt beside her and said, "What's wrong lass what has happened?"

Through her horrible sobbing I eventually managed to piece together what had happened. She had picked Snooky up from the floor and as she turned, her foot had caught on something and she slipped and Snooky had fallen from her arms and had crashed to the floor.

Accidents happen and there was nothing we could do about it. Roisin, also responding to Helen's urgent cries, joined us and did her best to control the distraught girl.

I had Snooky on the table and examined him expecting the worst and my face must have been as long as that of any Bassett Hound, when, to my amazement he smiled and wagged his tail at me, "Gosh! Did you see that Roisin?"

There was no answer; I was on my own as the girls had gone off to the office to find some support for Helen. Two minutes later Roisin returned and with a face even longer than Helen's she said, "The poor girl is so upset, this could have a . . ." She grabbed me by the arm and pointed, "Look!"

Snooky was struggling to stand.

Roisin flew to his side and there was great joy in her voice, "There you are you clever boy." She had her arms under him, supporting him and he stood up.

I was rooted to the spot, unable to react as we heard the Dangerfield ladies coming along the corridor towards us. As the door opened Snooky let out a strong woof of greeting and the excitement of their reunion was intense, and before I could interfere Becky placed Snooky on the floor and I could only shake my head on seeing him walking with a gait that resembled a drunken man, but at least he was walking.

Things began to settle down.

It took time for me to restore order to the dog, the nurses and the Dangerfield ladies and most importantly to get my own head together.

It was clear Snooky was going to make a complete recovery and amidst the excitement June said, "So sorry Alex for ever doubting you, so sorry."

Roisin and I lagged behind as the ecstatic throng headed along the corridor and my face was wreathed in smiles. Roisin looked at me and nodded with a sense of wisdom much beyond her years.

She said, "Amazing Alex, amazing, so it was a Fascist joint after all!"

CHAPTER 36

THERESA'S BED WARMER

EARLY MARCH WAS disgusting and we were stuck fast in a bitterly cold winter.

Every night the mercury dropped to sub-zero, and often hardly rose to positive territory during the weak daylight hours. Farm visits were a misery as the constant sleet was often horizontal and cunningly inveigled its way past the massive amounts of protective clothing I wore.

One Sunday morning a call from Dan of Ordsall Farm surprised me. He was far from his normal bouncy self and he began with an apology, "I am sorry to do this to you, I have dropped myself right in it. Me! The usually efficient one, I have a problem."

He outlined the problem and I said, "Gosh, I am on my way."

It was a Sunday morning.

The roads were thankfully quiet and I pushed the Saab as fast as I dared on the slippery roads; she enjoyed the challenge more than I did. I turned right into his driveway and then left up the farm lane and slithered to a stop, a lucky stop as I barely avoided hitting a barn wall. Dan pulled open my door and laughed, "Nice one Alex, you have only hit my wall once before and this was also pretty close."

"Don't remind me," I shook my head at that memory, and said, "So on with the business."

He pulled himself up to his five foot four inches which probably matched the ample waist that was hidden under the latest knee length jacket by Barbour. Its dark green colour was in marked contrast to the gay, yellow tartan Deerstalker into which his broad head was crammed. He spoke with a marked nasal, upper crust accent that was partly hereditary and partly related to a facial defect where his rather flat face and squashed nose were mementoes of a meeting with an angry cow and her calf at a tender age.

As we jumped into the Landi he advised me of the problem.

Dan had decided to out winter some big bullocks, "I was at Melton market last November, and could not believe how low the prices were." He inhaled hard through his front teeth, "Soooo, I bought forty big bullocks without considering where they would be housed."

For once his thought processes were incomplete as his cattle yards were already bursting at the seams. Knowing a large consignment of his own stock was ready for processing he reasoned that space could be found for the new batch from Melton, but Dan had miscalculated. The market price for fat cattle had indeed taken a drop and he could buy cheaply, but that meant he could only sell low, and he refused to take the knock that selling stock at a low price meant.

He shook his head and said, "No way was I going to take a loss on my fine bullocks so I came up with another plan," He smiled for the first time since commenting on my poor driving skills, "I decided to do a thing I have often thought about and made a plan to out winter the new batch of bullocks."

I interrupted, "That was a big step to take. One or two have tried it locally, and it has rarely been a success, what with the extra feed . . ."

"I hear you," His hand was in the air to stop me, "It's different for me as I have so much in the way of second grade vegetables and I reasoned that would keep my feeding costs at a reasonable level."

The early winter had gone well.

Dan's experiment appeared to be heading for success; cattle are in fact hardy animals and designed to survive outdoors under severe conditions, and the Melton bullocks benefited from the mild early winter which gave them time to adjust to what was to come. They grew long shaggy coats to insulate them from the cold and were well fed on the surplus vegetables from Dan's other large farming enterprise in Lincolnshire.

He continued filling me in as we drove over land that was very wet hard going, even in his Range Rover, "I even congratulated myself on how well the bullocks were coping," He made a sharp, impossible turn to the left and said, *sorry*, when he heard my head hit the window, then continued, "I am even considering how this system might become a regular part of my management practice, you will be surprised when you see the condition they are in."

"Have they lost much weight during this bad weather?"

"No! They have not lost weight and some are even gaining and it seems as though the exercise will be profitable."

The bullocks were running on land bordering the river that was old, mature, natural meadow that never seemed of much use for anything during the summer as it had a tendency to be boggy in places. It was, however, a place well worth a visit in spring when it nurtured a great variety of indigenous flowers and grasses. The river was the problem, and Dan confided he had not reckoned the fact flooding regularly occurred, "The rain has gone on and on, it is the most severe on the farm anyone can remember," He took both hands of the steering wheel and gestured extravagantly at the wet condition, "I am already sick of this winter and we may have months still to go."

My head was throbbing from the knock on the window, and my sense of self-preservation made me cling onto anything I could find in an effort to avoid further damage; and he said my driving was bad! "We are all in the same boat as it keeps going on and on," It was easy for me to agree, "I was on the phone last night to a friend of mine who is a dog vet. His biggest problem was how muddy his clinic floors are with wet dogs walking over them, can you believe that?"

"It's a different world for them."

Dan dived back into the subject.

"We check the cattle twice daily, but I never realised how badly damaged the river banks are." I was thankful he stopped talking to concentrate on getting us through a particularly rough and muddy piece then he risked a look in my direction, "The beasts do look well although I made a mistake with water. Instead of relying on them finding their own drinking water from the river I should have put in our own supply nearer to the gates on the higher ground."

"Please don't tell me you have lost cattle from drowning?"

"No! Thankfully I realised my mistake on Friday when I visited them myself and saw how badly the banks were cutting up. I spoke to my foreman, and told him to set up some water troughs back here on the cleaner land," He pointed over to our right where the action was taking place, "I was too late to help some of the bigger beasts." He paused as we slid through a muddy patch then continued, "However!" I sensed the punch line coming, "My foreman found three bullocks stuck fast over there in the mud." He described how they had managed to pull two of them to safety and had moved the herd to another field.

When we arrived the scene was akin to something from a modern disaster movie. That farm was blessed with a great deal of manpower and did nothing by half measure and there were Land Rovers and tractors and men aplenty, patiently awaiting my arrival.

The large red and white bullock was lying on his right side.

His bed was a wet, muddy, yet smooth hollow which his struggles had moulded to fit his body. His hind end was embedded in the mud and the rest of him was wet, bedraggled and exhausted. When I put my hands on his skin it was cold enough for me to be pessimistic, "He is suffering from advanced exposure and there is a real chance we might not save him."

"I agree he looks bad, but, as you are here we should at least try."

I examined him properly and found nothing to improve my opinion and more than anything it was his sad face with lifeless eyes that could barely hold me, "I hate that glazed look in his eyes as that often suggests them to be on their last legs."

"And if we slaughter?"

"That was my first thought, although it is likely his carcase will not pass the meat inspector."

"I agree with you. They will almost certainly fail him for human consumption so let's see what we can do."

"Now then you poor creature."

I knelt beside the bullock, and, as my examination proceeded it held no surprises, "His pulse is weak with a tremulous feel to it and that is not good." I suppose the bleak look on my face mirrored the sad expression on the bullock's face, and I reflected on what was happening; nature can be cruel, yet kind, and it was causing the bullock to slip gently into that state where death sneaks up in a quiet and almost sympathetic manner. I had nearly been there myself once, when exposure almost embraced me when I was caught calving a cow on a bleak hill in Dumfriesshire.

The sad beast was losing interest in life and hardly bothered to look at me when I injected large doses of drugs in an effort to reduce his shock and to prevent his system from being overwhelmed by the opportunist bacteria already infiltrating his system, "Let's stand back and give him five peaceful minutes."

The drugs worked quickly and the bullock shook his head and struggled in an effort to get his front legs going. The fatigue engulfing his body soon exhausted him and, although he sank back into his muddy bed I felt some hope, "That was an encouraging effort," I looked around me again at the men and the machines that were lined up to assist me, "Now is the time to get him out of this mess, bring me the ropes."

We passed a large, soft rope round the front of his body.

It was adjusted carefully until it fitted snugly onto his shoulders where it was then tied with a loose sort of a knot to prevent it from tightening round the major blood vessels and the windpipe. As I checked the knot I gave the foreman a nod, "That's it Bill. You take charge of his head and please take care as even the slightest bit of a throttling will push him over the edge." I knew Bill well and was confident he could be relied on to follow my instructions.

The remainder of the rope was passed along the ground behind the animal, and then fastened onto one of the front mountings of a tractor. The rope was positioned low, close to the ground, to give the maximum amount of pulling power and I said, "OK chaps we are almost ready to have a pull."

The men were hardy farm workers, well acclimatised to the vagaries of the weather and ready for anything, "You will take your commands from me and me alone, take up the slack and get ready." In a tight situation everyone feels obliged to offer their opinion, but there was no time for debate and it was necessary for me to emphasise the chain of command. Pulling heavy animals by tractor may not seem easy although it can be done effectively by people who know what they are doing.

We were dealing with flesh and blood that was in a fragile state and I continued to encourage the team, "I need you two men to stand on the rope behind him," I grabbed one roughly by the arm and repositioned him, "Sorry George, that's better and try to keep it as low as possible," The chaps I had singled out readied themselves and looked expectantly at me, "That's right, if necessary you can even sit on the rope, you will get a bit muddy, but that's life," They both smiled and George even gave me the thumbs up sign.

The men were ready.

I took another look around to satisfy myself the team were positioned exactly where I wanted them, then conducted a last check of the ropes, particularly where the knots and hitches had been placed, "That's it! Everything seems to be in place," We were ready to begin his rescue attempt, "Now lads let's see what we can do."

My hand waved in the air, commanding the tractor driver to move backwards. The big green John Deere machine started moving and displayed its awesome pulling power. On the one hand I hated them for what they had done to heavy horses, yet, on the other hand their power is special.

There was a plopping and sucking sound and when the beast began to move I felt we were not in complete control and issued further instructions to change the angle of approach, "You two, grab his head and pull it in my direction," I felt he was slipping away from me and that slight adjustment helped concentrate the power in the right place, "OK put a bit more pressure on the rope now."

The huge tractor tyres flicked up wet mud in every direction and the beast slithered towards us until, in a remarkably short period we freed him from his muddy prison. I signalled the driver to stop pulling and at the same time waved my arm at Bill inviting him to come forward to help me untie the knots, and remove the ropes.

Dan caught my arm and said, "Don't you think we should continue pulling him much farther away from the mire, he will be easier to work with."

I had considered that option and decided against it, "I agree with your thinking that it would be a disaster were he to rise and accidentally blunder back into the marsh," I was monitoring his pulse at that point and shook my head when I realised he was unfit to take any more pulling, and continued, "Rather let us be patient, in his weakened condition any further pressure with ropes might be too much, trust me on this one until he shows signs of recovering."

I was unsure.

My mind, although it vacillated to and fro about dragging him to a better place, was made up. His pulse had deteriorated and what was even more alarming was how his gums were taking on a muddy appearance with a purplish tinge. When pulse and gums deteriorate together they are good indicators of the failing state of an animal's circulation and the anxiety in my voice was clear as I said, "We are in danger of losing him," I turned to Joe, "Cover him up with everything you have and rub him down, I am going home for more equipment."

I faced the farmer, took him by the arm and said, "Come Dan, get me back to my car, quickly."

Land rover rides across boggy land are great fun and the slipping and sliding motion made our journey interesting and Dan was quiet until we reached my car when he asked, "Here we are and what you have in mind?"

I replied, "I have done everything I can at this stage. With a bit of luck his circulation will improve with time. Allow him ten minutes then pull him gently by his legs onto a sledge, get him back to the barn, drop him close to a power source and keep him covered," I was climbing into the Saab by then, "I will be back as soon as possible."

My journey home was a fast one. As it was a Sunday morning jaunt in the country and on a winter's day, the roads were almost deserted. Theresa and the children were not at home and that was lucky as I was dreading a discussion with her on the nature of the equipment I was collecting.

The return journey to the farm went smoothly and a cursory look satisfied me the bullock was still in the land of the living. I unrolled the equipment and wrapped it round the bullock.

Bill plugged in Theresa's electric blanket.

He draped the bullock in it and as he turned away from it he spoke to all of us, "Now chaps! What do you think of this fancy treatment?" Every head was nodding, and most faces were smiling at my unusual treatment. The dial, set to its maximum level, worked surprisingly quickly and soon generated enough heat to make steam rise from his still wet body.

We succeeded; if my management of the situation had been somewhat bizarre it was successful and after twenty minutes of heat therapy worked its magic he was a different beast.

I enjoyed a break for a mug of coffee and a bacon roll that hit the right spot and when I examined him again I said, "Would you believe that? His pulse and colour are much better, and his lungs have also improved."

"Well vet it is the first time I have seen this done. I think you are going to save him," That was accompanied by a big smile from Bill who felt the bullock's ears and continued, "I can feel his body getting back to normal, it looks like he might get up soon."

When he attempted to rise we tried to support his heavy bulk, and to push him forward onto his front legs. On the third attempt he made it and, as he stretched and shook himself he belched up a huge rush of gas that brought Dan back into the action, "Brilliant Alex, brilliant, I thought we would lose its and it looks as though you have saved his life." Dan the farmer was a happy chappy.

The bullock looked most odd.

He was still wrapped in Theresa's electric blanket and he reminded me of a hunter during a break on a hard hunting day in January. He shook himself again then wandered over to the manger where he pulled out a few wisps of hay and that made me smile and say, "I am happy with him."

"Brilliant!" The normally voluble farmer was short of words.

"Joe! Slip that blanket off now before he gets too strong to handle." As the tension of the situation dispersed, and I enjoyed another mug of steaming coffee and a jam doughnut, my thoughts slipped back to the family and I wondered if Theresa had returned from Mass and what she thought of the state of her bedroom?

Theresa was fairly loud on the subject.

Lest her thoughts be diminished by my only poorly recounting them, it is best she continues the tale.

We got home from Mass at the usual time. Alex was out on his rounds and my plan followed much the same routine. I popped the kettle on then went upstairs to the bedroom to change into a warm pair of slacks when the disarray in the bedroom shocked me and my hand went straight to my mouth, "Oh No! We have been burgled."

The bed clothes were everywhere, and the room was a long way from its usual tidy state. My next thought, as my imagination ran away from me, was to protect the children and I thought; what if the thieves are still in the house? I joined them downstairs and pulled them out of the house by the back door and we stood in the garden for a few minutes.

As time passed and all seemed in order my nerves settled and I began a systematic search of the house and from room to room and found the situation was one of its normal orderliness; it was only the bedroom that had been disturbed.

As we looked at the messy bed, an excited Andrew exclaimed, "They have taken the electric blanket."

The penny dropped, I knew my odd husband's mind! "It must have been dad, he must have come here and whipped the blanket off the bed to warm up some animal." The children smiled and were satisfied with that explanation and went about their normal business and that left me thinking; whatever will that daft man do next?

The bullock recovered.

All associated with the rescue session were in good spirits, and Dan in particular was most impressed when I said to him, "OK Dan. That's us finished I will pop this blanket into a bag and be on my way."

"I don't think so Alex," Dan smiled at me and continued, "I think this will now become a useful part of my own medical equipment, it will never be able to do the job it did previously."

"I guess you are right, it is well beyond being clean again," I shook my head and starred at the sorry thing that had given its own life to save the bullock.

"Yes! Leave it with me, I will be happy to replace it."

I set off for home.

I was content that at least I had not done too much damage to the Niven household. I popped my head round the door and called, "Hello everyone."

Without even the most basic of pleasantries Theresa launched into the attack, "What have you done with my electric blanket?" When she adopted that pose, both hands on the hips, and her chin straight out, she seemed a formidable lady.

I attempted to pacify her, by telling the family of the interesting experience I had been through. The children listen enthralled to my story; the wife less so. I finished by telling her that Dan the farmer would organise a new blanket and the good woman smiled and said to the children, "And that my dear ones, is simply your father."

Farming vets have a tough life.

God softened mine by giving me a special wife.

THE ARTIST

S ONIA MAROUN WAS born in Durban. From a young age, she had a vivid imagination and loved expressing herself with art. Sonia currently lives in Sydney, where, by selling her artwork privately, she is able to indulge her passion to explore a wide range of art styles. She also keeps her imagination in shape by making up new fairy tales for her two young girls.

Sonia's works may be found at *www.urbantonesgallery.com*

13364477R00144

Printed in Great Britain
by Amazon.co.uk, Ltd.,
Marston Gate.